Know!

TYME
&
TIME AGAIN

BY
STEFAN JAKUBOWSKI

To
Angela

Best

Published in 2011 by Zygmunt Stanley

ISBN 978-0-9554244-4-1

© 2011 Stefan Jakubowski

Cover illustration by Neil James
www.neiljamesartwork.co.uk

Cover and pages designed and typeset by
Rachel Jones
Absolute Design Solutions
www.absolutedesignsolutions.co.uk

Printed by Gomer Press, Wales

Jobbies
By
Stefan Jakubowski

*

Supernatural comedies starring Richard Ross
STRANGE RELATIONS
DEAD PECULIAR

*

Fantasy comedy nonsense
MISCREATION

*

Time Travel comedy starring Tom Tyme
ONCE UPON A TYME
TYME AND TIME AGAIN

THE AUTHOR

Originally from Reading Stefan Jakubowski moved to Wales in the latter part of the last century. (He wishes to point out that he is not as old as that makes him sound). He now lives in Pembrokeshire with wife Nia and their owner, Peaches the cat.

For Nia
For Peaches
For Fun
For Everyone

Special thanks to
Rachel Jones
and Neil James

THE GIST OF IT!

This is where I tell you how it is with Tom Tyme so far.

Tom Tyme is sixty-five and a time traveller – it runs in the family. He is not happy about it.

He has a familiar – something like a witch has – who has the job of training him.

He and his familiar have the task of righting wrongs.

He has a daughter called Lucy and two grandchildren; Kate and Marc.

Tom also has a famous son-in-law.

He also has a cat.

He also has a shed. He likes his shed. Sorry, he loves his shed!

He has a portable loo in his garden. It can transport him to any toilet in the world. It is also a time machine. And no, it isn't bigger on the inside.

He is sometimes told lies by his familiar; for his own good.

He never tells lies. Yeah, right!

Tom's best friend is Smokowski, a mysterious shop keeper.

Tom has a bit of a fear where grannies are concerned. (For more info on this, please read Once Upon A Tyme). But I'm sure he will get over it.

He can be an old fart at times. Make that most times.

He has a magical saver. It saves him. (At least it has so far).

Tom wears a cap, one of those that have flaps that can be worn up or down. It is silvery grey in colour. It is also a universal translator.

He wears a grey corduroy suit but the jacket doesn't match the colour of the trousers.

He likes the odd cuppa.

He likes biscuits.

He also likes the occasional pint

Tom doesn't like spending money.

He is about to embark on only his second adventure.

There, that is about it so far. Of course I haven't mentioned Excalibur, King Arthur, Catranna, or Rufus, or why Tom is slightly afeared by grannies. I don't want to spoil it for you when you read about his first adventure: Once Upon A Tyme.

So there you have it, the gist of it. So, onwards and upwards I say. Let's go see what trouble the old fool gets into this time!

'Whenever and wherever danger or peril might lurk,
be it in the shadows of hell or some unwholesome place of work,
we of the LISPS as one shall fight,
for justice, the weak, to put things right!'

Battle cry of the fighting LISPS's

CHAPTER 1

Tom let out a soft moan as the scenery beyond the glass whizzed past. Why? he thought for the umpteenth time. How could she have done such a thing to him, his own flesh and blood for goodness sake? He wrinkled his nose, let his gaze fall from the window and slowly cast a roving glance over his fellow travellers. Or was that fellow put upons?

There weren't many, perhaps fifteen of them, scattered like lost souls amongst the sixty odd seats, the old dears amongst them chatting inanely while the couple of old boys on board apparently muffled into submission by the scarves wrapped tightly around their faces, but thankfully they were all spaced far enough away from him so Tom could keep himself to himself. But for how long? he thought, as his eyes fixed on a buxom elderly lady of the blue rinse brigade whose eyes were also wandering, like manic butterflies, settling on each male soul in turn where they fluttered dangerously. Although, to be fair, there was no blue rinse, instead, a cloud of medusa hair not unlike a giant seeding dandelion clock, encased in copious amounts of hairspray. Tom quickly averted his eyes before he caught her attention and aimed them firmly at the passing vista outside. There was no way he was going to be turned to stone, or worse. But he knew there had been a fleeting moment of eye contact, just a smidgeon, as he had turned away, and now he felt the fear; the fear of the granny, and he'd had more than his fair share of granny trouble in his past.

Tom hunkered down into his seat and tried to become as invisible as possible. He had seen the like of the dandelion haired woman before. Likely seen off a few husbands in her time; a black widow. A woman not to be trifled with he didn't doubt, most certainly a stalwart of some institution or other. And talking of trifles, had the sound of a moving, rustling, crinoline dress tickled his ear drums? Tom held his breath and sank deeper into his seat.

Oh why, oh why had this happened to him? he thought, raising the collar of his tatty, grey cord jacket, which didn't match his equally tatty, grey cord trousers, except that is for the tattiness. He was a time traveller for goodness sake, a hero, a bastion of good against evil. He had been knighted by King Arthur, no less, didn't that mean anything? Tom assumed the foetal position best he could, it was difficult, what with the seat belt threatening to cut him in half. His eyes were just level with the rubber window seal. And where was that dang cat? One adventure and then nowt. What had happened to the promises? Blooming females. One promises adventures; ones, if he was totally honest, he wasn't sure about - and the other sends him on this! An adventure, bah! That's what his daughter had called it, but then he couldn't really blame her of course, she didn't know what he was. That dipstick of a husband could have said something, but no, under the thumb already that one. But still, she should have known better, he's sixty-five not eighty-five. He's too young, he had told her so; protested until blue in the face. But she had said it was supposed to be a surprise, booked ages ago, a late birthday present. What could he say to that? Especially when her face had wrinkled up like that; she had looked so hurt. Nothing he could do then and she would lose her deposit. That had been the clincher in Tom's eyes; no one should pay for nothing. But it was still a bitter pill to swallow, him, Tom, still but a young man, having to go on a blooming Turkey and Tinsel outing and a flipping mystery one at that! An adventure, bah! With those thoughts swirling in his mind and fear of the granny with the dandelion hair still fresh, Tom pulled his cap over his eyes, his special one, the one that doubled as a universal translator, and assumed the position that offered him most protection – the, I'm beginning to nod, position. Even older women of the buxom matronly persuasion knew to leave an old boy alone when he's beginning to nod off. An old man with the grumps is not a pretty sight. Tom started to nod.

CHAPTER 2

If Tom thought he was having it rough, then Cat, short for Catranna, Tom's magical familiar, tutor, companion, cat, was having it with knobs on. She was on trial!

It happened, not often, blue moon territory, but it did none the less. The charge: Cat had broken the code. Or a code. One of the codes. Anyway, she had broken something, which wasn't hard really, considering the amount of codes there were in her existence. There had to be where time travel was concerned, especially so when magic was involved.

Not all familiars were magical – there were codes covering them too – but all possessed something extraordinary. Cat of course was magical, which was covered by the more stringent of the codes. Not that she was on trial for that. The charge concerned her latest companion, Tom. It was complicated. Some say unnecessary. Trumped up was whispered. Cat smelled a metaphorical rat. But someone, one of the Travellers, so the rumour ran, had raised an objection to Cat's behaviour as to the use of Tom. This in a nutshell was the charge. The idea was being frowned upon by all the familiars, who knew just how hard it could be when running in a newbie, along with most of the Travellers, all had heard about Tom and there was a certain amount of sympathy for Cat, but an accusation had been made and according to the rules of code, Cat must be judged, and therefore guilty until proven otherwise – and if upheld, banishment could be on the horizon.

'How do you plead Catranna?' asked the Chief Traveller and, in the circumstances as was accustomed, judge. His face, as it was with all the Travellers in the courtroom, was covered when in the presence of other travellers. The identity of a Traveller was highly secret, even amongst themselves. Only familiars knew Travellers' true identities. Whether that was just their partner or all Travellers, they didn't let on.

13

'Not guilty, Your Honour,' said Cat.

'Not even a little bit?'

'No, Sir.'

Someone whispered in the Chief's ear.

The Chief cleared his throat and spoke, 'It would appear that the members of the jury should strike my second question from their minds.' He turned to the whisperer, 'Are you sure?' he whispered.

The whisperer nodded.

Frowning, the Chief turned back to face the courtroom, 'Then let the trial begin.' The Chief then tapped the gavel he was holding on his desk and caused a stir by making an unheard of announcement, 'But first,' he said, narrowing his eyes as in warning, even though no one could see them, 'I feel that it would be in everyone's interest if Catranna was allowed to inform Mister Tyme that she will be unavailable as familiar and tutor for the foreseeable future, and so that his next assignment goes unaffected by these events as much as possible, she introduce to him a replacement familiar.'

'Catranna,' said the Chief, sounding grave, 'I hereby give you leave to visit your charge and introduce him to your replacement.'

There was a gasp from the courtroom followed by a building furore of complaints and questions and shouts of "unheard of" echoing throughout. Replacements were only used in the direst of consequences, the worst in fact; the demise of the familiar. The usual course followed in these circumstances was for the partner Traveller in question to be withdrawn from duty until a replacement was found.

The Chief Traveller called for quiet. He explained that in Tom's case, as his next project was already underway and very important, and as this was extraordinary circumstances, the show should go on. It was in the codes if anyone wished to look. A fair amount of shaking heads greeted the news.

The whisperer, whispered in the Chief's ear again who immediately held up placating hands and called for more order. 'The replacement is of course temporary,' he shouted above the raised voices, 'and Cat will have a restraining collar fitted.'

This managed to placate most in the courtroom. As for the others who were still unhappy and making a noise about it, the Chief decided it best to ignore these and had Cat led from the dock. The Chief met her in the judges' chamber.

'Catranna,' said the Chief, 'please turn round, the collar has to be fitted. I know you don't like it but nor do I.'

Cat, who had been giving the Chief, the old one eye, an ancient cat insult, turned, '*You* don't have to wear it!' she snapped.

'You wouldn't be able to see Tom without it,' said the Chief, 'and besides, once you are back it will be removed. I thought I was helping.'

The Chief was a good old stick at heart, but this didn't help where Cat's dignity was concerned. Cat though decided to say no more on the subject and asked her leave. She was duly escorted from the chamber by two ushers under the proviso that she returned as soon as she had introduced her replacement to Tom. With a growing feeling that that rat she had smelled earlier might be bigger than she first thought she fell in step with the ushers.

As she walked, she played the events of the previous day over and over in her mind. None of it made sense. She hadn't done anything out of the unusual. In fact, Cat thought she had been over lenient with Tom on occasion. Perhaps that was it, she had been too easy on him, too light, too casual in her approach. No one had as yet come right out and said which code she had broken, but then she was guilty until innocent, she had few rights; not knowing what you were charged with until the day of the trial was the norm in these cases. Perhaps she was going to be made an example of. The old school feeling threatened by the new up and comers; showing their authority? But to what end? She *was* one of the old school. No, something was up. And that something had a rotten smell about it. Her cat intuition was seldom wrong. What she needed to do now was find out what was going on, and if there was something underhand afoot, find out who was behind it, and to do that she needed to escape, get home to the pyramid. But before she finished playing along and that chance of escape presented itself, there was something else she had to do.

'Okay,' said the senior of the two ushers, who had considered Cat's request doable because of the collar around her neck, 'but be quick.'

Cat nodded, smiled appreciatively and wandered into the ladies.

CHAPTER 3

A small jolt stirred Tom from the sleep he had fallen into when pretending to fall into just such a sleep. That jolt was immediately followed by a second; this one verging on the edge of violent. So much so that Tom's cap slipped over his face.

Tom instantly drew on the assumption that something wasn't right and replaced his cap, whereupon his eyes, wide and suddenly fearful, backed up his supposition. He blinked a couple of times until the obvious came into focus; the light in the coach had changed. Not your forty to sixty watt sort of change, more your reality to not quite so much reality sort of change. A light that was not technically light anymore – more dark. A reddish dark, to be precise. Tom did some more blinking, sat up and peered through the window, to be faced with two sights guaranteed to make ones blood run cold. One was his reflection, sleep dribble running down his chin – the other, an inexplicable absence.

No longer low lying green topped with blue and white of the fluffy persuasion, it was now red, red and more red, from top to bottom, as far as the eye could see. No trees, no houses, no nothing, nothing but barrenness. A red, desolate barrenness. Red desolation.

Tom pressed his face against the glass and stared at the alien vista. For that was what it was – alien. It stank of alien. It stank of trouble. Not that Tom was an expert of the first, but he had been given a book a couple of years back about the solar system, chock full of his preferred medium, pictures. And one of them came to mind now – Mars! The second observation he could be reliably relied upon due to the feeling that was at that moment invading his nether regions; his bowel and bladder were seldom wrong where trouble was concerned.

Tom sat up even straighter, that of the bolt upright. But it couldn't be. He was on a coach, not a rocket. Another thought struck home. Tom sniffed. He was still breathing. From what he could remember Mars didn't have an atmosphere, did it? But the point was, whatever, it

16

wasn't breathable. This set Tom off on a frantic search of his pockets. Panic started to sink in, it wasn't there – the saver. Tom tried to get a grip. Contain that panic – for the moment. A test! That's it. Cat was testing him. A "what will Tom do now scenario". Part of the training. That ol' Cat. But why take the saver? It's the first thing ol' Tom would have reached for in a situation like this, that's why. Panic squeezed a little harder. But if it is then the passengers and driver must be in on it. With frantic eyes Tom surveyed his fellow travellers.

If outside had been unnerving, what Tom saw now was downright disturbing. The passengers were all staring dead ahead – he couldn't see what the driver was doing from where he sat – their faces blank, unconcerned with their predicament. All staring forward as one, a strange smile fixed on their lips; those lips he could see. But it wasn't the smile or the blank looks that had caused the hairs on the back of Tom's neck to stand on end. It was the response those faces had made when Tom had looked at them. As one they had turned and looked back at him. Fifteen or so faces staring, their smiles turning to grins; false gnashers abounding in frightful unison.

The hairs on Tom's neck started to cower, hoping they hadn't been noticed, as a new turn took to the stage, one that had Tom following his neck hair's example. One of the old dears had got to her feet and was bearing down on him along the aisle. It was the buxom lady – the human dandelion – moving towards him with a determination that had worrying worried.

On she came, relentless, marching to where Tom sat, wide eyed and trembling. Each step and movement almost mechanical. Her grin had progressed to a sneer and then she opened her mouth as wide as it could go.

Tom, knees knocking, bladder pulsing, expecting a laugh on the level of the seriously manic – or someone usually readily identifiable with such actions – tried frantically to merge into the fabric of the seat. But, no laugh came. Instead the dandelion lady turned and pointed to the front of the coach. She then spoke, a high pitched strangled noise, 'It's coming,' she said, 'It's coming.'

Knees now pulled to his chest, Tom, more than slightly perturbed, disturbed and perplexed, stammered at her, 'What is?' he said, almost beseeched.

'The vortex,' said the dandelion lady, her voice now a growl. 'The vortex,' she repeated, and now came the deranged cackle Tom had expected earlier.

'The vortex?' said Tom, still with the stammering.

The dandelion lady turned, bloodshot eyes staring. 'You deaf?' she snarled. She held out a liver spotted hand and offered it to Tom. 'The vortex,' she repeated again. 'You have to see it. It wants to see you.' Her hand reached for Tom's.

'No!' wailed Tom, a little higher than he had meant to, 'I don't want to.' But the dandelion lady was having none of it. She reached down and clutched at Tom's arm.

'You haven't a choice,' she said. Behind her the other passengers were gathering.

CHAPTER 4

The door of the post office cum mini-mart swung open. The proprietor of said post office cum mini-mart looked up from what he was doing and arched an elderly eyebrow.

'Good morrow,' said the door opener.

'Good morning,' said the proprietor, tidying away the business he had been about.

'The swallows fly alone this summer,' said the door opener, cryptically.

The proprietor of mentioned premises now arched his other eyebrow and in doing so, with both eyebrows arched, he took on the look of the somewhat surprised. But the owner of the arched eyebrows, who was also the proprietor of mentioned premises, was not so much surprised as befuddled. 'What?' said he.

'The swallows...'

'I heard what you said,' said the proprietor, 'I mean, *what is it* you are going on about?'

The door opener closed the door behind him and gave a furtive look both left and right that suggested conspiracy was afoot. When certain he and the proprietor were alone he spoke again, this time in a whisper. The door opener was of the opinion that one could never be too careful. 'It's code,' he said.

'For what?'

'For...' Here the door opener stuttered to a stop. His forehead furrowed. His bottom lip stuck out. He looked at the proprietor of the shop. 'I... er.'

'Still watching too many films eh, Darren?' said the proprietor, revealing the door opener's identity. 'And may I point out,' he continued, 'if you want to communicate through code you should inform the intended recipient of that code and the proposed usage of it, otherwise the point of the exercise is rendered pointless.'

'What?' said Darren, mouth hanging open.

Envisaging the imminent arrival of another pointless exercise, the proprietor decided against elaboration and went straight for the jugular, 'What can I do for you, Darren?'

'Do?' said Darren, who was still trying to work out what had been said to him before this question.

'Yes, do. I take it you came in for something other than to engage in inane statements.'

Darren's frown deepened for a moment before dispersing in a burst of understanding, 'Ah,' he said, 'I'm here.'

'I can see that.'

'It's my first day.'

For thinking? thought the proprietor, somewhat cruelly. 'For what?' he asked.

'For here,' said Darren, 'It's my first day here.'

An eyebrow that had recently relaxed now went back into arching action. Does he mean what I think he means? thought the proprietor, hoping upon hope that he was wrong. He wasn't.

Darren produced something white and folded from the man bag he was shouldering. 'Ta-da,' said Darren, flourishing it. 'Lucy bought it for me just in case you didn't have one in my size.' He gave the folded item a shake and there, in all its glory, was an apron – the greengrocery type.

Grief, thought the proprietor as a light went on in his mind, illuminating something his sub-conscious had obviously hidden away. Was it today? But how could he possibly have forgotten about today? About the day that Darren, otherwise known as the legend, Arthur King of the Britains, but only to a select few, which didn't include Lucy, Darren's wife, was to start work in his humble premises. He had forgotten because he had been dreading it, that's why. As a king and warrior, Arthur had no equal. As a twenty-first century man called Darren… well… it must be something in the air. How had Tom talked him into taking him on? Because Darren was Tom's son-in-law he supposed. But Tom knew he worked alone. It was no good, he would have to send him on his way.

'What do you want me to do first, Mister Smokowski?' asked Darren, donning apron on muscular frame, a massive smile spread across his handsome face, lantern jaw jutting, innocence exuding from every pore. He was trying to please – putting the history between them behind him.

'Tea, I think,' said Smokowski, bowing to the fates, 'Let's get that kettle boiling.'

CHAPTER 5

'Waaaa!' screamed Tom.

'Waaaa!' screamed the dandelion haired lady.

Tom's first instinct was to jump up but the seat belt held him firmly so his movement was restricted to a pathetic hunched stoop.

The dandelion lady, surprised by Tom's sudden hunched stoop, fell backwards across the aisle and landed in a heap on the seat opposite.

Back across the aisle Tom, not quite back with the world, was holding his chest. Inside, his heart was auditioning for a role – a drum roll, the one where something pretty damned dramatic happens when it stops.

The coach suddenly lurched sideways, all was in panic. Hell was breaking loose. Scarves that had fallen from faces were frantically being replaced, worried looks created fearful crossing of legs, handbags were clutched, knitting unravelled, flowered hats that had only moments earlier been worn at a jaunty angle, now covered eyes.

The coach driver, appearing in a red faced and flustered state stomped up the aisle and stopped beside Tom expecting the worst; whatever that was. 'Wuz-up – wuz-up?' he demanded, 'Who pressed the emergency button?'

An elderly lady, her hairnet perforated by a knitting needle, gingerly held up a hand. The driver frowned at her – she took fright and delved headfirst into the sanctuary of the large bag she was carrying.

'Now,' said the driver, happy his authorative look had done its job, 'what was all the shouting about?' He aimed this question at Tom as the lady of the dandelion hair was indisposed at that moment, and quite upside down. 'Darn near gave me a heart attack, that buzzer. Did an emergency stop.'

'He was snoring,' said a voice from below the seat opposite Tom.

The driver decided to lend a hand and pulled the dandelion haired lady upright. Once sitting, she was immediately consoled by a lady whom Tom suspected as being her lieutenant, or sergeant, or something.

'And then,' said the dandelion lady, sniffling, 'he started to shout and scream as I tried to wake him and…' And now she realised what it was she was saying. The mistake she had made. Never, ever, try to wake a snoring man. A gentle cajole into shifting, tease into moving, use tricks and ruses, introduce altogether downright underhandedness, but never give him a shake, never attempt to wake him. She had overstepped the mark. Head now bowed, she let her lieutenant or sergeant or whatever lead her back to her seat.

'Are we all done then?' enquired the driver, who appeared to be much calmer now. A much calmer driver with a beady eye trained on Tom.

A brow knitted Tom nodded. It had been a dream. Mars! Vortex! What a fool. A much relieved one, but a fool none the less.

'Good,' said the driver, satisfied he could return to his seat, 'We'll be getting on our way then.' He went to walk back down the aisle but stopped when he realised all the recent commotion may well have its consequences. 'And, if anyone feels the need for a comfort break, I will be making a mystery stop in about,' he looked at his watch, 'half an hour. In the meantime please feel free to use the facilities provided.' This said, the driver returned to his seat and propelled the coach back onto the motorway.

In his seat, Tom was deep in thought, brooding on his lot. The blame for his reaction when woken couldn't all rest on the dandelion lady's shoulders. There were other factors in play, two ludicrous ones – ones he never thought in his wildest dreams would ever affect him, one more ludicrous than the other. The first was deep in his psyche – a scar on it. It was silly. It was irrational. It was a fear of grannies. Sure, he had feared them before, which man of his age didn't, but this was more than just fear, something far more deep seated – terror almost. Whenever he saw one and they moved in a way he hadn't expected, he would openly flinch. He half expected them to draw a weapon, or start clicking. No, perhaps it wasn't irrational. Would he ever get over it? He doubted it. And then there was the other factor – perhaps the worse of the two. Something that had recently started keeping him awake at night. Something that had him looking under his bed and in the wardrobe for things that weeks ago wouldn't have been there. Tom shuddered as he thought about it. He had always thought it a terrible thing to have. Had been glad he lacked one. But now he wasn't so sure. Oh woe was he. Had he developed an imagination? Oh double woe was he.

Tom rubbed at tired, troubled eyes and decided he needed the toilet. He supposed he could wait for the mystery stop, but his legs felt stiff; time for a stretch. Tom unclipped his seat belt, slipped from his seat and made his way to the toilet at the back of the coach, taking care not to make eye contact with any of the ladies present, especially the dandelion lady. On reaching it he saw the lock was on green so he pushed on the door.

'Blow,' he groaned under his breath as the door failed to move. He tried again, but again it wouldn't shift. What now, he thought, fearing more trouble on the horizon.

'Give it a bit of a shove – it sticks,' said a muffled voice from behind Tom.

Tom turned and saw that the voice had come from a scarf covered old boy. Beside him, his female companion was fast asleep. 'Thanks,' said Tom, tipping his cap.

'My pleasure,' said the old boy.

Tom put his shoulder to the door, shoved, watched with satisfaction as it swung open, then yelled the yell of the greatly startled.

CHAPTER 6

Job done, the ushers resumed their duties and escorted Cat to the intended destination, a door with sign that read waiting room. Inside, she met her replacement.

'Brandy!' exclaimed Cat, surprised.

'Cat,' said Brandy, expressing equal surprise, 'what's going on?'

'Don't you know?' said Cat, again surprised, she thought everyone would have known by now. She cast a glance at the ushers, but they were staring straight ahead, their faces expressionless.

'I know nothing,' said Brandy, now looking perplexed. 'I've been in here for ages, waiting. I was beginning to think I had done something wrong. I haven't, have I?' She took a lipstick from her bag and started to apply it.

'No one has said anything to you?' Cat again looked at the ushers – again the same response.

'Only that I was needed for another op, hush-hush and all that.'

So I've got to do my own dirty work have I, thought Cat. 'You've got to take my place for a while. Work with my Traveller on his next mission.'

'Why?' Brandy looked shocked.

Cat looked at the ushers, again no semblance of interest. What did she say, especially as it appeared they had kept Brandy in the dark for whatever reason? Had to be careful what she said she supposed, didn't want to incriminate herself, someone was bound to be listening. Okay then, 'The Chief has something else lined up for me, something that needs my talents.' No change from the ushers, so far so good, she hoped.

'That's different, I didn't think that sort of thing happened while their partner is still alive and kicking, but hey-ho, how is Rufus? Still a pain in the old you-know-what?'

Cat's turn to look shocked. 'Rufus is no longer with us,' said Cat, 'I'm looking after Tom, his great-nephew now.'

'Oh,' said Brandy, 'I didn't know. That's what comes with working on the edges – mostly one way traffic. Any news usually takes an age to filter through, unless it's of ultra importance that is.'

'I can imagine,' said Cat.

'So, when do I start?'

One of the ushers suddenly broke his silence and spoke, 'As soon as you've been briefed on your Traveller's next mission, Catranna will introduce you to him when we return. This way please, Miss Brandy.' The usher opened the door to the room.

Brandy slipped from the table she had been perched upon, put her lipstick away and fluttered extra-lash mascara eye lashes. 'I'll see you later then,' she said, clutching her handbag to her chest.

'Look forward to it,' said Cat.

Brandy, escorted by the usher that had spoken left the room, leaving the other usher looking after Cat.

Cat sat for a moment, then leapt onto a chair and made herself comfortable. All she could do now was wait and think.

CHAPTER 7

'Well don't just stand there catching flies, get in before someone sees me.'

It took a second or two, but Tom finally regained his senses and shuffled into the coach loo, scanning the nearest fellow passengers to see if his squeak of surprise had aroused attention. All looked quiet, so he quickly closed the door behind him.

'Where the heck have you been the last couple of days?' said Tom, venting some of the frustration he had been building up, 'And what are you doing in here?'

'Nice to see you too,' said Cat, who was sat on the toilet seat not looking the least bit happy.

'Yeah, well,' said Tom, calming a little as he noticed Cat's mood, 'It's just…'

'Look, sorry to interrupt, but I haven't got much time and I need to tell you something, and this isn't me, it's a projection, I'm in the ladies at head office.'

'Projection?'

'Listen please.'

Tom closed his mouth, something in the way Cat was acting worried him.

'I've got to go away, but before I do I've a few things I've got to tell you.' Tom went to interrupt again, but Cat stopped him. 'Firstly, the time machine, the loo, you don't have to flush it every time you want to go somewhere, my little joke, sorry – you only need to think yourself there.'

This time Tom couldn't contain himself, 'But the doorway in time you make.'

'The loo doesn't need one, it's self transporting, sorry – though I can make doorways in time if needed.' What was she doing? 'Look, Tom, let me say what I've come here to say. You've a new mission, but I won't be going with you.'

27

'What? But…'

'You're to be accompanied by someone else. Just until I get back that is.'

Tom's mind was swirling. He didn't want to listen anymore. 'Back from where? What the heck is going on Cat?' he demanded. And he had thought his day couldn't get any worse.

'I'm sorry Tom, I've got to go. I'll explain later. Give Smokowski a call and tell him to pick you up from wherever you are and take you back to the cottage, I'll meet you by the loo.'

'But who's this someone else, Cat?'

But Cat had gone, disappeared back to from where she had come from, leaving Tom wondering what the hell was going on. A new familiar, is that what she meant? He sat on the seat now vacated by Cat and pondered. That wasn't like Cat, but then again, he realised, he hadn't really known her that long. Perhaps this was the way of things. Perhaps he should keep an open mind. Perhaps he should just stop thinking. His head hurt. Who knew how things operated in this new world he was now part of, the strange, quirky, sometimes scary, very scary, world of time travel. He put hand to chest, his heart had started to beat a little faster again, but this time it had nothing to do with fear, well, perhaps a little bit, but more to do with the thought of an imminent adventure – his new found Traveller blood gearing up for it. He stood up, thoughts of why he had come to the toilet in the first place forgotten for the moment, and opened the door.

Back in his seat he played what had just happened through his mind again, what Cat had said. Something about something she had said was playing on his mind. Didn't have to flush it, thought Tom – at least that sounded like the Cat he knew. He afforded a quick smile at that, but it wasn't what was nagging at him. Then it came to him, and with that realisation the blood drained from his face. She had said someone else was going with him, which meant that someone had to be a familiar, didn't it? Had to be. But Cat had told him that Traveller and familiar were together for life until the worst happened – Rufus was an anomaly. Grief, what wasn't Cat telling him? He needed to use the phone, call Smokowski. Flipping mobile phones, worse than the normal ones, an intrusion Tom thought. He scrabbled in the infernal man bag his daughter had given him. Where was it? Ha-ha, he thought, triumphantly holding it aloft – now, what the flip was Smokowski's code?

CHAPTER 8

The phone rang.

The only occupant in the room went to pick it up, but walked into a chair. The room was in complete darkness you see. Dark walls, dark carpet, even the furniture was dark, all blending in nicely with the darkness encompassing it. Plus it didn't help that the only occupant also had their face covered. The only occupant blindly found their way round the chair and walked into the desk.

'Blast,' cursed the only occupant, feeling for their knee. It was stupid, all this darkness. The only occupant thought so and so did just about everyone else that knew about the room, but anonymity was everything; once your identity was blown it was all over, literally sometimes. So the only occupant rubbed their knee and got on with things and eventually found the phone.

'Yes,' said the only occupant, speaking into the earpiece. 'What, speak up, I can't hear you. Hang about. There.' Phone now right way round, the only occupant listened intently to what was being said to him.

'And you could win one of a number of holidays or the cash equivalent,' said the voice on the phone.

'What?' said the only occupant, 'No I don't want the chance to win one of several small prizes. How did you get this number? I demand…'

The line had gone dead.

Seething at the cheek of it all, the only occupant slammed the phone back into its cradle. Then tried again, and this time succeeded. The phone immediately rang again. Snatching it back up, with earpiece in the right place this time, the only occupant let rip, 'I told you, keep your money and I most certainly don't want one of your small ones!'

There was stunned silence on the other end of the phone for a moment before a voice that the only occupant knew broke it.

'Oh,' said the only occupant, 'yes, well, I, send him straight in. No, yes, no I don't need financial help, thank you – no, now please forget what you just heard and send him in, thank you.'

CHAPTER 9

The phone rang.

Darren and the only customer in the shop looked up. Mister Smokowski picked it up.

'Hello?' said Mister Smokowski, in his voice reserved for business. Suave, he thought it. Bordering on the creepy, it was. 'Smokowski's mini-mart, Smokowski speaking. How can I help you?' Then it was back to normal, 'Oh, it's you.'

'Blah-blah!'

'What? Now?' Smokowski's eyebrows did a bit of raising.

'Blah-blah.'

'But the…'

'Blah-blah.'

'Did she?'

'Blah-blah-blah!'

'Okay, where are you?'

'Blah.'

'Take a couple of hours there and back.'

'Blah!'

'No, you know what the old van's like.'

'Blah-blah-blah.'

'See you in a little while then.'

'Blah!'

'Okay, it won't be a little while.' Mister Smokowski replaced the receiver and started to take off his apron.

'Is everything all right?' asked Darren, who still wasn't sure about the object that answers you in a small voice when you speak into it.

Yes, thought the only customer, tin in hand, ear suddenly straining. A local retired farmer that didn't get out much and had come in for his paper, milk, bread and a small tin of alphabetti spaghetti for his toast – beans gave him wind – but knew the value of a good piece of gossip.

'I've got to go out,' said Smokowski, taking off his apron and hanging it on a coat hook on the back of the storeroom door, 'I won't be long.'

A look of horror appeared on Darren's face, 'But I heard you say a couple of hours!'

A couple of hours at least, thought the only customer, something must be up. He edged a little closer to the counter.

'You'll be all right,' said Smokowski, reassuringly. 'You're... you know.' Smokowski had nearly let Darren's secret out.

'But it's my first day,' said Darren, knowing full well who he was, but that wasn't going to help a whole lot; what was he going to do, grab a sword and have a go at the customers? Having said that, the old boy lurking with the tin in his hand looked the sort you might have to take the flat of a sword to. Darren glowered at the man, who didn't notice as he was too busy being nosy, then turned a pleading face towards Smokowski, 'But what if it gets busy?'

'It's Thursday, it never does, you'll be fine.'

'It's Monday,' said Darren.

Monday! thought the only customer, blimey I thought it was Friday.

'Whatever,' said Smokowski, grabbing his jacket, 'I've got to go and you're in charge.' Smokowski didn't like the idea of a greenhorn handling the greenbacks, but he didn't have much choice – duty called.

He looks like he's got something on his mind, thought the only customer.

As Smokowski got to the front door he thought about turning the closed sign face out, but Monday, if it indeed was Monday, was quite busy. Instead he gritted his teeth and left.

'What was all that about?' asked the only customer, as the door closed, 'Sounds like summit's up.' He peered at Darren, all ears and eyes, waiting for the knowledge to fall from the tree.

But, before Darren had the chance to wonder where he might get a sword from, the door to the storeroom opened and out walked Smokowski looking a couple of hours older.

'Ah,' said Smokowski, sensing all was not right. His return to the storeroom was a darned sight quicker than his entrance had been.

33

'Did you see that?' said the only customer, his eyes now even wider and his ears picking up Smokowski saying something about it being the wrong time as the storeroom door closed.

'See what?' said Darren, trying as hard as possible to think on his feet.

'Smokowski,' said the only customer, staring at Darren as if he were mad, 'He came in through the back – almost came back before he'd gone.'

'Oh, would you look at the time,' said Darren, mimicking someone from a film he had watched, and only now understanding the use of the phrase, 'Time to take the stock somewhere.' Something else he had picked up from the small silver screen, but what shopkeepers did with the stock they were taking, he hadn't yet fathomed.

'You ain't got a watch on,' observed the only customer, glaring at the wrist Darren was looking at, 'You're mad.'

'I'm not the one seeing things,' said Darren, not doing too badly on his feet, considering the rocky ground he was on, 'How could Mister Smokowski be in two different places at once?'

'I never said he was in two places at once. I said… I said he was there and…' The only customer glared, 'There's something not right going on here,' said he, now wondering just what it was he had seen, but he was sure he had seen something.

'Do you still want that tin of spaghetti you're squeezing?' asked Darren, beginning to feel oddly pleased with himself.

'Blast you, I know what I saw, I'm not the crazy one.'

'Yeah, and I'm King Arthur,' said Darren.

'Mad I tell you,' ranted the only customer, slamming the tin of alphabetti spaghetti on the counter, 'and I'll not be shopping here again. I'm off to the pub.'

'Are you sure you haven't already been there,' said Darren, throwing in a low punch for good measure, but not really knowing he was.

'Pah!' said the only customer, who then turned and left the building.

''Bye then,' said Darren, who, as soon as the only customer had left, hurried over to the door, turned the open sign to show closed, locked it and then made a bee line for the storeroom and cautiously peered inside. But there no sign of Smokowski – he too had left the building; for a second time.

CHAPTER 10

Marc, Tom's grandson, Lucy's son, Kate's brother, was busy trying to ignore the apparition, which had appeared in the shadows by the school hall and which, at that moment, was franticly waving at him for all it was worth. It was giving him a strange feeling, as if he had been in this exact same situation before. What did the grown-ups call it? Dayjar flu? There was certainly a lot of flus about, what with pig flu and bird flu; was no animal safe? But Marc couldn't remember hearing about a flu that made you think you had done something before, he was sure he hadn't heard about it on the news. Marc put hand to forehead – no temperature to speak of. Whatever, it was giving him the creeps and the apparition was still there, even though he had opened and closed his eyes a couple of times, so he couldn't be imagining it. How had he got in?

'Marc?'

Marc started at the sudden interruption to his attempted apparition ignoring, but then he always started when he heard his sister's voice.

'What are you doing?'

'Nuffink,' said Marc, immediately feeling guilty, though on this rare occasion he wasn't actually up to no good – up to no good being a prerogative for any eleven year old boy – or so they will tell you.

Katie stared hard at her brother as the uneasy feeling that for once he might be telling the truth, crept over her; it was quite unnerving. 'Well,' she said, frowning at her brother, 'when you've finished doing "nuffink" remember there's a rehearsal of the school play in ten minutes, don't be late.' Why he had to be in it she just didn't know, bound to do something stupid and spoil everything. Katie had landed the lead role alongside the school heartthrob. She gave her brother another searching stare, then, without saying another word, spun on her heels and left him to whatever it was he wasn't doing.

As is sometimes the wont of little brothers, Marc was screwing up his face and making good with the old ritual of the poking out of the tongue. Why did *he* have to be in the stupid play? Stupid teacher saying he should support his sister as it was her first big role and she had such talent. What did she know? Marc returned his tongue to his mouth and started thinking. What he needed was an excuse to get out of it. Perhaps he had one? He looked at the apparition, who was now picking up the tempo on the waving front, then again, perhaps not. Still, he had better go over and see what the apparition wanted before it had a heart attack or something.

CHAPTER 11

Smokowski's van stuttered to a stop outside Tom's cottage, Hope End.

Tom liked the name. He liked his cottage. He loved his shed which sat all unassuming at the bottom of his garden. He was even beginning to think better of the monstrosity which sat beside his shed – the portable toilet. And it was there that Cat had said she would meet him – her and that someone she had mentioned.

'You coming?' said Tom, peering in through the passenger side door.

'You sure?' said Smokowski.

'You're an aide, ain't you?'

'A what?' said Smokowski, clambering from his seat.

'My helper, you know, like you did with Uncle Rufus.'

'Oh – suppose,' said Smokowski, locking his door.

'Then come on.'

'You locked your door?'

''Course I have,' said Tom, pulling on the handle and falling backwards as the door opened.

Smokowski raise eyes skyward, went round, locked Tom's door and started to follow him through the back gate. He would help, be an aide, but that didn't mean he had to like doing it – too dangerous by half what some of these Travellers did. Rufus had been crazy – the jury was still out on Tom. Yes, he had known Tom for years, but not as a Traveller – there was a difference. Besides he hadn't quite recovered from Tom's first adventure yet – still couldn't look a granny in the eye. But having said all that, there was something about all of it that got the blood coursing. Smokowski closed the garden gate behind him. As long as the blood wasn't coursing outside of his body, and all the coming adventures he guessed he was to be part off, weren't as dangerous.

Being four or five paces ahead of Smokowski, Tom was the first of them to notice the door to the portable toilet stood open and Cat was sat outside looking in. It appeared she was in conversation with someone or something inside. Tom shuddered. Please don't let it be a something, thought Tom, his new found imagination getting the better of him.

'Cat,' said Tom, thoughts of the something dispersing as he noticed how far removed she appeared from her old self. Should he say something? He thought he should. 'Nice collar.'

If looks could kill, Tom would have been a smouldering pile of ashes right then. 'Tom,' said Cat, 'Smokowski, how are you?'

'Hello, Cat,' said Smokowski, catching up with Tom, 'Fine thanks.'

'So,' said Tom, putting on a grave expression that would have looked grave on anyone other than him, 'what's going on?'

Cat stood up, 'I'll explain everything in a moment, but first I want to introduce you to someone.'

A rather long, bare, tanned leg, with a four inch stiletto attached to its foot emerged from the loo, followed by another one equal to the first.

It took Tom a second or two to notice to what they were joined to, but he got there eventually, helped by a low gasp from Smokowski that broke through his trance. When he did, he too gasped. The long tanned legs were topped by a short skirt that hardly covered the essentials. A skirt so tiny that it could have easily been described as a belt if one thought about it. Tom and Smokowski weren't, at least not about it being a belt.

A bare, tanned, midriff appeared above the skirt, a bejewelled belly button flashed purple as sunlight caught on the amethyst embedded there. Above the midriff came the chest parts. Here, Tom's mind went to mush, turned by the array of hundreds of coloured sequins, sparkling and heaving before him – a sparkling sea of colour giving way to the slenderest of necks. A perfect neck, sat on perfect shoulders, leading to a face with perfect, the most perfect, lips. Red, rosy, full, pouting lips that – that…

'Tom?' said Cat, wondering for a moment why Tom's mouth was hanging open as, at the same time realising why. '*Tom!*'

'What?' said Tom, snapping to, colouring and quickly raising the drawbridge on his tonsils.

The lips Tom had just been mesmerised by emitted a giggle. The sort of giggle attributed to French maids – or those dressed like them. The sort of giggle that could tantalise the strongest willed amongst men. They now parted and their owner spoke, 'He is funny.'

Yeah, thought Cat, funny in the head, the besotted old codger. 'If you've got a moment,' she said.

'Yes, Cat. Sorry about that, bit of a surprise,' said Tom, making excuses.

'He-he,' giggled the owner of the lips, 'you said he was…'

'Tom – yes,' said Cat, quickly, 'now if everyone has quite got over the initial meeting, I've got a few things I need to say and not a lot of time in which to say them.'

The giggling stopped. Tom got hold of himself. Smokowski, whistling in an embarrassed manner did likewise, but luckily had his back to everyone. So now, at last, Cat had her chance to tell Tom what was going on.

'But that's not fair,' uttered a flabbergasted Tom, when Cat had finished.

'Like I said, Tom, it's the code,' said Cat, shrugging shoulders.

'But why are you on trial?' said Tom, trying to get his head around what he had been told.

'That I can't tell you,' said Cat, thinking it might be wise not to divulge the reason. She doubted Tom would understand – she didn't.

'Why not?'

'I just can't.'

'This flipping code thing I suppose.'

'I've told you all I can, Tom, it will have to suffice,' said Cat, wishing it were all just a bad dream, 'and now I really have to go.'

'What about her?' said Tom, resigning himself to what he had been told, but none the wiser on the replacement front.

So caught up was she on the trial and its implications, and avoiding telling too much to Tom regarding her thoughts and fears, Cat had all but forgotten introductions.

'I'm so sorry,' said Cat, as she returned to the portable loo and the patiently waiting Brandy, 'this is Brandy, Tom, your temporary familiar, she's a BIMBO.'

Tom was aghast. He could hardly believe what Cat had just said, even though the thought had briefly flitted between his ears when he had finished ogling the poor girl earlier. But thinking was one thing, actually saying, well! 'Really, Cat,' Tom admonished, his own guilt at thinking it adding heavily to the chastisement, 'I hardly think…'

'It's her job,' said Cat, removing Tom's soapbox.

'My name is Brandy,' said Brandy, chipping in chirpily. 'I picked it myself.'

'It's an acronym for the organisation she works for,' explained Cat.

'Organisation?' said Smokowski, now recovered from his embarrassing moment.

'I was going to say that,' said Tom.

'Who is the other funny man?' asked Brandy.

'Mister Smokowski,' said Cat, 'a trusted friend.'

Smokowski bowed his head.

'So funny,' giggled Brandy.

'Organisation?' said Tom, stepping in between Brandy and Smokowski.

'BIMBO stands for The Edge and Field Intelligence Division, of which I am told, is a very professional body, as is Brandy,' said Cat.

Certain thoughts rearing ugly heads quickly suppressed, Tom proceeded to give forth the impression of a puzzled man in deep thought, which of course he was. 'How's BIMBO an acronym for that?' he said, 'Shouldn't it be T-E-F-I-D or something?'

'I was going to say that,' said Smokowski, moving out of Tom's shadow into the light of Brandy's gaze.

'The organisation is top secret so it's in code,' explained Cat.

'Makes sense,' said Smokowski, although looking doubtful.

'I was going to…'

'*Tom*,' said Cat.

'But…'

But Cat didn't have any more time for old men's foolishness. 'Time for me to go,' she said, cutting Tom off in mid whine, 'or I fear someone will come to get me.'

'Let them try,' said Tom, chest puffing.

'Ooo,' swooned Brandy, 'he's so brave.'

'I…' Smokowski began, but on catching Cat's eye decided it might be wiser to adopt a less said the better attitude.

'And you too, Mister Smokycoughski,' said Brandy, putting the world right.

'Now I really do have to go,' said Cat, 'You're in safe hands, Brandy knows what she's doing.'

'But am I?' giggled Brandy.

Tom shot Brandy a worried look, he still wasn't sure about all that was going on, 'But Cat…'

But Cat was gone.

'She's gone,' said Smokowski.

'Gone,' said Brandy.

'I can see that!' snapped Tom, more uncertain than angry.

For a moment Brandy looked hurt, but she rallied, 'And soon it will be our turn to go – we have a job to do.'

Tom knew that, but it wasn't at the top of his list of priorities right then. He turned to speak to Smokowski, but Smokowski was halfway to the garden gate, heading for his van. Worried he might have offended him with his snapping, Tom went after him.

'Tom?' said Brandy.

'Back in a mo,' said Tom, 'there's tea in the kitchen.' He pointed towards the backdoor to the cottage.

Brandy wondered if there was something stronger.

Tom caught up with Smokowski as he was putting key to ignition. He pulled the passenger door open. 'Where are you going?'

'I've got to get back Tom, Darren's on his own in the shop and I've already been away longer than I thought.' Smokowski turned the key, but nothing happened.

'But you're my aide, my friend,' said Tom, 'Give it a bit of gas.'

The key turned in Smokowski's hand, but still nothing. 'I am, Tom,' said Smokowski, getting out of his van, 'a friend always and an aide in times of trouble.' He joined Tom on the pavement, 'Dead as a dodo.'

'This *is* times of trouble,' said Tom. Tom relayed to Smokowski what Cat had told him.

'This isn't trouble Tom,' said Smokowski, who, as Tom's Great-Uncle Rufus's aide when he was a Traveller, had seen worse things, 'just sounds like someone in higher authority throwing their weight around. Cat knows what she's doing and she'll cope a lot better if she hasn't got to worry about you.' Smokowski kicked the van.

'But she's got to go to court,' said Tom. 'Perhaps it's the battery.'

'And we've got to carry on as normal as possible,' said Smokowski. 'Old age more like.'

Tom looked crestfallen.

'But you can help me, old pal,' said Smokowski, trying to lighten the load resting on Tom's shoulders.

'But I don't know anything about shops,' said Tom, 'besides, I don't think her in doors would let me.' He thumbed over his shoulder at the cottage.

Smokowski laughed. 'You're an old fool Tom; I mean give me a lift now the old van's gone and given up on me.'

Against the odds a faint smile managed to appear on Tom's lips. 'I suppose I could,' he said, the smile broadening.

'Good man,' said Smokowski, slapping Tom on the back.

They returned to the garden.

'You know that if things do go belly up, you've only got to call,' said Smokowski.

'And you know that if that son-in-law of mine doesn't pull his weight you can call on me; these boots aren't just for walking you know.'

Smokowski laughed. And he and Tom were still laughing when they walked into the kitchen.

Raised eyebrows greeted them, 'Everything okay?' asked Brandy, surprised to see Smokowski still on the premises.

'An old friend needs a lift, that's all,' said Tom.

'Ah, a threesome it is then,' said Brandy, all straight faced and fluttering lashes.

Wreathed in awkward silence, Tom and Smokowski quickly made pace to the portable loo before further embarrassing moments could arise.

CHAPTER 12

'Hel-lo?' enquired a voice, as its owner entered a very dark room.

'Come in,' answered the room's only occupant from somewhere within.

'Ow!'

'Careful of the furniture, it's antique.'

'Can't we turn a light on?'

'You know that's not possible.'

'How do you know it's antique?'

'Everything in here is antique.'

'Must be worth a few bob then?'

'As a matter…' The room's only occupant – the one that was there when there wasn't anyone else in the room, stopped what he was saying and let out a disgruntled snort. 'Look here, let's get to the point, is everything ready? And more to that point are you?'

'As much as it can be,' said the now other occupant of the room, the one that had just entered, 'as am I, Sir.'

'Don't call me that, you don't know who's listening!' snapped the occupant that had been in the room before the other one. 'No one is supposed to know who I am.'

Funny, thought the other, slightly puzzled, occupant, the one that had just entered, on hearing that, as he thought he did know. 'Sorry.'

Satisfied with the apology the first occupant of the room questioned his visitor further, 'Any news on the, *you-know-what*?'

'The, you-know-what?'

'Yes.'

'No.'

'Oh.' The original occupant, the one that had been in the room before the one that had just entered, had entered, wasn't surprised. If there had been any news on the, you-know-what, he doubted he would be having this stupid conversation. 'Tell them to keep me posted.'

'Will do. Is that all, Sir?'

'DON'T CALL ME THAT!!'

'Sorry, S–. I'll be off then.'

'Better had, we don't want to keep her waiting.'

The room fell silent. The only occupant now rose from behind a desk. A few steps were taken. Something wasn't right.

'Ow!' said the only occupant suddenly.

'Ow!' said someone, who should have left the room already.

'Why are you still here?' asked the only occupant, who wasn't for the moment, and who was nursing a bruised ankle, and who had wondered why the door hadn't opened when the visitor should have left.

'Sorry,' said the other occupant, nursing a bump on his head, 'I couldn't find my way out.'

The door to the dark room opened a tad, letting in just enough light to show where it was.

'Here.'

'Thank you.'

The door closed again.

'I'm still here.'

The only occupant, which wasn't strictly true at the moment, grumbled and opened the door again. 'There.'

'Thank you.'

'You out yet?'

'Nearly. Okay.'

The door slammed shut. The only occupant of the dark room sagged against it. Was he doing the right thing? He hoped so.

CHAPTER 13

'Order! ORDER!' demanded the Chief Traveller, as the courtroom rippled with discontent. The reason: rumour was awash that the jury had been nobbled, which, under the code, true or not, meant the Chief Traveller would alone draw a verdict. It was this he was about to announce.

The room gradually settled. The Chief Traveller surveyed it through his mask from atop the raised dais, upon which his desk was sat. Familiars were crowded on the pews to his left, those that hadn't found a seat and could, were clinging from wall and ceiling. To his right sat the Travellers. At the back, a mixture stood waiting. He hoped there wouldn't be trouble when he announced his verdict. His eyes settled on the accused who was licking herself in a most unladylike fashion.

'Ah-hum,' coughed the Chief, politely trying to get her attention.

Cat looked up from beneath her leg to find the whole courtroom focused on her. She stopped her licking and sat up. So this was it, she thought. How was it going to go now the Chief had the final say? A miscarriage of justice? She suspected so, for whatever reason, she had the idea someone was out to get her. Who was behind it? She could only guess. But one thing was for sure, she wouldn't stop until she found out whom. Of course, she might be pronounced innocent. Yeah and a snowman had taken up residence in hell.

With Cat and the courtroom's attention now on him, the Chief got to his feet. A black cloth he had been handed now hung on the front of his desk; the verdict was about to be announced. He cleared his throat. 'I have made my decision,' he announced, 'And after carefully considering all the facts, the accused is found guilty!'

Well there's a surprise, thought Cat.

The room erupted. A few applauded the verdict, but most were loudly opining the travesty of it.

'Quiet please, order!' shouted the Chief, banging on his desk for all he was worth with his gavel. But as it looked doubtful he would be getting anything that he was asking for any time soon, he continued proceedings anyway.

'Catranna,' said the Chief, looking stern under his mask – at least she was paying attention, 'it now falls on me to lay sentence upon you. From this day forth you are hereby stripped of your duties as a Familiar and your membership of the Travellers Aide Guild, and for as long as you so shall live, you shall be banished from the world of the time traveller. Please take her away.'

Cat went willingly enough – she had to if her plan was to work. Stepping from the stand she positioned herself between her escorts and was led from the courtroom. The door to the room Cat had been ensconced in since the trial began came into view. She readied herself, but this time they walked on past it. Instead they continued walking until they stopped in front of a door of solid steel. Cat guessed it was lead lined – a defence against the use of magic; the walls would be too. It was time to act. Bolts were drawn, the door was opened and the first escort walked inside, followed by Cat and the second of the escorts; the door slammed shut behind them. Cat watched them go.

It hadn't been hard to re-wire the collar the Chief had presented to her – a simple programme that maintained a solid projection of her body for as long as the collar's power lasted. As she and her escorts had approached the steel door, Cat had simply slipped from the projection before going though – a simple glamour being sufficient to hide her from the escort's eyes. The hard bit had been not to laugh as she hitched a lift in it Trojan horse style; it had tickled for some reason. The lucky bit had been the collar; without it escape would have been difficult. Any use of magic would have been cut the instant her escorts closed the lead lined door; the alarm would have quickly been raised – so difficult, but not impossible. This way though, she had time, and time is just what she needed. Head down, and with a sudden chill clinging to her back, Cat made her escape.

CHAPTER 14

'It's the wrong time,' hissed Smokowski, as he hurried back to Tom and Brandy, who were thankfully still in the toilet.

'Wrong time?' said Tom, looking at his watch.

'Nearly got here before I'd left,' said Smokowski, squeezing in beside them.

'Anyone see you?' asked Brandy.

'Don't think so.'

'Better try again then,' said Tom.

Darren's head slowly appeared around the storeroom door. He peered inside. Nothing-nada-zilch – completely empty. Perhaps he *was* going mad!

A couple of minutes later – Tom time line – and roughly two and a bit hours later – Smokowski time, it was Smokowski's turn to poke a wary head around the storeroom door. Darren was alone. Smokowski turned and gave Tom the old thumbs up and went into the shop.

Darren, who had been busy doing nothing the past couple of hours, looked up from whatever it was he was doing as the storeroom door clicked closed.

'How're we doing?' asked Smokowski, as he took his apron from the back of the door.

'Just fine,' said Darren, a strange look on his face, something between worry and perplexity, 'if you count the only customer of the day being driven to drink and your assistant seeing things as fine.'

'Did he buy anything?' asked Smokowski, deftly avoiding the other issue.

'No.'

'Only customer you say?' said Smokowski, suspicions aroused, his attention seeking the front door and the sign hanging from it.

'It's Thursday,' said Darren quickly, as his eyes followed Smokowski, 'wasn't busy'.

'Thought you said it was Monday?'

'Shall I put the kettle on?'

'Capital idea,' said Smokowski, 'and while you're about it, I'll turn the sign on the door to open.'

Darren headed for the storeroom, huffing as he went. The man had deliberately ignored his mention of seeing things. How dare he keep him out of the loop, he was a king for goodness sake, and it wasn't as if he didn't know about Tom and his travelling. He would have a chat with Tom later and sort things out. In the meantime he thought it wise to keep his head down and make with the tea toot-sweet.

Smokowski watched Darren go with a wry smile on his lips. So he had seen the early arrival had he? Best keep what's going on, on a need to know basis for the moment though. As for the lack of takings, he would take that up with Tom later – Darren working in the shop was his idea after all. Still smiling, Smokowski turned the sign round, unlocked the door and opened it, all the while blissfully unaware of what was waiting for him on the other side.

CHAPTER 15

There was a tentative knock on the door. The knocker of the door was new to their job.

'Come in.'

The door opened, but the knocker of the door didn't – he had heard stories – met people who had been injured.

'Well?' asked a voice from within the very dark room.

'I've been told to tell you that he is on the job,' replied the person standing in the doorway.

'Good. And does she suspect?'

'We don't think so.'

'Ah.'

'Sir?'

The owner of the voice in the dark room sighed, why did he bother? Did no one listen? 'Yes.'

'Will that be all?'

'Have you anything else to tell me?'

'No I don't…'

'Then, if I were you, I'd stop dithering betwixt and between and shut the door behind you before you let the dark out.'

The door was quickly and quietly closed.

CHAPTER 16

Brandy's perfume wasn't of the cheap persuasion, but it was certainly lacking in subtlety. As a coughing Tom could attest to, as he staggered from his bathroom where the portable loo had deposited them after dropping Smokowski off at the shop. But it wasn't only the headiness of Brandy's perfume that had him a staggering – her inane constant nattering had contributed a large part to his present condition too. He just hoped, to whichever deity that happened to be closest, as he made for the kitchen, that it wasn't the norm for Brandy – that she was just overcome by first day nerves, excitement, or something. He doubted he could handle her if it wasn't. A strong cuppa was way overdue.

Half a cup of good old char later, Tom started to relax a little. Add to that the relative quiet coming from Brandy's corner of the room as she sipped at hers, and things were starting to look sort of normal again – or as normal as it could be in the world Tom now inhabited. But that didn't mean Tom had accepted the day's events thus far – far from it. Tom had questions, ones he hoped Brandy might be able to answer. Cat had given an explanation, but it had all sounded a little sketchy. He wanted to know more.

'So,' said Tom, in that matter of fact, man about town, suave sophisticated gentlemen of action air, all men thought they possessed when in the presence of an attractive woman – any woman.

But before he could lay on the charm any thicker or sound and look even more ridiculous, Brandy cut in. 'Cat said you were silly,' she giggled.

'What?' said Tom, poise slipping.

'No,' said Brandy, putting a finger to her lips, 'I mustn't say more.' And before Tom could say more she turned her attention to the cup in her hand and tutted, 'Where are all the tea leaves?' she asked, staring into the cup.

'There aren't any,' said Tom, brow furrowed, wondering how the conversation had swung so, 'I used bags.'

'Then how am I going to tell our future?' said a pouting Brandy.

Not a bimbo, thought Tom, but definitely blonde – a blonde-blonde. Tom was not being sexist here, not politically incorrect, or any of the above that lurked waiting for the unwary, he was just making a personal observation. He himself at times experienced blonde moments, or in his case, grey ones. But putting those thoughts aside, he thought he now saw an opportunity to get back on track, while her mind was on other things, and ask those questions.

'About Cat,' said Tom, diving in. He wanted answers. He wanted them now. He wanted... He... He was staring at Brandy's eyes. He hadn't noticed her eyes before. Were they blue? Yes blue, but more than just blue, deep blue like the ocean, azure like a clear, deep blue sky. No, they were more than that, they were electric, they were...

'Tom?'

'Eh?' said Tom. 'Oh,' said Tom, as the tea he didn't realise he had been spilling, now seeped through his trousers.

'Your tea, Tom,' giggled Brandy, 'it looks as if you have had a little accident.'

Tom grabbed for a tea towel. What was he doing? What had he been thinking? Get a grip man. He placed his cup on the drainer and started to dab at his trousers.

'Let me get that for you?' said Brandy, finding everything Cat had told her to expect where Tom was concerned, dead on the money.

'You what?' said Tom, suddenly frozen to the spot.

Brandy, a couple of sheets of kitchen roll in her hand, left her seat and headed for Tom. 'The floor, there's a small puddle of tea on it. It's dangerous you know, when it gets wet.' She fluttered those eyelashes at him again.

'Oh – yes,' said Tom, rubbing away like a mad man. His neck felt hot. Why did his neck feel hot? Maybe he should open a window.

'You'll make a hole,' said Brandy.

Tom instantly stopped his rubbing. Grief, he thought as Brandy wiggled her way to the waste bin to throw away her tea sodden tissue paper, working with her is going to be hard work. He threw the tea towel onto the worktop, sat at the kitchen table and tried to ignore the damp patch at the top of his leg.

'So,' said Brandy, taking a seat opposite Tom, 'perhaps we should think about the mission we've been set.'

If only it was that easy, thought Tom. Why did she have to wiggle like that? And those eyes and lips and…

'Tom?'

Tom sat up; he wished Cat was there, but she wasn't. He would just have to pull himself together. She was just a woman; like any other woman. But she wasn't, she was a familiar. Did that mean she wasn't human? There was a sobering thought, perhaps he should hang onto it? 'Mission?' said Tom, hanging onto the thought like it was a life-belt.

'Did Cat tell you anything about it?'

It was working. 'No,' said Tom, regaining a little of his old self, 'She said she hadn't been privy to it, said you'd know the ins and outs.' Perhaps it best to hang fire on trying to find out more about Cat – find a moment later.

Across the table, Brandy was smiling at him, her lashes fluttering.

Across the other side Tom waited.

Brandy inspected her nails.

Tom started to wonder if he should say something.

'Oh,' said Brandy suddenly, as if Tom had just popped up in front of her. 'Sorry, I was miles away, do you like my nails?'

'Lovely,' said Tom, not really looking.

'Cost a fortune you know. Now, where were we?' Brandy tilted her head, thinking. 'Ah yes, the mission, did Cat say anything to you about it?'

Tom couldn't believe his ears and was just about to embark on some serious eye rolling when Brandy giggled.

'Only joking,' she said, 'Cat said you were a little...'

'A little what?' said Tom, about to get on the nearest high horse.

'Impatient,' said Brandy, smiling, and lying. She gave her nails a quick glance. 'We've got to visit some artist inventor fella.'

Tom was fuming. Was she playing with him? If so, why? Or was it her way of sounding him out – testing the water. Funny old sticks those intelligence people. Perhaps she wasn't so blonde after all. But how did he know? Still, at least they were getting somewhere.

'Do we know which one?'

'De Kaprio,' said Brandy, finger on chin, 'I think.'

The name rang a bell with Tom, but where had he heard the name before? Ah, he thought, as recollection rang that same bell. Wasn't that the name of a horse he had had a bob or two on or… was it the name of some actor? Hadn't Darren been watching one of his films the other night? But something didn't ring right.

'You sure you got the name right?' asked Tom.

Brandy took on the look of the constipated as she took a moment to cogitate. 'I'm sure it is,' she said, 'it definitely started with an L.'

'An *L*?' said Tom. Another bell rang. 'Wouldn't be Leonardo you're thinking of by any chance would it?'

'That's it,' grinned Brandy, her face lighting up, 'I knew I knew it.'

'And I think he's called Da Vinci, Leonardo Da Vinci,' said Tom.

'Is he?' said Brandy, all wide eyed. 'You are clever.'

Tom's eyes did the opposite, narrowing just slightly. Had she done it again – tested him somehow? He was beginning to think the blonde thing was just an act. Had Cat said what Brandy's speciality was? He couldn't remember. But she had to have some tricks up her sleeve or she wouldn't be allowed the job of familiar, or in intelligence for that matter. Perhaps she was a master wind-up merchant?

'So why have we got to go pay Mister Da Vinci a visit?' said Tom. Did he really just say he was going to visit Da Vinci?

'Well,' said Brandy, leaning forward, 'rumour has it, he's doing a lot more now than ever he did, if you get my drift?'

Tom certainly had, and he'd had to divert his eyes pretty sharpish to stop them bulging. 'What do you mean?' he asked, while wilfully staring at the table.

'Something is not tickety-boo down there in De-'

'Da.'

'-Dakaprioland.'

'Da Vinci land.'

'Yes, records of his achievements are growing each day. New theories of his are appearing in documentation. New paintings are being discovered, some are changing. We have to find out what is going on back there and if we can, stop it and put things right before it starts to affect the world in other more dangerous ways. It's an urgent one.'

'How can paintings change?' said Tom.

'All things can change Tom, can be tampered with if you can travel in time – even you.'

Tom didn't like the sound of that one bit, being tampered with, but he understood what she meant, he'd had experience, but not much. 'But how do we know if something's changed, if it's changed in the past?'

'You are new aren't you?' said Brandy, smiling. 'The punters don't.'

'The punters?'

'Ordinary people, but the ripples of change can be felt if you know what you're doing and what to look for. You'll catch on in time.'

Was she being ironic? Tom wasn't sure. 'Will I?'

'Certainly.'

Tom thought he would have to take her word for that. 'So we have to pay Leonardo Da Vinci a call then and see what he's been up to?'

'That's about it.'

'So where and when do we find him?'

Brandy stared at Tom as if he had dropped a silent one. 'That's your job. I'm the pretty one in this partnership.' She put her elbows on the table, steepled her fingers, rested her chin on them and fluttered those lashes.

'Better get to work then,' said Tom, standing, 'if it's as urgent as you say.'

'Can we do something first though?' said Brandy, smiling her most innocent smile.

'What?' said Tom, bracing himself.

'Can we pick up my magazine first, only it comes out today and it's *so* very popular, I would just hate to miss it.'

Urgency forgotten for the moment, a relieved Tom readily agreed. It was only a magazine after all.

CHAPTER 17

That was easy, thought Cat, as she arrived home after escaping the halls of justice. Home being a secret room, which lay undiscovered – not counting Cat – deep beneath one of the great Egyptian pyramids. She sat and took stock. Maybe a little too easy for her liking. More fuel for her idea that all was not as it appeared. But before she could get stuck into finding out just exactly what was going on, there was a little job near at hand that needed her immediate attention.

'Okay,' said Cat, 'you can come out now. I know there's someone here.'

The tomb, for that was what Cat's home was, stayed as quiet as it should do.

'I won't ask again,' Cat warned.

The room stayed silent.

'Okay,' said Cat, 'but don't say I didn't warn you.' Those words said, a small carton started to magically rise into the air from atop a welsh dresser – Cat was a collector of many things – then slowly drifted across the room. It came to a stop a few feet from the ground, a few feet to Cat's left and started to tip its contents onto the floor below.

At first the silence of before continued – then a sudden rush of expletives, that would have had an old seadog red with embarrassment, reverberated from the tomb's walls. Cat let the carton fall. But it didn't drop to the floor. Instead it appeared to hover in midair about three inches from it.

'Ow!' said someone yet unseen, 'Add insult to injury, why don't yer.' The carton now flew across the room. 'It's given me a paper cut on me head, right near me bruise.'

'How are you enjoying the itching powder?' said Cat, smiling.

'What are you, a child? Flipping itching powder, it's below the belt.'

'I hope so,' said Cat.

The voice changed tone. 'How did yer know?'

'I felt a cold chill run up my spine.'

'Drat,' said the unseen interloper, 'Knew I was waiting around too long.'

'I should see someone about that if I was you.'

'Comes with the territory, being cold an' all.'

'And now that we have been partially acquainted, I have a few questions for you,' said Cat, no longer sporting a smile. 'I'll start by asking you who you are, let's make it a formal acquaintance?'

The room would have returned to its former silence but for the sound of someone scratching.

'Cat got your tongue?' said Cat.

Now there was the sound of a hurried movement.

'Oh no you don't,' said Cat, waving a paw.

A sudden yell of pain, accompanied by the whack of bare flesh against hard floor was followed by the noise of something metallic rolling towards Cat. As it reached her, it rose in the air and headed for a sterilization unit Cat kept for such events.

'Not fair,' groaned the unseen interloper, who was now rubbing as well as itching bodily parts.

'Now can we talk?' said Cat.

'Never!' yelled the unseen interloper, suddenly making with the fast movement of tiny feet.

Cat sighed and did another wave of the paw. This time an empty pickle jar took to the air. It flew banked, swooped low and engaged its target. There was a scream.

'No!' screamed the unseen interloper as the floor was taken from him. But there was nothing he could do.

Job done, the jar gently landed upright on the floor. Cat ambled over to it and peered in. It appeared empty, but Cat knew otherwise.

'You ready to talk yet?' said Cat, to apparently nothing.

'Let me out?'

'If I do, will you talk?'

'I might.'

'I could always fill the jar to halfway with iced water,' said Cat.

'What sort of fiend are you?'

'Do we have a deal?'

The jar was quiet for a moment. 'Oh, okay then, but I know me rights, the Geneva convention and all that.'

'Okay,' said Cat, who wasn't as naïve as the jar's invisible occupant hoped she was. 'But first.' A small pot accompanied by a sachet of liquid, which had been quietly hovering out of sight now came into play. Each emptied their contents into the jar.

'Unfair,' yelled the jar's invisible occupant as glitter and lurid purple body paint enveloped him.

'Just a little bit of a shake, there, all done. Good grief man, you're naked, turn around!' Cat averted her eyes.

The jar's occupant did some quick covering. 'Told you – comes with the territory.'

'Here, put these on.' A set of clothes from Cat's collection of Victorian dolls arrived in the jar.

The jar's occupant glared at the clothes, but put them on. 'It's torture, that's what it is,' he complained.

Cat laughed as her gaze returned to the jar, she couldn't help herself. It wasn't often one saw a three and a bit inch tall, purple painted, glitter encrusted man, dressed in a Victorian pageboy outfit.

Now visible, the tiny man was tipped from the pickle jar. He sat for a moment, getting his bearings before scrambling to his feet. He stood there, looking at his hands. 'I hope this stuff comes off,' he said, rubbing them together to see if it had any effect; it didn't. The little man grumbled under his breath.

'Don't worry,' said Cat, a huge smile on her face, 'I'll get rid of it for you *Bob,* as soon as you spill some beans.' The flinch was slight, but there as she mentioned the small man's name.

Her hunch proved right. He was known as Invisible Bob – for obvious reasons. She had heard tell of him. A failed familiar because of the accidents – the Travellers kept tripping over him and leaving him behind amongst other things – he had joined the ranks of the BIMBO's – a job he took to like a duck to orange, again for obvious reasons. An invisible man was worth his weight in gold to the intelligence corps, especially one so small.

The small man stared up at Cat; it would appear the game was up. 'You know who I am?'

'I wasn't sure until I said your name.'

'Gave it away, eh? Wouldn't have happened if I'd still been invisible.'

'Well?' said Cat.

'Well what?' said Invisible Bob.

'Are you going to tell me why you were following me?'

Bob gave this some thought. Why not? His cover was blown, he wasn't going anywhere and he didn't know. 'I don't know,' said Invisible Bob.

Cat sniffed the air and narrowed her eyes. She could usually smell a liar a mile off – literally. Bob though wasn't lying. That was strange, she thought. Or was he? Perhaps the gift of invisibility wasn't the only talent the little man possessed. Perhaps his mind and body complimented each other – one you could see through, the other you couldn't. The jar started to rise.

Bob saw it and started to back away. He hated confinement – he was purposely early as a baby. 'It's the truth, I tell you,' he said, his gaze never leaving the jar.

The jar lowered. Cat was ready to believe him.

'Okay,' said Cat, gearing up her next question, 'say I believe you, who sent you?'

Ah, thought Invisible Bob, this was going to be difficult – wasn't going to sound good. 'I don't know that either,' he admitted. He was right, it didn't sound good.

The jar started to hover. 'So you don't know why and you don't know who?' said Cat, picking up confused signals.

The little man was suddenly feeling uneasy; he was in a tricky situation. He realised he was in the field agent's worst case scenario; nowhere to run and no one to vouch for you. If Cat stopped believing him, he could be in big trouble. Eying the jar nervously, Invisible Bob decided to come clean – as was possible.

'I was called to a dark room and met someone who told me to tail you and report back at intervals with what I saw, but I'm afraid I'm confused about who it was I met, but I could tell you who I thought it was,' said Invisible Bob, hardly able to believe he had caved in so easily.

'No need,' said Cat, a rough idea forming in her mind as to who that someone might be and allowing Invisible Bob a sliver of face saving into the bargain. So, she thought, I *am* being played, but why? She mused on the idea of the dark room. She had heard rumours of one; a place purported to be the centre of operations for all involved with time travel. But she had never, until now, had any reason or need to find out if such a place did exist. If it does though, it means she has been set up at the highest level, which could only mean...

'So, I've been set up,' said Cat.

'Don't know about that,' said Invisible Bob, who didn't.

'And I suppose you don't know why,' said Cat.

Invisible Bob shrugged tiny shoulders. 'Not officially like,' he said, 'but might have heard something on the QT. Could be nothing.'

'Try me,' said Cat.

'There was a ripple,' said Invisible Bob.

'And?' said Cat, unperturbed by Invisible Bob's disclosure, as ripples were always happening. That's how the familiars knew there was a problem somewhere in time.

'But this one was different,' said Invisible Bob, lowering his voice, 'No one felt it.'

'Impossible,' said Cat, 'I would have felt it, even the slightest of ones.' But she knew, as incredible as it sounded, Invisible Bob was telling the truth.

'But you didn't, *did* you,' said Invisible Bob, 'and from what I hear, that's what's got the boys at the top in such a tizz. You never miss one. Got them worried.'

Cat was suddenly aghast. 'Are you saying someone thinks I had something to do with it not being reported?'

'Like I said,' said Invisible Bob, looking at his feet, 'I know nothin'.'

The very idea of her not being trusted was like a sledgehammer blow in the guts, but even as she reeled from the thought another struck her. 'But how does anyone know about it if it didn't register?' she asked.

'Gawd knows,' said Invisible Bob, shrugging those little shoulders again.

Cat's brain suddenly started to whirr as she played everything through her mind. Moments later she had come up with the only two scenarios that made sense. The first had everyone that matters thinking she had something to do with it, the real reason for wanting her locked up, using a jumped up charge as an excuse to lock her up without worrying everyone with the truth. The second one had them hoping that if they could somehow peak her well known curiosity it would get the better of her and she would try and find out what was going on for them. But which made more sense? Perhaps she was clutching at straws? Perhaps it was nothing to do with a ripple; could just be hearsay. But a new feeling was clawing at her guts that something about it rang right. She needed to think harder and the best way for her to do that, when she needed serious concentration, was when she was at her most relaxed – when she was asleep. Leaving Invisible Bob to his own devices – he wasn't going anywhere, Cat leapt onto the welsh dresser and curled up to think.

Less than five minutes later, Cat woke up, problem not solved, but a darn sight clearer. If those that mattered really thought she had something to do with a rogue ripple, if that is what all this is about, she wouldn't be away and free to think about it. Even they wouldn't be stupid enough to hope that if she was guilty, she would lead them to whatever it was she was up to. No, that would be crass stupidity, too dangerous. It had too many holes in it. So that left scenario two. She cocked an eye at Invisible Bob who was busy falling backwards over an old Zulu spear Cat had collected. Perfect, she thought, send someone to watch her, knowing full well they would be caught, and better still, carrying nothing in the way of knowledge – except for a whiff of a rumour to hand as a hint of what was going on. All the time using the court case to cover their tracks so no one outside of those that knew, knew that Cat was on the prowl and looking for answers. And at the same time, keeping their hands well and truly clean. If she was right, she had to hand it to the old codgers, they certainly knew what they were doing when it came down to underhand shenanigans. The only doubt – were they really that clever? Only one way to find out. Cat decided it was time to move, but she had a problem; what to do about the little guy? A little guy who was now dangling from the tip of the Zulu spear he had fallen over. What could she do?

There wasn't a lot of choice really. So, working on the adage of, "keep your friends close and the idiots even closer", and who knows, he *might* even prove useful, Cat unhooked him, spelled him clean and then allowed an invisible again Bob to climb on her back. It was time to find out just what was going on. First though, before she got her paws dirty, there was something she wanted to do and to do it, she would need some help.

CHAPTER 18

Tom was a little confused, which wouldn't have surprised anyone who knew him. Brandy had wanted a magazine, one he knew Smokowski stocked, because Katie, his granddaughter bought it from there, so that is where he thought they would be going after he mentioned it. It was closest after all, but no, Brandy had wanted to pick it up from her usual shop. And where was that shop? Miles away, that's where. But, as she had pointed out, as they were going to get there in a blink of an eye anyway whichever shop they went to, did it really matter? No, not really, but *what* was with the queue? Surely the magazine wasn't that popular. He popped his head out of it and noted the front didn't appear to be getting any shorter and behind him it was now noticeably longer. Head popping back again, Tom thought he would broach the question of the magazine's popularity.

'Popular this magazine then?' said Tom.

'Magazine?' said Brandy, all of a twitter.

Tom had never seen anyone getting so excited about a glam rag. 'Something free with it is there?' said Tom, not knowing of anything more exciting than getting something for free.

'Oh, the magazine,' said Brandy, standing on tiptoe to see if she could see the front of the store yet, 'we'll get that when we're finished.'

Finished? Finished doing what? thought Tom. Should he ask? Maybe it's some sort of competition – who can queue the longest. He was going to ask. 'Finished what?' asked Tom.

Brandy turned and gave Tom the sort of look that questioned his sanity.

Tom shrivelled a little under her gaze. 'I was only asking,' said he.

Brandy's features softened a little. 'Sorry, look, once I've got my book signed, we'll grab the mag and hightail it out of here. Promise.'

She rose on tippy toe again. 'Shouldn't be much longer now, looks like something's moving up front.'

Book? Colourful confusion turned to equally colourful puzzlement, then mixed, and rolled, and fused together and turned into a small brown mess inside Tom's brain. 'But you haven't got a book,' he said, attaining observational mastery.

Brandy looked down at Tom as a mother would a child as it tried unsuccessfully to understand the simplest of tasks. 'That's because no one has brought one out yet,' she explained, in that most patient of ways only a mother can achieve. Yet the hands she placed on hips when she returned her attention to the front of the queue displayed a distinct lack of that patience. 'What's keeping them?' she said.

Tom didn't know. Tom felt he was in the dark about a lot of things just lately. Tom supposed all would be revealed in good time. Tom jumped as Brandy suddenly let out an ear piercing squeal.

'It's here – it's here,' squealed Brandy, gripping Tom's right arm with both hands.

'What is – what is?' squealed Tom, as the feeling in his right hand started to drain from it.

'Oh!' squealed Brandy, now jumping up and down on the spot.

'Oo – Ow!' moaned Tom, as he shook like a rag doll in Brandy's grasp.

Brandy, excitement growing to fever pitch as the trolley bearing books she had spotted drew closer, squeezed on Tom's arm even tighter. 'What shall I ask him to write? Oh, gosh, I'm all shaky. Are you shaky?'

Tom was, and on the verge of losing consciousness, or so he would have anyone that asked believe, but still he managed to wriggle free of Brandy's mauling mitts. 'Who?' he asked, briskly rubbing feeling into his arm and hand and not really in the least bit interested in *who* that who might be.

'Leslie Poppett,' said Brandy, fairly dribbling over the name. 'Got to be something cool.'

'Leslie who?' asked Tom, wondering why he was bothering to ask and putting it down to the blood that hadn't been going to his hand, clogging up his brain.

Brandy, who had calmed down enough to rummage in her handbag, started at Tom's question and looked at him as if he had just arrived on the blue moon special from outer space. 'You... you haven't heard of Leslie Poppett?' Tom shook his head. Still in dumbstruck mode, Brandy continued. 'You must have.' Another head shake from Tom. 'But he's famous, he... he's world famous.'

'What did he do?' said Tom, chancing Brandy's ire.

Brandy looked fit to emotionally burst. 'What did he do? What doesn't he do?' She hugged her handbag to her bosom, her eyes glazing over. 'Oh Tom, if only you knew. He's an actor Tom, a supermodel, a romantic novelist, an artist, a poet, a dancer, a lover, a meteorologist, a world renowned horticulturist.' She looked at Tom, her eyes full of the pity she saved for the hopelessly ignorant. 'Need I say more, Tom, need I really say more?'

No, thought Tom, who had had more than enough already thank you very much. But before he could think up a way of tactfully saying that, a voice took Brandy's attention away from him.

'Book, madam?' enquired a spotty faced, lank haired youth, pushing a trolley.

'Two please,' said Brandy, Tom and his ignorance now forgotten as she reached for her holy grail – grails.

'For you and your... um,' said the youth, trying to be tactful, you just never knew with relationships.

'No, I don't want one for my *um*, they're both for me.'

'Sorry madam, but only one per customer I'm afraid; policy.'

I'll policy his... But thankfully, Brandy maintained control of her emotions. 'How much?' she asked, teeth not quite clenching.

'Seventeen ninety-nine please,' said the youth, holding out a sweaty palm.

'Tom?'

'Yes?' said Tom, who had been temporarily mesmerised by the youth's spots and was idly wondering what would appear if you joined them up.

'Can you pay this dear sweet man,' said Brandy, snatching her book, 'I seem to have come out without any wonga.'

'Wong-what?' said Tom. The youth's sweaty palm was now thrust under Tom's nose. 'But...'

'Seventeen ninety-nine please,' said the youth, eager to move on.

Grief, thought Tom, glancing at Brandy, hoping to plead, but she was away in her own little world, book lovingly held in her arms. Drat. With shaking hand Tom delved into one of his deep pockets and removed his wallet. He took from it a crisp, barely seen the light of day, twenty squid note. Daylight robbery, thought Tom. 'Gold leaf is it?' he asked, as the youth took the money.

The youth gave Tom a blank stare. 'No,' he said, 'hardback.' He then took a notelet from a pad on the trolley and handed it to Tom. 'Make sure your granddaughter puts down exactly what dedication she wants Mister Poppett to write in her book before handing it to him.' With policy covered, the youth moved on.

A speechless Tom stared after him. The cheeky little… granddaughter indeed! He looked at the change in his hand, two British squid and a penny tiddler. Blooming daylight robbery; be half the price, come Christmas.

'We're moving,' squealed Brandy, as the queue did just that.

Tom, still bemoaning the assault on his wallet, shuffled along with it. 'This is yours I believe,' he said, handing Brandy the notelet.

'Ooh yes, ta,' said Brandy, whisking it from Tom, 'Don't suppose you've got a pen?'

'No I haven't,' said Tom, a tad testily. What did she think he was, a packhorse?

'Never mind,' said Brandy, ignoring Tom's tone, 'I think I've got one, here hold on to my book.' She popped two fingers down her top and fished around. Tom looked away. 'Ah-ha! Thought I had one somewhere,' she said, producing what she was searching for. 'Here Tom, look at this.' Tom was afraid to, but did anyway. 'It flashes and plays a tune when you write with it.' A smiling Brandy brandished her pen in front of Tom's nose. 'I hope he likes it.'

I'm sure he'll love it, thought Tom. The queue shuffled forward again, Tom with it. When it stopped again, he gave the cover of the book a cursory glance and wondered what it was about. He read the title "Lovey Dovey". No, don't go there, he thought, don't want to know. He should give it back really, it was quite heavy for one thing, but when he looked up Brandy was busy scribbling on the notelet, instead he sighed and idly opened it.

'Never gave them his real name you know.'

'Sorry?' said Tom.

'The publishers,' said Brandy, free to harass Tom again as she had finished with her scribbling. 'He was already famous as a horticulturist you see, and actor of considerable ability, and a model and his doctoring was well documented, so he wanted to be appraised on his talent, not his name.'

That's a new one, thought Tom. 'What did he doctor?' he asked, intrigued.

'People, silly,' said Brandy.

'Ah,' said Tom.

'There are some people you know,' said Brandy, 'as there always is, who say that it's all so much bullshit, him not telling them, you know, the publishers. I personally think he's above that.'

Yeah right, thought Tom, ever the cynic. He cast a perusing eye over the published by page and paused when he read the part about not doing things without the author's permission. That's strange, he thought, reading the author's name. Harold Scratch? Leslie Poppett must be a pseudonym. 'Not his real name then, Poppett,' said Tom.

'Course it is,' said Brandy.

'Who's this then?' said Tom.

Brandy took the book from Tom and stared at the page he had been reading. 'Who, where?' said Brandy.

'Here,' said Tom, pointing.

'Oh him, that's the author,' said Brandy, jiggling her head, amused. 'Leslie is far too busy with other things to have time to write, he has the ideas see.'

Tom was flabbergasted. How did the public put up with such goings on? And then have it flaunted in their faces? Now Tom couldn't wait to see this Poppett character, see what sort of person openly accepts the plaudits for someone else's work. Tom's gander was well and truly up. He despised people like this. Worse than overpaid telly presenters, they were. Can't be happy doing one thing, oh no, they have to have their podgy little fingers in every pie going. Chase the fame, that was their little game, flaming so called *celebs* clogging up the works. This is what Tom thought. He was most upset.

'Tom?' said Brandy, looking concerned, 'You all right – you've gone a funny colour?'

CHAPTER 19

'Waa!' wailed Mister Smokowski in surprise.

'Waa, to you too,' said Cat, who was sat on the welcome mat that sat just outside the shop entrance, 'but good timing Mister Smokowski, may I come in?'

'Catranna,' said Smokowski, recovering from his shock, 'what are you doing here?'

'Well that's a nice way to greet an old friend,' smiled Cat, squeezing through Smokowski's legs.

'I'm sorry, I mean...'

'It's okay, I'm joking,' said Cat, springing onto a stool behind the counter. 'Wait!'

Smokowski instantly froze mid door closing.

'You in?' said Cat.

'What?' said a confused Smokowski.

'Yeah,' said a voice somewhere near Smokowski's feet.

'You can shut the door now Mister Smokowski,' said Cat, lifting a back paw to her mouth.

A puzzled Smokowski did as he was asked.

'And you had better lock it too.'

Smokowski locked the door and turned the closed sign to face outside. As he did the storeroom door opened.

'Waa!' said Darren, when he saw Cat, the contents of the two mugs of tea in his hands swilling, but thankfully not spilling.

'Hi Darren,' said Cat.

'That him?' asked a voice from somewhere.

'It certainly is,' confirmed Cat.

'Don't look much of a king does he?'

'Okay,' said Smokowski, peering at the floor, 'what's going on?'

Darren handed Smokowski his tea.

'Got one for a thirsty amigo?'

'Who said that?' said Darren.

'Cat?'

'Mister Smokowski, Darren, meet Invisible Bob.'

Invisible Bob took a bow for all not to see.

'Where is he?' said Smokowski.

'Where are you?' said Cat.

'Down here,' said Invisible Bob, waving. No one saw.

'Where's Tom?' said Darren, peering over the counter at the floor.

'You've not told him then,' said Cat.

'Told me what?' said Darren.

'I thought you were in court,' said Smokowski.

'I was,' said Cat, 'I'm also supposed to be behind bars.'

'They found you guilty?' gasped Smokowski.

'Who did?' said Darren, desperately out of the loop.

'Then banishment.'

'That's ridiculous,' said Smokowski.

'But true,' said Invisible Bob.

'Mister Smokowski?'

'Not now Darren,' said Smokowski, keen to hear more of what Cat had to say.

And Cat didn't disappoint. The story was told.

Afterwards Smokowski was flummoxed.

Darren was still mystified.

Cat was brooding.

And invisible Bob was, well, still invisible.

'So what are you going to do now?' said Smokowski.

'The only thing I can do,' said Cat, 'find out what is true and what isn't.'

'And you think this ripple exists?'

'I don't know, but if it does I need to find out what caused it.'

'Throws up a disturbing fact though, don't it,' said Smokowski.

'It sure does,' agreed Cat.

'What does?' said Darren, trying, yet failing miserably, to keep up.

'That no one at the top knows who they can trust,' said Cat, 'of which I'm included, hence the BIMBO tail.' Cat suddenly stretched her neck. 'Talking of which, where is my little invisible friend?'

'What's that noise?' said Darren.

'It's coming from the pick and mix,' said Smokowski, he too taking a turn at the neck stretching. He went to investigate. 'Grief!' exclaimed Smokowski when he arrived.

'What is it?' said Cat.

'He's in with the chocolate covered peanuts.'

'Bob?' said Cat, arriving beside Smokowski.

There came a muffled reply that sounded like someone trying to say hungry, but couldn't because their mouth was too full.

'Begad,' said Darren, getting his centuries mixed up, 'it's sorcery.'

And so it could well have been, as they watched a chocolate covered peanut disappear bite by bite into thin air – but it wasn't.

'Oh no,' groaned Smokowski as he remembered what Cat had told him, 'he's naked in there, isn't he?'

'Sorry Smokowski,' said Cat, grimacing.

'The stock,' wailed Smokowski.

'Will it shut?' said Cat, looking at the Perspex flap Invisible Bob had climbed through.

'There's a latch,' said Darren, who had familiarised himself with certain aspects of stock control while Smokowski was away.

'Good, shut him in.'

'But the stock?'

'*Really?*' said Cat.

Perhaps not, thought Smokowski, already reeling from a so far unproductive day. With heavy heart, Smokowski turned the latch.

'Is it secure?' said Cat.

'I suppose,' said Smokowski.

'Good, at least we'll know where he is,' said Cat. 'Now, sit down, I've got something important to ask you.'

CHAPTER 20

A harassed, dazed Tom stumbled from the shop, a book called "Lovey Dovey" tucked under his arm.

'Wasn't he lovely?' oozed Brandy, cuddling her book to her as if it was Poppett himself.

'Was he?' muttered Tom, wondering what the heck had just happened.

'Those gorgeous eyes and that tanned body,' fawned Brandy.

What Tom remembered was finally getting to the door, then the sudden surge, which was caused mostly by Brandy, followed by having to fork out another exorbitant amount for a book as you couldn't see Poppett without one, which he didn't want to do, and from which he didn't get any change as another surge had swept him away, and then there he was, the Adonis adored, standing in front of him, all bright white teeth, slicked back black hair, less than five foot tall, wearing gardening gloves and an orange suit that clashed violently with his skin tone – bottle bronze.

Tom at first sight had thought someone was pulling a fast one and what he was seeing was an orang-utan, but then the man spoke, asked for Tom's notelet, scribbled something in the book Tom didn't want, flashed a smile, and asked for the next admirer to step forward. Tom couldn't even remember getting a notelet, let alone writing something on it.

'What's yours say?' said Brandy, grabbing at Tom's book.

'I don't know,' said Tom.

'Give it here.' Brandy took Tom's book from him, opened it and read the hand written dedication. 'To my friend *Grants Notelet Company*, kind regards Leslie.' Brandy frowned and handed the book back to Tom. 'That's weird, why did you want him to write that?'

'Thought I'd be different,' said Tom, wondering at the insanity of it all.

'Well it's boring, mine's much better, here read it.' Brandy handed her copy to Tom.

With heavy heart, Tom opened it. He read it. He went to hand it back.

'Aloud,' said Brandy, 'I want to imagine him saying it to me.'

Tom screwed up his face and swallowed hard, did he have to? He supposed he had, if he wanted any peace. 'To Brandy,' a little cough, 'the most beautiful girl in the world and beyond, love and kisses, your prince, your servant, your everything, Leslie.'

'Don't forget the kisses.'

Tom reluctantly did three kissing sounds.

'Isn't it lovely,' said Brandy, all doe-eyed.

'But you wrote it,' said Tom, ever the romantic.

'Did not,' said Brandy, 'that's not my handwriting.'

'I meant on the note you gave him.'

'He's a very busy man; it's what he would have written. Besides I only wrote two kisses.' At this juncture Brandy snatched her book from Tom and gave him his back, winding him.

'Fair do's,' gasped Tom, more than happy to let the matter lie. 'Shall we head back to the loo now?'

'Why not,' said Brandy. 'Oh, hang about, I forgot to pick up my magazine. Be a love, I'll hold your book for you.'

Stunned by the sheer cheek of the woman, Tom wandered back into the shop. He found it, picked it up, joined another queue and realised how much he missed that darned cat. They had only been on one mission together, and had only known each other a short time, but darn it, there was a bond. She was his familiar and he was her Traveller; more than that they were friends. Tom bit on his bottom lip, he wished she were here now, on this mission. Without her he didn't have his heart in it. The queue moved a pace forward. Tom heaved a deep sigh. But he had to put all that aside, he was a Traveller, he had responsibilities; like it or not. He released his bottom lip and stiffened his top one. He had a job to do. He had a visit to make.

Cap first, Tom stuck his head from the loo into the room beyond. All was quiet. Would luck be on his side as it had before? He hoped so, especially as this time he didn't have Cat watching his back. He looked back at Brandy, she was holding up a small mirror, tending to an eyelash. Thank goodness she had stopped prattling on about that orange short-arsed jumped up gardener. Would she watch his back? He thought she would, it was her job. But it didn't stop him feeling he was on his own where this mission was concerned.

'Psst!' whispered Tom, attracting Brandy's attention, 'all clear.'

Brandy, perched on the shelf Cat usually laid on, snapped her compact shut, uncrossed her long tanned legs, straightened, what she called a skirt, and wiggled up beside Tom. 'That's good isn't it?' she said, trying to peep over Tom's shoulder.

She's winding me up, surely? thought Tom, rolling his eyes. But he was starting to get the feeling that whoever it was who had decided on the name of Brandy's department was secretly having a quiet laugh to themselves somewhere. Acronym, my aunt Bessie! He was also beginning to wonder if the whole BIMBO thing wasn't just an excuse to keep the less talented of the familiars out from under everyone's feet. He did expect Brandy to possess a talent, they all did, but he had the horrible feeling it might have something to do with hair products. No, he shouldn't be so mean. She'll probably do something that will make him choke on his own thoughts.

Feeling a tad guilty for thinking such things, Tom left the safety of the loo and stepped into the room, Brandy followed.

'Where are we?' said Brandy, as they moved across it towards a closed door.

'The men's toilets I hope,' answered Tom, glad his friends couldn't hear him say that. There had been a lot of things he had said, and done, lately that he hoped they would never hear of, or find out about.

They reached the door and Tom opened it. It led into a corridor.

'Should I be in here?' said Brandy, feigning horror.

Ignoring her Tom slipped silently into the corridor. 'Just follow me and keep quiet, I've been here before.'

'Lurking in men's toilets?' whispered Brandy, grinning behind Tom's back.

'No,' said Tom, lips tightening, 'Marc and Katie's school.' Perhaps he should have told her to wait for him in the loo?

Progressing slowly, but progressing all the same, and with only one "back as close to the wall and hold your breath moment" along the way, they duly arrived at the double doors that Tom knew would lead them outside, not far from where the grounds man's hut stood. And as it was Monday, the day the ground staff had their weekly area meeting up at the council offices, the coast would be clear.

Tom cautiously peeped through one of the door's windows. Was it Monday? That's the day his coach trip had been booked for. Strange day for a trip, Monday. Then he remembered, it was cheaper on a Monday. Good girl Lucy, thought Tom, like father like daughter, tight as a ducks... 'What're you doing?'

Brandy was wrist deep in her handbag and making a noise of it. 'Looking for my lippy, I can't find it.'

'Forget your lippy,' whispered Tom, glancing away down the corridor, sure someone would appear wondering what all the clamour was about. 'You won't need it here.'

The look Brandy gave him would have frozen Niagara Falls. 'Now look here, you might be happy going around looking like a tra... ah, here it is. Well most of it.'

If the look had not scared Tom half stiff he would have probably been wondering what it was she had been about to say, but as it was it went over his head. Tom made a mental note to self, never come between a woman and her condiments if you like being in one piece. He also made a note, that if ever they were in a tight spot and surrounded by nasty pieces of work, to goad them into saying something derogatory about her appearance – that should see them safe.

'There, what do you think?' said Brandy, all bright and breezy once again.

'Think?' said Tom, backing away from Brandy's advancing lips, and suddenly hoping her talent wasn't of the mind reading kind.

'The colour,' said Brandy, 'It's cherry cola with a twist. It's a one off, bespoke, made especially for moi, you like?'

'Lovely,' said Tom. Mad as a box of biscuits, he thought.

'Great,' said Brandy, popping lipstick and compact back in her bag. 'Shall we get going then?'

A more than happy to get on with things Tom pushed one of the double doors open, and after scouring the immediate area and deciding all was well, sidled outside. Keeping close to the wall he and Brandy made for a corner of the building they had just left. There they would have a clear view of the school playground.

'That's him,' whispered Tom, pointing Marc, his grandson, out to Brandy.

Brandy went to take a step forward.

'Wait,' said Tom, stopping her, 'he'll see you.'

'I thought that was the point,' said Brandy, looking puzzled.

'Yes... yes,' said Tom, 'but so will everyone else.'

'Ah, undercover, I like it undercover.'

'Yeah,' said Tom, not entirely sure what that meant, 'and we're not really supposed to be here. It's a school remember, we'll get into trouble if someone sees us.'

'What do we do now then?' said Brandy.

'I'll attract his attention.' Tom waited for the right moment and then waved for all he was worth. This went on for a little while.

'Hasn't he seen you yet?' said Brandy, who was killing time with a spot of on the spot manicuring.

'No, do you think I'd sti... drat.' Tom stopped his waving.

'What is it?' said Brandy, suddenly crouching low and adopting a stance only seen by the public in the very best of martial arts films. As she was behind Tom it went unnoticed by him, which was a shame. It might have put his mind at rest. Then again...

'Katie's talking to him.' Tom joined Brandy in the shadows of the building.

'What's he doing?' said Brandy, relaxing.

'How do I know,' said Tom, back flat to the wall, 'I'm hiding.'

'But shouldn't you be watching what happens?'

Everyone's a critic, thought Tom, but she was right. It was almost as if Cat was back – almost. Tom popped his head back around the corner. Marc was alone again and looking straight at him. Tom decided it needed both hands waving this time. 'He's coming.'

Thank goodness for that, thought Brandy, who had money on Tom doing himself a mischief had he carried on waving the way he was.

'What you doing here Granddad – aren't you supposed to be on a trip?' said Marc, arriving after a cautious mosey across the playground, 'And you know you're not allowed on school property.'

Brandy gave Tom a quizzical glance.

'It was cut short,' Tom said. He turned to Brandy. 'He means anyone, not just me.' Feeling obliged to explain.

'Oh,' said Brandy, making a play of sounding unconvinced, 'okay, if you say so.'

Tom scowled at her.

'Cor Granddad!' exclaimed Marc, spying Brandy for the first time, eyeballs on stalks, brain turning to mush, forgetting all about Tom's trip, 'who's yer lady friend?'

A clearly rattled Tom, who had clean forgotten to steer Brandy to the grounds man's hut where she could lay low, suddenly had to think fast. Think man, he thought. 'This is Brandy, she's… she's my home help,' said Tom, hoping his teeth would take the strain of him lying through them.

But Marc wasn't convinced and gave Brandy the once over. 'Looks more like an au pair,' he said, subconsciously running a hand through his hair. Looks like every schoolboy's fantasy has landed, was what he was thinking.

'Look,' said Tom, stepping between Marc and all the birthdays the lad thought had arrived at once, 'I need your help. I've entered a competition.' The excuse had worked before, so why not again, thought Tom, a big fan of tried and tested. Not that the boy would remember; it was another time.

But Marc wasn't listening, his mind was on other things as he tried to see past Tom.

Okay, thought Tom, only one thing for it. He didn't want to do it, it would hurt, but the lad was forcing his hand.

'There's a cash prize,' said Tom, biting the bullet, the pain flowing at the thought of his wallet taking another hit.

'What sort of competition?' said Marc, as if woken from a dream.

The last time Tom had answered that question it had caused problems – complications – it had been an off the cuff reply. This time he was ready. 'A book competition,' said Tom. There, much better than a gardening one. He was feeling confident.

'But you don't read. Mum says you're a bad example to us,' said Marc, deadly serious.

'Ah,' said Tom, squirming. Brandy giggled. Marc took the opportunity to try and catch another glance of Brandy.

'That's why I... I've entered it,' said Tom, endeavouring to redeem himself.

'Okay,' said Marc, giving up for the moment on the Brandy front, 'Say I can help, what's in it for me?'

'Satisfaction in helping your old Granddad?' ventured Tom.

Marc gave Tom the old sideways look.

Nothing changes, thought Tom, but at least I tried.

'A couple of squid sound okay?'

'Five?'

The pain was going to be worse than he thought. 'Deal,' said Tom, spitting on his hand and offering it to Marc.

'What do you want me to do?' said Marc, quickly folding his arms.

Wiping his hand on his trousers Tom told Marc what he wanted to know.

'That's an awful lot of questions about Da Vinci,' said Marc, looking doubtful. 'When do you need to know them by?'

'A-sap,' said Tom.

'A-what?'

'This afternoon?'

'I'll try, could ask to use one of the computers in afternoon break.' Marc's forehead acquired a couple of creases. 'How am I going to let you know what I find out if you need the answers this aftie?'

'Use your mobile,' said Tom.

Marc paled. 'You know Mum doesn't let me bring my phone to school.'

'I'll make it a tenner,' said Tom, making a mental note to find out if there was some way he could claim back today's expenditure.

'Done,' said Marc, 'but you won't tell Mum will you?' Tom vowed he wouldn't. Happy with that assurance Marc attempted one last look at Brandy, which failed, before turning tail and making with the quick skedaddle to join his sister before he was late.

'He's a good boy, our Marc,' said Tom, watching his grandson disappear.

'Sounds an expensive one to me,' said Brandy, smiling.

'He's an entrepreneur, that's all.'

'Can we go now?'

'Onwards and upwards,' said Tom.

CHAPTER 21

'You want me to what him?' stammered Smokowski, seriously taken aback by what was being asked of him.

'Tail him,' said Cat, repeating what she had just said.

'But why?' Then a horrible thought bubbled up in Smokowski's mind. 'Surely you don't think he's got anything to do with what's going on?'

'Don't be silly.'

'Then why?'

'I want to keep an eye on him, he could be in danger.'

'But he's got Brandy…' Another horrible thought, this one draining the colour from Smokowski's face. 'Grief Cat, surely you don't think Brandy might do something to him?'

'No, she's a BIMBO. I'm just afraid that if there is something going on and whoever's behind it discovers that I'm on the job, they might use him to get to me.'

'There's a lot of ifs and buts flying about there, Cat,' said Smokowski, wondering if perhaps she was overreacting.

'Better safe than sorry.'

'Then we should tell Brandy what we know.'

'Best not. If she suddenly goes on the defensive it might attract unwanted attention.'

'You think someone might be watching him, who?'

'I don't know, as you said, there are so many ifs and buts, but we can't go leaving things to chance, we need to cover all our bases.'

A thoughtful Smokowski picked up his tea, sipped at it and grimaced, it was tepid. 'Darren.'

Darren, who had long lost interest in trying to keep up with what Cat and Smokowski were going on about, was standing beside the pick and mix, mesmerised by the rapidly disappearing chocolate peanuts within. For a little chap he sure had a healthy appetite.

'Darren?'

'Yes.'

'Any chance of another?' said Smokowski, holding his cup aloft. 'I'm afraid I've let it go cold.'

'Right away,' said Darren, tearing himself away.

'And have one yourself, anything for you Cat?'

'I'm fine thanks,' said Cat, although chicken was never far from mind.

Darren took Smokowski's cup and headed for the storeroom. While he was out of the way, Cat – deciding it might be best for Darren to be kept on a need to know basis only – took the opportunity to tell Smokowski her plan for him and how he was to do it.

'A *hitchhiker*?' said Smokowski.

Cat went on to explain that the hitchhiker was how BIMBO's travelled through time if they weren't magical. Using it to snag the time stream wake left by a time machine, they were effectively dragged along for the ride. 'You can use Bob's; he won't be needing it for a while.'

'And you expect me to do that, be dragged through time?'

'It's not dangerous if used properly.'

'And if it's not used properly?'

'It's ninety-nine point nine percent safe. There's only ever been one accident,' said Cat.

'What happened?'

'We don't know, we haven't found him yet to ask.'

That was enough as far as Smokowski was concerned. He didn't mind giving the odd lift now and again, but travelling haphazardly through time, that was insane. 'I see,' said Smokowski, rising from the stool, 'but as tempting as you make it sound Cat, I'm afraid you'll have to excuse me this one, I've a shop to run. Here, in this time.'

Cat had half expected Smokowski's reaction, what sane person wouldn't baulk at such an idea, but she had also half hoped he might have said yes straight away, because she would now have to put her paw down, and firmly.

'I had hoped it wouldn't have come to this but, you are his aide – with the responsibilities.'

Smokowski stopped pretending he was doing something and

turned to face her. He knew he had no choice, but time hopping, there had to be another way?

'Okay, Cat, you're right, but isn't there another way? Couldn't we plant a bug or something on him?' said Smokowski, preparing one last throw of the dice.

'You'd never get near him without Brandy knowing.'

'When she's asleep?'

'Had spy training have we? Besides we don't know that she does sleep?'

'I have actually,' said Smokowski, letting those dice go.

Of course he has, thought Cat, forgetting the training Travellers' aides go through, but it still was nowhere good enough. 'Yes, but times that training by one hundred and you have Brandy, she's about the best there is.'

The dice threw up snake eyes. But Smokowski wasn't beaten yet. 'What if I can't find a time machine to latch onto?'

'You'll be following Tom's.'

'But what if I get squished?'

'Squished?' said Cat.

'By the pressure.'

'Pressure?'

'When I'm towed along in the slip stream.'

'Ah,' said Cat, catching on, 'the hitchhiker protects you – forms a barrier round you. Here, catch.'

The small object that Cat had confiscated from Invisible Bob in the pyramid materialised in Smokowski's hand. Smokowski gave it a doubtful look and turned it over in his fingers. The hitchhiker was miniscule, silver in colour, resembling a compass and measuring no more than a couple of millimetres in diameter. 'I'll lose it,' said Smokowski.

'Not if you keep it somewhere safe. Invisible Bob didn't. You squeeze it to travel, release to stop.'

Until now, thought Smokowski. 'Doesn't the little man have a small bag or something to put it in that I could borrow?'

'Something,' said Cat.

'Something?' said Smokowski, puzzled.

'Somewhere,' said Cat, helping Smokowski along.

'I don't under... ugh!' groaned Smokowski, dropping the hitchhiker on the floor in disgust. 'You're kidding?'

'Where else would a small naked invisible man be able to keep it?'

Smokowski stared at his fingers and started for the sink in the storeroom.

'It's okay, it's clean,' said Cat, grinning, 'I sterilised it.'

Smokowski stopped midway through the gap in the counter. 'You sure?' he said.

'Yes,' said Cat.

Smokowski gave a little shudder. 'It's just the thought,' he said.

'Then don't think about it,' said Cat, her smile growing. 'It's on the floor at the foot of the counter, by your feet.'

Still not keen on the idea, Smokowski bent down and gingerly plucked the hitchhiker from the floor. He quickly placed it in his pocket.

'Time to go, I think,' said Cat, acting before Smokowski threw up further objections.

Subconsciously gulping, Smokowski attempted to gird his nervous loins. 'I'll tell Darren we're going then, shall I?'

'I'll get Bob.'

CHAPTER 22

Tom had arrived at a decision – he was going to buy Brandy a present, some perfume, any perfume as long as it was subtle, understated, didn't stink. Which one he hadn't the foggiest, but he couldn't go on like this, continually breathing through hands clasped over his nose and mouth every time they travelled in the loo. As for his ears, he doubted there was anything he could do about her constant nattering, unless he wore ear defenders or clamped a hand over her mouth that is. But he doubted she would take kindly to either idea. No, his ears would have to put up with it. So, pushing these latter thoughts from his mind, Tom alighted from his bathroom where the loo had taken him and laboured towards the kitchen. Brandy tagged close behind, her wiggle pronounced, her sense of smell cast iron.

'Cuppa?' asked Tom, opening the kitchen window and breathing deeply.

'Please,' said Brandy, placing both hers and Tom's copies of "Lovey Dovey" on the kitchen table. She positively purred as she stroked the cover of her book. She then gave Tom an appraising glance. 'You should do more exercise,' she said.

'Me?' said Tom, lungs purged, so now filling the kettle.

'Yes, you Sir,' said Brandy, 'making a lady carry your book for you.'

'It's my back,' said Tom, giving his teeth another battering as he lied through them again, he wasn't going to tell her the truth – that her perfume was draining his strength. 'Was it milk and sugar?'

Whether she believed his excuse or not, she said nothing about it, instead giggling as she told him how she liked her tea. 'You know I take it as it comes,' said Brandy, more giggles.

Tom managed to spray water on his shirt as a minor case of the shakes made him miss the hole in the top of the kettle.

'Tom?' purred Brandy, her tongue sliding along the top of her bottom lip.

'Yes?' said Tom, who was well versed in the wonts and wiles of women, having a daughter, a granddaughter and having once been married, so noticed the subtle, yet dangerous change in tone to her voice.

'I was just wondering if we were going to see Mister Vinci anytime soon?'

With just a slight tremble to his hand Tom plugged the kettle in. 'As soon as Marc calls, why?' Where was this going? he thought.

'Well,' said Brandy, hanging out her words like clothes on a line, 'if we've got time, and it's okay with you that is, would it be okay if... and you can say no, if we had a bath?'

Tom almost dropped the cups. 'We?' he spluttered, putting the cups down before he did.

'I mean me,' said Brandy, giggling. 'I'm sorry, it's the way I say things.'

You're not wrong there, thought Tom, trying to get a grip on his nerves. 'I... I can't see why not,' said Tom. He doubted Marc would phone before three.

'Goody,' said Brandy, clapping her hands. But her show of delight was suddenly cut short. 'But I haven't got any bubbly,' she said, suddenly looking glum.

Grief, thought Tom, tea not good enough for her now? Who does she think she is, a C celeb or something? Champagne in the bath, whatever next?

'Have you got any?' asked a pouting Brandy.

'Don't think so,' said Tom, wondering if there might be some cider left over from his last birthday party.

'Shall I go look?' Brandy got up. 'If not perhaps that nice Mister Smokowski might have some in his shop.'

'Be my guest,' said Tom. And he doubted Smokowski would have any, but he agreed to go anyway if need be. But, to his surprise, instead of heading for the fridge like he had expected her to, Brandy disappeared into the hall. Scratching his head Tom followed her and found her emerging from the bathroom, wreathed in smiles. She was holding something in her hand.

'It says here that it'll relax you with gentle caresses and sweep away your aches and pains.' Brandy showed the bottle she was holding to Tom. 'I don't know about you, but I could do with a good caress,' she giggled.

Bubble bath! Blimey! Tom felt a twinge of guilt over what he had been thinking earlier. 'Ah,' he said.

'I'll have my tea first though, if that's okay?'

'No prob,' said Tom, back peddling both in mind and body.

As Brandy soaked, Tom sipped at a fresh cuppa, thoughtful like.

He wondered on the wheres and whys of the day so far. How he had got from there to here? When would Cat come back? What was going on with her? What would he find back in Da Vinci's time? This thought produced a small shudder as he recalled his first adventure in the past. If he remembered right, and there was no guarantee, as it was well over a week ago, or so, he couldn't quite recall, there had been a certain amount of bondage involved. He tried to think more cheerful thoughts. At least he would try. He touched the book he had bought. He expected he would look back and laugh at it all one day, maybe. His mind turned to how excited Brandy had become at the thought of meeting the orange midget. He thought of Brandy. He thought of Brandy in the bath.

'Brrr,' said Tom, quickly standing. It was a thought too far. He hurried over to the sink. He would busy himself. Wash his cup up even though it was still half full. And where was that grandson? he thought. Should have called by now. But when Tom looked at the clock it was still only just past two o'clock, plenty of time yet. Plenty of time for more idle thinking. Tom squirted detergent and quickly filled the sink with hot water.

CHAPTER 23

'But I've made more tea,' groaned Darren, when Smokowski told him he had to leave again.

'Can't be helped,' said Smokowski, shrugging, 'Cat needs my help.'

Darren followed Smokowski through the shop, the cups of tea still in his hands. 'But what about me?' he asked.

'You can try and keep the sign the right way round for one thing,' said Smokowski, 'and I mean open. And if you've got a moment, disinfect the pick and mix.'

'Ready?' asked Cat, who was waiting by the shop door.

'I suppose,' said Smokowski, looking every inch a King Ethelred.

'Good,' said Cat, 'got the hitchhiker safe?'

Smokowski patted his pocket. 'Yes.'

'Remember what I said?'

'Squeeze to travel. Release to stop.'

'Good man, but use release only in an emergency.' Cat cast a glance in Darren's direction. He was stood glaring at the pick and mix and didn't appear to be taking any interest in what they were saying. Cat lowered her voice further, just in case, 'You'll stop wherever Tom has stopped.'

'I wish I had your faith,' said Smokowski.

Cat smiled at him. 'You ready Bob?' She felt a chill on her back.

'Ready boss,' said Invisible Bob.

'We'll be off then,' said Cat, stepping outside.

'Wait!' said Smokowski, suddenly, 'You haven't told me how to contact you.'

But Cat was gone.

'Drat,' said Smokowski under his breath. He closed the door and found a puzzled Darren staring at him.

'I thought you said you were going too?' said Darren.

'I am,' said Smokowski, walking past him, heading for the gap in the counter.

'But...'

'No time to explain, I'll see you later. And remember the sign.' Smokowski removed his apron, hung it on the back of the storeroom door and went in.

'Yes, but...' But Darren's appeals fell on deaf ears, or to be more precise, fell on the empty space where the ears had been, but not knowing this as yet, Darren put the cups he was still carrying on the counter and followed Smokowski into the storeroom.

'But Mister Smo...' The words died on Darren's lips as he saw the storeroom was empty. He quickly opened the back door to the yard, but the yard was empty as well, no way could Smokowski have got through the back gate before he had got to the yard door. Darren scratched his head. The loo! Darren closed the back door only to find that the loo was empty too. Darren's mind was suddenly filled with dread – no one had shown him where the disinfectant was kept.

CHAPTER 24

The sound of the phone ringing wouldn't ordinarily make Tom nearly jump out of his skin, but as he had his nose deep in his copy of "Lovey Dovey" in a desperate bid to keep his mind off a certain bathing beauty, this time it did.

'Waa!' said Tom, rocking on his chair and losing his place and his bearings.

The phone rang again.

'Waa!' said Tom, this time because Brandy had just walked into the kitchen.

'Heard the phone and thought you might be outside,' said Brandy.

Tom, his eyeballs on stalks, waved a hand and managed to mutter something incoherent Brandy's way.

A frowning Brandy, puzzled by the sight of the flailing pensioner, asked if he was okay, then pointed out that perhaps someone should pick the phone up as it rang for a third time.

Somehow Tom managed not to lose his eyeballs, regain his bearings, and not give two hoots that he had lost his place in "Lovey Dovey". He even managed to find his voice, 'There's a towel in the airing cupboard,' he spluttered.

'Phone,' said Brandy, putting a hand to her head.

'Towel,' said Tom, putting a hand over his eyes to shield them.

'What's wrong with this one?' said Brandy, all innocent like.

'It's a flipping flannel,' said Tom, now up and feeling blindly for the phone.

Brandy gave a deep sigh, walked over to the phone, handed it to Tom, then wandered off to find this towel he was so adamant she find.

Tom, for his part, nearly choked as the phone was handed to him, but he did manage to take it. 'Hello,' he gasped into it as Brandy turned away, 'buttocks Brandy! Good grief.' He attempted to compose himself. 'Tom speaking.'

'Granddad?' said the intrigued voice of his grandson, on the other end of the line.

'Boll... Marc,' said Tom, cringing, 'how nice to hear from you.'

'You okay, Granddad?'

'Er... yes, tickety-boo, you?'

There was a moment's pause on the other end of the phone as an eleven year old digested what he had heard. 'I've got that info you wanted,' said Marc, a sudden unpleasantly confident air about his voice.

'You what?' said Tom, interference on the line, a pounding noise, threatening to drown out their voices.

'I said, I've got that stuff you wanted me to get,' said Marc, wondering if perhaps his granddad shouldn't get one of those hearing aids he had seen advertised.

'Hang about a minute,' said Tom, who took a couple of deep steadying breaths as he realised the pounding he had been hearing was in fact the sound of his blood pumping like the billio.

'Granddad?'

'Here,' said Tom, the pounding lessening, 'What did you find out?'

'Not much.'

'What's not much?'

'Well I know when Da Vinci was born, where he lived, when he died and bits and pieces like that, oh... and did you know he was supposed to have invented the helicopter and computer games?' Marc sounded quite excited by that last piece of information.

Tom actually did know a little about the man having watched a documentary on him once, the kind you half watch half doze to, but he couldn't remember anything about computer games being said. That didn't mean he didn't though, it could have been mentioned during one of the doze moments. 'You sure?' said Tom.

'That's what it said on one of the websites.'

Tom had heard of these websites, didn't know what they were, hadn't asked, so he remained doubtful. 'And that's all?' asked Tom.

'There is one other thing,' said Marc.

'Go on.'

'I know that Brandy's got buttocks.'

There was a couple of seconds of coughing before Tom was able to find his voice again, 'What?' he said.

'I heard you say it on the phone,' said Marc, the entrepreneur in him thinking of trying his hand at a little blackmail – not that Marc knew it as that.

Grief, thought Tom, he'd had to think hard today, but how did he get out of this one? 'No you didn't,' he said, buying time.

'Did too,' said Marc, who hadn't had the hindrance of a noisy blood supply.

'No you didn't, what you heard was…' What could he tell him he had heard? What was plausible? Then he had it, there was life in the old dog yet. 'Butter!' said Tom.

'Butter?'

'Yes,' said Tom, finding it hard to hide his relief. There would be serious questions if his daughter found out about Brandy. Scrub that, when she found out and it would be a whole lot harder to come up with an excuse if Brandy's buttocks were brought into it. 'Brandy's making toast and asked me what I wanted on it.' Phew!

'Butter?' said Marc, the earlier confidence beginning to wane.

'Yes, yummy,' said Tom, laying it on perhaps a little too thick.

On the other end of the line Marc had decided to cut his losses, he couldn't be totally sure what his granddad had said, not with those teeth of his. Marc took it as said that Tom wore dentures, he didn't know for sure. 'Still a fiver though?' he said.

'Still a fiver,' said Tom, getting his equilibrium back. 'Right, let me get a pencil and I'll jot down what you've got.'

Five minutes later, three minutes after Marc had rung off, Tom was still staring at the sheet of paper in his hand. There wasn't much, but was it enough. Marc hadn't had a lot of time to gather it together to be fair, shouldn't really involve him, but what else could he do? He needed the information. How else would he get it? Unless he got one of those darned computer thingy's. Tom's heart sank, he had always turned his nose up at the idea, at technology. The only one piece he had embraced and thought of as truly useful was the widget breweries now incorporated in their beer cans – can't beat a good frothy head.

As Tom drank down that pint in his mind's eye, Brandy returned swathed in the largest towel she could find – couldn't have her Traveller having a cardiac arrest, could she now. She had been drying her hair. 'Was that Marc?' she asked.

'It was,' said Tom, relieved at not being able to see so much of her, 'but there's not much to go on I'm afraid.'

'Have to visit a library then,' said Brandy, her hair swishing as she turned about. 'I'll go and get dressed.'

A library! Why hadn't he thought of that? Because he was a silly old duffer, that's why. They're bound to have loads of information about Da Vinci to look through. Right, wait for Brandy to get dressed, pop the ol' jacket on and… Where was the closest library? Would it be open? Phone book! Tom went for the phone book and within minutes was gearing up for his first visit to a library in… he couldn't remember when.

CHAPTER 25

The sound of a muffled yell of surprise was quickly followed by the dull thud of something large and heavy falling to the ground.

'What's going on out there?' demanded a voice from within.

There now came an impatient rapping on the door of the dark room.

'Who's there?'

But instead of an answer, the door burst violently inwards – which was a surprise to the occupant of the dark room as it usually opened outwards. Then something strange happened, the light went on.

'Yah!' yelled the dark room's occupant, frantically trying to pull a mask from his desk's drawer.

'Surprise!' said Cat, as she jumped up onto the desk before the mask could be donned.

'Outrageous!' bellowed the naked faced Chief Traveller. 'It's an affront! You're in trouble now, Catranna.'

'I thought I already was,' smiled Cat, casually licking a paw as the Chief roared disapproval.

The Chief finally managed to slip on his mask, but was horrified to find he could no longer see. 'What have you done to me?' he yelled. 'I'm blind, you've blinded me!'

'It's on the wrong way round,' said Cat.

'What?'

'The mask,' said Invisible Bob, happy to discover the voice in the dark who had given him his orders was owned by the person he thought owned it.

'Is that you Invisible Bob?'

'In the flesh,' said Invisible Bob.

'Sadly,' said Cat.

The Chief turned his mask the right way round to show eyes wide with surprise. 'You told her about our meeting?'

'Yeah, sorry about that.'

'But you're a BIMBO.'

'Nothing I could do,' said Invisible Bob, shrugging, 'she covered me in itching powder and purple paint and then confiscated my hitchhiker.'

'Gad!' said the Chief, his mask hiding his shock and, it has to be said, slight amusement.

'So,' said Cat, 'what's going on Chief?'

'I don't know what you mean, Catranna. Bob, call the guards.'

'I can't,' said Invisible Bob, keen to see where all this was going.

'Can't or won't?' demanded the Chief.

'Can't,' said Cat, gesturing to the floor outside the dark room's door, where two bodies lay, one on top of the other.

'Should have used BIMBO's,' said Invisible Bob, instantly regretting the remark as he wasn't exactly a shining example.

'Are they all right?'

'Sleeping,' said Cat.

'All right, Catranna, you clearly have me at a disadvantage what is it you want?' said the Chief, sitting.

'Why have I been fitted up? And don't try to lie.'

'She'll know,' said Invisible Bob, who was quietly enjoying another discovery, that there wasn't a single antique in the room – unless it came flat packed.

The Chief Traveller sagged into his chair, his shoulders looking to admit defeat, but then he suddenly sat bolt upright and was all smiles. 'Well done, Catranna,' he said, making Invisible Bob jump with the suddenness of it all, 'knew you wouldn't let me down. Didn't expect you this quickly though, but damn good show none the less.'

'You expected her?' said Invisible Bob, all agog.

'High hopes of it happening,' said the Chief. 'And now you are here, let me tell you what has been going on and why you are here. A merry tale it makes too.'

Cat and Invisible Bob listened as the Chief told his tale.

At the end of it, Cat's suspicions had been proved spot on. She *had* been set up, but for the right reasons. The rumour of the unfelt ripple wasn't a rumour, the unthinkable *had* happened. Cat's help was needed but a direct approach to her with what was known had been felt a dangerous move to make, perhaps alerting those responsible, so a plan was devised to make it appear that Cat was out of the picture, but it was still too dangerous to contact her as only a small inner circle knew of the ripple and they didn't know who to trust outside of it. They needed another plan, they needed to arouse her curiosity further, beyond jumped up charges, make her come to them, and that's where Invisible Bob came into the picture. He had been used to try to feed that curiosity, the rumour fed to him by the inner circle in the hope Cat would hear about it and latch onto it when she discovered him. They had great faith in her. They also needed her as she was the best and most trusted familiar there was. Thankfully it had worked.

Cat had listened and then nodded approval, but she had a couple of burning questions which she put to the Chief when he had finished, 'I take my hat off to you, Chief,' said Cat, genuinely impressed, 'but why wasn't the ripple felt?'

'*You used me,*' said Invisible Bob.

'We don't know for sure, but suspect a glamour was used on the main wall and you familiars.'

'*Unbelievable,*' said Invisible Bob.

'Magic?' said Cat, surprised by the suggestion. The mystery had just deepened considerably. The use of magic for time tampering was unheard of, mainly because magic was beyond the reach of mortal man.

'*It's a disgrace,*' grumbled Invisible Bob.

'We can't think how else it could have been done.'

First question sort of answered, now for the second. 'But how did you discover there even was a ripple?' said Cat.

'Hello! Disgruntled BIMBO with a grievance here.'

'Purely by accident,' the Chief admitted. 'One of the cleaners discovered an alarm flashing on a disused area grid in a disused office. We used hundreds of them before they were incorporated into one single wall. Just by chance the supervisor had decided to start using it as a storeroom. It hadn't been disconnected so was still listening in, but luckily not connected to the main wall grid, so not under the glamour's influence.'

'Suit yourselves then,' said Invisible Bob, starting to accept the situation that no one was listening to him.

'You suspect an inside job then?'

'Worse, we think a Traveller and his familiar may have gone rogue for some reason.'

'I'll just shut up then, shall I?'

Cat couldn't believe what she was hearing. A Traveller yes, it's happened, but with their familiar, it was unthinkable. The sooner this mess was sorted the better. 'You had better show me which point in time the ripple occurred so I can find out what is going on?'

The Chief shook his head. 'It's not as easy as that.'

'But why not?' said Cat.

'The alarm that went off just indicated that there was a problem somewhere, not where it was exactly.'

'Zipping it.' Invisible Bob zipped it and slumped cross legged onto the desk top.

'Then we're looking for a needle in a haystack?'

'Not quite, as I said the alarm went off in an area grid, so we have a rough idea.'

'Didn't you try feeding that into this main grid to see if you could narrow it down?'

'We did, Cat, and if you would like to follow me I shall show you what happened.'

Cat jumped from the desk and looked to head for the space where the door had been.

'Not that way,' said the Chief Traveller. He reached behind him and pulled on a wall sconce. There was a scrapping sound as the desk started to move backwards. 'Hop back aboard, Catranna.'

Cat did and watched intrigued as part of the wall, directly behind the desk, began to slide aside.

The desk continued its movement until it had turned full circle and was facing the gap the sliding wall had left. It now moved towards it and through it.

A sudden exclaim of surprise from the disgruntled and ignored Invisible Bob as he spied what lay beyond the gap, heralded confirmation of what Cat had already suspected, a secret centre of operations existed. But the dark room had only been the tip of the iceberg.

When the desk came to a halt the Chief Traveller got up and walked across the room they had entered – which wasn't in the least bit dark. Cat stayed sat, taking in the sights. The room was busy, dotted with masked men and familiars moving here and there. Cat guessed the masked men had to be elder Travellers and the familiars' BIMBO's. She could be wrong, but it wasn't often that she was. A few of them had glanced her way, but if they were surprised to see her there they didn't show it. Expecting her no doubt, she thought. The Chief Traveller had stopped by the far wall and beckoned for her to join him.

'The operational wall,' the Chief announced.

It took a lot to strike Cat speechless, but for the moment she was dumb as she stared at the wall, awestruck. The wall was huge, way too long for the room it was part of. It appeared to go on and on. And on it, thousands, perhaps tens of thousands of small light bulbs, some of which flashed and pulsated.

'Points in time,' explained the Chief, pointing to the bulbs. 'The flashing ones are ripples. The coloured pins beneath are the Travellers attending.'

'Which of them is Tom?' said Cat.

'Beatrice,' called the Chief. A lithe creature, which any human not in the know would have instantly and wrongly assumed to be an elf, wandered over.'

'Yes, Chief?'

'Catranna wants to see her traveller's position on the grid.'

Beatrice gave a clipboard, which had materialised from nowhere, a brief look over then studied the grid for a moment. 'Ah yes, there he is,' she said, starting to float into the air, 'section fifteenth century.' She pointed to an amber pin with 007 written on it.

'Way to go man,' exclaimed an impressed disembodied voice from somewhere at the foot of the wall. A voice that, thanks to all the shiny and bright, was starting to forget his earlier grievances.

But as Beatrice pressed on the pin, a holographic number ballooned beside it, reading: 00742965498329746185-N.

'Bummer!' exclaimed that same disembodied voice.

'Would need a ruddy big wall if we didn't shorten it what?' said the Chief, chortling.

Bigger! thought Cat.

'What does the N stand for?' asked Invisible Bob from below.

'Newbie,' said Beatrice. 'Anything else I can do, Chief?'

'I want to show Catranna what happened when we fed the info we have on the unfelt ripple into the main grid.'

'Certainly,' said Beatrice, 'light protective goggles everyone.'

Everyone in the room started to don dark goggles. Beatrice managed to produce four pairs from the same place she had got the clipboard and handed a pair each to Cat, the Chief, and after a couple of seconds of voice trailing, to Invisible Bob.

'Sorry,' said Invisible Bob, after trying any which way to put them on and failing, 'they're too big for me.'

'Beatrice...'

But Beatrice was already on it and produced a welder's mask and helmet, which she placed over Invisible Bob.

'All right in there?' queried the Chief.

'Can't see a thing.'

'Good... good. Now, if you please Beatrice, could you insert the area grid's information stick.'

Beatrice began to float again and hovered over to a pin reading "Information Input". Below it was a small aperture. In this she placed a small crystal, rectangular in shape. She pressed the pin, and the second she did, a brilliant light instantly engulfed the room as every single bulb on the wall lit up as one.

But it was only for an instant. The room then fell just as quickly into total darkness. But again this didn't last long. There was a click from somewhere and everything returned to how it had been before the light.

'I see what you mean,' said Cat.

'Pretty,' said Invisible Bob.

'We think the main grid was rigged to respond in this manner, all bulbs flashing instead of one should the unfelt ripple be somehow stumbled across by accident, thereby making any attempt at definitive identification of the exact time it had occurred impossible, an insurance policy if you like. We haven't been able to pinpoint the cause so all we have to go on is that area grid.'

'Was anyone hurt the first time it happened?'

'Luckily no, Beatrice had been working alone and had managed to blink from existence the very moment it happened, otherwise we think she may have lost all or some of her sight.'

'I was lucky,' said Beatrice, removing her goggles, 'but it fused the mainframe the first time it happened.' She removed the crystal.

'It took quite a few hours to put that right,' said the Chief.

'Why didn't it fuse this time?' said Cat.

'Beatrice put in a failsafe so the grid wouldn't be harmed should things change and we decided to try again.'

'So, where does this leave us?' asked Cat.

'As I said, with the area grid, it's not much, but it does help to narrow down the possibilities.'

'How many?' said Cat, expecting the worst.

'Beatrice, can you load the area grid's area and show us the possibles?'

Beatrice placed a new crystal in the input slot and pushed the pin. The wall changed again, with most of the bulbs going out this time, those that stayed twinkling were the possibles.

'And these are all ripples?' said Cat.

'Yes,' said the Chief, but not all were showing on the main grid just now. Those that were, were obviously known about so we can dispense with those. Can you turn those off please Beatrice?' Seven bulbs stayed twinkling.

'You mean these are *all* unfelt?'

'Again, we don't know, could be. We just don't know, could be an elaborate ploy to hide a single one, but this we do know, there is at least one and it's up there somewhere, staring back at us.'

CHAPTER 26

Smokowski hurried to the loo. He could hear Darren in the shop. There was no time to worry. A deep breath, some strange feelings in the tummy region, gritted teeth. Here goes. Maybe he… no, too late, too late to worry now. Smokowski had pressed the hitchhiker between thumb and forefinger. What happened next was indescribable – for Smokowski. He had never seen the aftermath of an explosion in a sixties psychedelic wallpaper factory.

There was a whooshing noise. Then there were the colours, a myriad of them that encased him in a multi-rainbow ball. He was propelled forward, picking up speed as he went, until he was no longer in a ball, but a multi-coloured tunnel that trailed away behind him, stretching far into the distance. Broad lines of colour all around that as they stretched, grew thinner and thinner and thinner until they were so thin they looked about to disappear completely. Which they did, suddenly, causing Smokowski to land with a thump.

It was dark, but at least he was on terra firma, he could feel it, even though he couldn't see it. His eyes hurt. Why did they hurt? The area around them hurt. What had happened to him? Where was he? What hellish craziness had Cat landed him in the middle of? What unseen nightmarish landscape surrounded him? If only he could see! Then, through the terror Smokowski was gripped by, there spoke up a voice of reason from somewhere in the depths of his mind, 'It might help if you stopped screwing your eyes up so tight and opened them!' it said.

Feeling sort of foolish, but weighing against that the excuse that he had been scared shitless, Smokowski unclenched his eyes and took in the nightmarish vista that *did* surround him.

Right away he knew where he was. The garish sixties carpet, the wallpaper that almost matched, but in some strange way also clashed, the browns and oranges of both wall and carpet combining to assault the senses. He was in Tom's hallway. Well it worked, thought Smokowski, making sure the hitchhiker was safely tucked away in his pocket, but noted it wasn't one hundred percent accurate. He had expected to arrive in Tom's bathroom, not outside it. That could be tricky if he landed somewhere crowded.

For now though he was just happy to be safe and sound and thankful none of the nausea he had been half expecting had materialised. Smokowski felt fit enough, apart from the strained eyebrows and eyelids that is, to strike on.

With the stealth that years of training the skills of stealth brought, Smokowski stealthily moved along the hall, listening all the time for any movement from the other rooms. He had to be careful, if he was discovered there was no way he could make up a plausible enough excuse for why he was there, let alone how he had got there.

He reached the kitchen door and was relieved to find it standing ajar. He carefully peered in. It was empty. He gave a small sigh of relief and went in. But what did he do now? He spied two empty cups on the draining board, one with lipstick on the rim. Ah-ha, thought detective Smokowski, they've been here. Which if he had thought about it was why he was there. Donning his detective hat again Smokowski further deduced that they weren't there now, which meant they were somewhere else. He congratulated himself on his deductions and went over to the cups. What he did next he had seen done on telly.

He had noticed that one of the cups, the one without lipstick on it, still had tea in it, about a third of a cup. He stuck a finger into it – stone cold. They had been gone a while. This returned him to his previous quandary, what did he do now? Should he hang around, conceal his person somewhere on the premises? Or did he return to the loo and give the hitchhiker another squeeze and see where it took him?

After a moment or two of toing and froing with what to do next, Smokowski plumped for sitting firm and waiting. Another moment passed and it occurred to him that as he was supposed to be tailing Tom, it might be better if he did that – who knew when he would be back.

'No,' said Smokowski. Oops, he thought, realising he had spoken out loud. No, he would go back to the hall.

Hitchhiker in hand, Smokowski crept warily back to the hall, listening for movement, the last thing he wanted was to bump into Tom coming out of the bathroom. This in mind he decided it best to give the hitchhiker a squeeze at the point he had landed instead of going into the loo as he had back at the storeroom. What could happen? He squeezed the hitchhiker just as the thought – what could happen – was superseded by – he could be dragged through the bathroom wall, that's what! Luckily for Smokowski, he wasn't. He was dragged through the bathroom door instead.

CHAPTER 27

As Tom waited for Brandy to get dressed, he gathered together everything he felt necessary for his foray into the library – a pencil and a pad of paper. On the top of the first page of the pad he had written: ICNIV AD. He had figured it wise to write Da Vinci's name backwards as a sort of code against nosey parkers looking over his shoulder trying to see what he was doing. It made sense to Tom. Soon, with pencil and paper snug in his jacket pocket, which he was now wearing, Tom was set and ready to rumble.

Five minutes later he was still set, but the rumble had turned to something of a grumble. Ten minutes and a couple of shouts to enquire whether Brandy was ready yet later, and Tom was all grumble. Twenty minutes later Tom was worn out from all the grumbling and enquiring and was trying hard to keep his eyes open.

Where is that woman? thought Tom, head on arms, arms laid on the kitchen table, eyelids batting as they fought a losing battle against gravity – it hadn't been this bad when he was married.

'Tut-tut, you sleeping on the job, Tom?' asked Brandy, who had arrived that second at the kitchen door.

Tom's head jerked up at the sound of Brandy's voice and the eyes that had just been on the verge of defeat suddenly leaped open and wide. Tom's jaw dropped. 'Where did you get those from?' he stammered, referring to the clothes she was wearing, or hardly wearing, as was the case.

'My wardrobe of course, sweetie,' giggled Brandy, delighted with Tom's reaction. She did a little twirl for him so he could fully appreciate her ensemble. Which Tom did, judging from the saliva gathering at the corners of his mouth and the beads of sweat forming on his brow. 'You like?'

He didn't know what to say, but given a moment, like many a man before him throughout history, once his brain had given up trying to multi-task, looking, thinking and talking at the same time, and not wanting to appear overly enthusiastic, he spouted those immortal man words every woman, who has spent simply ages getting herself just so, hates to hear, 'It's all right, I suppose.'

Brandy's face took on the look of thunder. 'Just all right!' she growled, her lips curling in a snarl that would have had any man, woman, child, bird, animal, anything with the slightest sense of self preservation, scurrying for cover. Tom on the other hand just sat there wondering how she had managed to get a wardrobe into his cottage without him knowing.

But lucky for Tom, she couldn't be angry with him for long, fifteen seconds to be precise, he was only a simple man after all, and a silly mortal at that. Instead she proceeded to instruct him on the fashions of the day and on how she had most of them in her wardrobe. Tom, mesmerised by her "all right I suppose" clothes, or lack of them, was half listening, but enough to be wondering if her versions were in miniature.

When Brandy had finished her lecture she asked him if they had time for a cup of tea before they set off to the library, because talking always left her parched. Must have a tongue like the Sahara, thought Tom, rather unkindly. He said, "why not?"

Tom watched as Brandy set about the tea making, drinking in the vision before him. Yes he had said "all right I suppose", but what he had meant to say was "COR!" All men mean to say "COR!" He wasn't too sure about the beads in her hair, but he did appreciate the low cut top, lovely material. The teeny shorts that had replaced the skirt/belt but still barely covered her seating arrangement brought a tear to his eye – thinking how tight they were, they were bound to chaff. But at least she was wearing sensible boots – black leather ones that travelled past her knee, although he wasn't sure how comfortable that would be.

Tea ready, Brandy brought the cups to the table. 'I just remembered,' she said, handing Tom her tea, 'I haven't shown you this.'

Tom nearly spilt his tea. 'You've got a pet,' he said, staring at it, 'a pink one.'

'Silly,' said Brandy, 'what do you think?'

Is it still alive? thought Tom. 'Lovely, what is it?'

Brandy's lips twitched, but only for a second. 'It's my handbag. It's Vera.'

Thank goodness for that, thought Tom, who had been certain Brandy had dyed a hamster. 'I knew that,' said Tom, 'and that's a lovely name you've given it.'

For most of the next five minutes and nearly all of the instant it took to get to the library, Brandy managed to nearly hardly speak to Tom at all.

CHAPTER 28

As Smokowski passed through Tom's bathroom door which, as luck would have it, no longer existed in the same temporal plane as he did, so no harm done, the multi-coloured tunnel took hold and rushed him to his next port of call.

I'm getting good at this, thought Smokowski, who had managed to land this time with only one eye tightly closed. The one eye that had bravely stayed open saw that Smokowski had landed in a brick toilet cubicle. His nose, adding input to the optic information already received, told Smokowski it was very likely a cubicle occupying space in a public convenience.

Smokowski wrinkled his nose, thanked his deity for having the grace to land him in an empty cubicle, and then popped his head around the door. The place was empty. To his left, more cubicles ending at a wall, to his right, a small sink at the foot of a staircase. He headed for the staircase. When he got there he could see daylight filtering in from above. Up he went.

As he climbed the steps, it struck him just how difficult his job was going to be. Pressing the hitchhiker and rainbow hopping was all well and good, and took him where he was supposed to be, but actually finding Tom at the end of those rainbows so he could tail him was another thing entirely. Smokowski reached the top. What now? In front of him a square, people were milling, there were seats, a café, a parade of shops, a queue outside one of them, Tom and Brandy, a couple of trees, pigeons… Tom! Smokowski immediately flattened his body against the entrance to the public lavatories. He couldn't believe it, Tom was standing less than thirty feet from him. What to do? What to do? Smokowski was in a dither, but dithering was no good. Hold firm man, he told himself, hold firm.

It took a second to compose himself, but Smokowski managed it, his training coming to the fore. He headed for the nearest tree and hid behind it, making sure Tom and Brandy were in view. They hadn't seen him. He needed time to take stock. He decided he needed to merge, to blend – done the right way you could become virtually invisible. He was going for the end of the queue. Adrenaline pumping, Smokowski waited for the right moment. Not yet. Not yet. Not…

'You okay mate?'

Smokowski nearly ended up in the branches above him. A dishevelled king of the road, who had wandered from the other side of the tree while Smokowski had been gearing up to go, was looking him up and down.

'Pardon?' said a shaken Smokowski.

'Only you don't look too good mate, yer shaking,' said the hobo. 'You 'iding from someone, toing and froing behind that tree like that?' The hobo peered round the tree to see what he could see. He saw a queue, but not much else. 'You gonna push in over there mate?' The hobo let out a laugh, the sort that attracted attention.

Smokowski *did not* want attention. He had to do something and now. Smokowski cast a quick glance to see if anyone was looking. No one was. He spoke to the hobo, 'You are getting sleepy,' he said, and before the distracted hobo had a chance to wonder what Smokowski was going on about, Smokowski reached out a hand and squeezed certain pressure points on the hobo's neck. Then, with eyes darting everywhere, Smokowski manoeuvred the unconscious man against the tree. Man now propped, and the coast looking clear, Smokowski grabbed hold of the hobo's shopping trolley and nonchalantly wheeled it across the square, away from people, trees, seats, pigeons, and most importantly, Tom.

When he deemed it safe to do so, out of Tom's line of vision, Smokowski returned to his normal shopkeeper self. He was shaking as he joined the end of the queue. Grief, thought Smokowski, looking at the tree he had just come from, the hobo had started to slowly slide down it, had he really just done that? It never left you, he supposed.

The queue started to move, Smokowski with it, a sharp eye trained on Tom and Brandy. He wondered what was going on and whether the queue was worth reporting. Better to report everything, just to be on the safe side. How he was going to do that though was another thing, Cat disappearing like that.

He was still mulling over that particular bump in the road when he noticed a youth pushing a trolley leave the shop and start walking alongside the queue. He was stopping and chatting to people as he went. He stopped beside Tom and Brandy. The youth handed something to Brandy and Tom wasn't looking at all happy about something. It appeared Smokowski had something worthwhile to report back at last. He pressed forward, eager to try and see what it was that had made Tom so unhappy.

'Oi! Who do you think you're pushing?' enquired a stern faced, leather clad lady in her sixties, sporting an "I Love Poppett" scarf, round her wrist.

'Oh,' said Smokowski, backing away, 'I do apolo...'

'Oi!' said a voice behind him, 'you just stepped on my foot.'

Smokowski turned to apologise and came face to face with a woman who bared a striking resemblance to the lady he had just accidently pushed, only this one had two Poppett scarves; one tied round each wrist and an "I Love Poppett" button badge pinned to a leather biker's cap.

'He giving you trouble, Madge?' said the lady with two scarves, glaring menacingly at Smokowski.

'Nah, he's just a bit over excited that's all,' said Madge, batting eyelids, heavy with mascara, in Smokowski's direction, 'I think he might be a virgin.' She winked at the other woman.

'A what?' spluttered Smokowski. 'Now look here...'

'A first timer eh?' said two scarves, 'We better look after him then.'

'Bagsy first dibs though,' said Madge, smiling at Smokowski, her lashes causing a breeze.

'Seems fair to me,' said two scarves, winking, 'but I bagsy any leftovers.'

Laughing heartily, the two ladies each took hold of one of Smokowski's arms in theirs and gave them a hug.

'Don't you worry,' whispered Madge, as she nuzzled Smokowski's shoulder, 'everyone gets first time jitters.'

But he did and was, and further so as the danger of being smothered by two leather clad ladies looked increasingly likely. He craned his neck, he couldn't see Tom, but he could still see Brandy who looked excited about something. But then the queue shuffled forward again and she too was lost from view.

Drat, thought Smokowski, his worry increasing further at the idea of losing them so soon after finding them. He tried to break free of the ladies' grip, but he was clamped tight as if in a vice. What did he do now?

'Book, madam?' enquired the youth with the trolley, who had just arrived.

'Ooh... please,' said Madge, going for her faux zebra skin handbag.

'Me too,' said two scarves.

Madge pulled a faux leopard skin purse from the depths of her faux zebra skin handbag. 'Here, I'll pay for them.'

'Are you sure?' said two scarves, who had taken her faux turtle shell shoulder bag from her shoulder in a faux attempt at paying. She quickly replaced it. 'You're a doll, Madge,' she said, taking her copy of "Lovey Dovey". 'I'll get the coffees.'

With the two ladies otherwise preoccupied, their grip loosened, Smokowski saw a chance of escape, but all his attempt at wriggling free did was draw attention back onto him.

'Oh,' said Madge, 'we're forgetting you. Do you want one? Silly question, 'course you do, wouldn't be here otherwise. I'll get yours too. One more please.'

The youth handed over another book.

'Madge had it off last light,' whispered two scarves, tapping her nose.

'Yeah,' said Madge, laughing, 'thank goodness for two fat ladies.' Madge handed the youth a bag full of fifty pence pieces. 'There's more than enough for three,' she said, placing it in the youth's outstretched hand.

The youth looked at the money in his hand then looked at Madge, he appeared to be on the verge of saying something.

'Problem?' growled Madge, menacingly.

'Eh... no,' said the youth, stepping back from the leather clad lady that was filling his view with her face, 'More than enough, I expect.' He quickly stashed the money amid horrible visions. He could see it now, in tomorrow's headlines, "ANGRY GRAN MUTILATES

BOOK BOY! READ ALL ABOUT IT!" "PICTURES!" He quickly moved along the line to the next eager punter.

'Keep the change!' Madge called after him. 'No need for thanks,' she said to Smokowski, thrusting a book his way, 'we oldies got to stick together, right?'

'Er... right,' said Smokowski, hugging his book and wondering what to do with the notelet Madge had given him.

The queue started to move again, taking with it a stricken and bewildered shopkeeper called Smokowski. The doors drew closer. And closer still. And as the doors finally loomed large, Tom and Brandy reappeared from within. Smokowski just had time to duck back and nip behind Madge to hide. He watched as Tom and Brandy approached the square. He watched as they stopped halfway across and words were exchanged. He watched as Tom started walking back to the shop. Oh no, thought Smokowski, he'll see me for sure, but the door had been reached and another surge was about to take place, this time fronted by Madge and two scarves. It easily breached the already harassed security defences and Smokowski was bundled inside, out of sight. Tom missed him, he missed Tom. Smokowski also missed Tom queuing for Brandy's magazine. He missed Tom rejoining Brandy. He missed them stopping beside a tree where a small crowd had formed. He missed them disappearing into the public lavatories. What he didn't miss was what he at first took to be an orang-utan. Oh woe is me, thought Smokowski, as the orang-utan took his book, he had been so close.

CHAPTER 29

'So,' said the Chief Traveller, 'what do you think?'

'I think it's about time someone let me out,' said Invisible Bob, from the confines of the welder's mask and helmet.

'Beatrice, if you wouldn't mind,' said the Chief, nodding at the mask.

Beatrice picked up the mask and lifted Invisible Bob from the floor.

'You do know I'm naked?' said Invisible Bob.

'Rubber gloves,' said Beatrice, smiling.

'Ah,' said Invisible Bob, warily. 'Don't suppose you've got any chocolate?' He had developed a hankering for it after his adventure in the pick and mix.

'Chief?' said Beatrice.

'Take him to the canteen.'

'I'll see what I can find,' said Beatrice, whisking Invisible Bob away.

'Not sure,' said Cat, who had been studying the wall. 'Could be connected, or red-herrings. Talking of which, got any chicken?' Listening to Invisible Bob she realised it had been a while since last she had eaten.

'I've some tucked away in the fridge,' said the Chief.

'Good man,' said Cat.

'But connected you say, how so?'

'Just a feeling, all of them on the same grid like that,' said Cat, 'could be a path to the ripple.'

'A path?'

'Leading us to it or up it,' said Cat. 'Whoever did this either made a mistake, purposely left us clues for reasons known only to them, or just wants to lead us on a wild goose chase.'

The Chief Traveller studied the wall. 'Well,' he said scratching his head, 'you see more than I do.'

'Like I said, just a feeling.'

'But sadly we have to check all that's left, and as that's why you are here, Catranna, which do you fancy visiting first?'

Cat gave the bulbs some thought. 'A trip to the Greenwoods I think.'

'Anything I can do to help, just ask.'

'Some chicken would be nice.'

The Chief laughed and led Cat to the canteen.

'So, what's going *down*?' said Invisible Bob, as they entered, his voice emanating from a fast disappearing chocolate egg on one of the tables.

'Down?' said the Chief.

'What's happening,' Cat explained.

'Ah,' said the Chief, as he took some chicken from the fridge. He carried it to the table Bob was on and placed it in front of Cat.

'Thank you,' said Cat, mouth watering.

As she ate, the Chief filled Invisible Bob in as to what was going down.

'Cool,' said Invisible Bob, 'can I finish my chocolate first?'

'I'm sorry,' said the Chief, 'but I'm afraid your part in this is over Bob. Catranna can't be worrying about you.'

'Cat?' said Invisible Bob, a piece of egg dropping to the table top. He thought Cat and he were a team.

'He could be handy,' said Cat, keeping with her thoughts while in the pyramid.

'You really think so?' said the Chief.

'Got me here, didn't he?'

'Yeah, I got her here, didn't I?' said a miffed Invisible Bob.

'If you're sure?' said the Chief.

'I am here you know,' said Invisible Bob.

Cat finished her chicken and licked her whiskers. 'He won't be a problem.'

'Okay then,' said the Chief, far from sure himself. 'Anything else I can do before you set off, Catranna?'

There was, but it was more what he could do while she was away. Cat told the Chief Traveller what she wanted.

'Already in hand,' said the Chief, smugly.

'It is?' said Cat, puzzled.

'Oh yes,' said the Chief, tapping the side of his nose with a finger.

And as it seemed the Chief wasn't going to elaborate, Cat took her leave. 'We better get started then.'

The Chief Traveller escorted Cat and Invisible Bob, who was sat on her back, back to the dark room and wished them luck as they left through the broken door.

Cat took it, she had the feeling they were going to need a lot of it.

'So where in the Greenwoods are we going?' asked Bob.

'To the Hood first, I think,' she replied.

'Hey dude, that's cool, hanging wit me bruvvers an' all.'

'Not that kind of hood you imbecile,' said Cat, thinking perhaps the Chief had been right, 'the one dressed in green.'

'Cool,' said Bob.

CHAPTER 30

'Hush!' hissed Brandy, holding a finger to her lips.

'What?' said Tom, who had been whistling.

'We're in a library remember.'

'And?'

'You have to be quiet.'

'Do you?'

'Just how long has it been since you were in a library?'

'Can't remember,' said Tom, thinking about it. 'Think I was a kid, got thrown out for talking.'

'There you go then.'

Tom went to whistle again, but thought better of it. 'Where do they keep Da Vinci then?' he asked instead.

'Under D or V, I expect?'

'Where's that?'

'As I said,' said Brandy, fluttering her considerable lashes, 'I'm the beauty round here. Why don't you ask that stern looking lady sitting at the desk, the one glaring at you?'

Wow, thought Tom, after looking round and meeting the woman's gaze, must be a hell mouth needs guarding around here.

'Go on,' egged Brandy.

'You go,' said Tom, not fancying it one bit.

'I can't,' said Brandy, already drifting in the other direction, 'I want to see if they have any Leslie Poppett books.'

'I'm scared,' said Tom. The woman was still glaring at him.

'Tough, I'm off, see you in a mo.' Brandy breezed off in search of Poppett.

Tom was on his own. Tom was far from happy about it. Tom was damned if he was going to ask the hell mouth gatekeeper for anything. Tom stood there for a moment or two. Tom was adamant.

'Excuse me,' said Tom, just after the second moment had passed.

'Yes?' said the stern looking lady behind the desk cum gatekeeper to hell, perhaps, her glare intensifying.

'I… er… I was…'

'Dithering? Whistling? Talking loudly? Accosting a young lady? All of the above?' said the stern looking etcetera, etcetera.

'Now you just wait a darn tooting minute there,' said Tom, mustering up, although not realising it, a rather good impression of the late great James Stewart.

'Da Vinci is it?'

'Wha…'

'You're looking for information regarding Leonardo Da Vinci, yes or no?' said the stern etcetera.

How did she know? Tom was taken aback and a little perturbed by this mysterious turn of events. Was she magical? Did she read minds? Perhaps she was a witch? For a man who had once boasted a mind of little imagination it was now playing a blinder. 'How?' said Tom, his mouth working on automatic for the moment as his brain was otherwise occupied.

'I heard you talking about him?' said the etcetera, etcetera.

'Oh,' said Tom, imagination back in its box.

'What is it you are looking for in particular?'

'Well, to be honest, I'm not entirely sure,' Tom admitted.

'Have you tried the computers? There's a lot to be found surfing you know, although you can't believe all you read. Safer with a well thought out book on the subject.'

'You have computers?' said Tom.

'Oh yes, five of them,' said the etcetera.

'Five.'

'But for how long I don't know, what with the budget cuts and people swopping books on the internet willy-nilly. We're a dying institution. A dinosaur of the twenty-first century you could be led to think, but we're so much more than that, we're an information centre, a hub of learning. We'll fight them. We're not finished yet. With the backing of the public and high profile authors we'll fight our corner, just you wait and see.'

'Five,' said Tom, eyes glazed over.

'Are you okay?' The stern looking lady looked concerned. 'I could phone for help if you want. Have you a name tag?'

'A name tag?'

'From the institution or care home that takes care of you. Was that young woman you were talking to your carer?'

'Carer?' What was the woman going on about?

The back to stern looking lady stood up, causing Tom to flinch. 'I'm a busy woman you know,' she said moving from behind her desk, 'and I've got better things to do than sit around joking with you all day. Come with me.'

Joking? thought Tom, who seemed to be finding it increasingly difficult to string a sentence together either verbally or mentally. Tom followed the woman like a lamb to slaughter.

'This,' said the stern looking lady, showing Tom a door, 'is the computer room. Any problems, please give me a whisper and I'll try to help.'

'Computer room,' said Tom.

'Ah,' said the stern looking lady, 'a sequence. Isn't education a wonderful thing? Passwords can be obtained at the desk.' She returned to her desk leaving Tom to it.

'There you are,' said Brandy, suddenly arriving at Tom's shoulder and making him jump.

'Don't do that,' said Tom.

'Do what?' said Brandy.

'Creep up on me like that.'

'How do you want me to creep up on you?'

Tom narrowed his eyes, he wasn't in the mood for tomfoolery. 'Do you know how to work one of them?' he said, casting a thumb at the computer room door.

'A door?'

'A flaming computer!'

The stern looking lady glared at Tom.

'Ooh,' said Brandy, 'she *has* got your knickers in a twist.'

'Who?' said Tom, knowing full well who Brandy meant.

'Yes.'

'What?' said Tom.

'I do know how to use a computer.'

'Can you show me how to use one?'

'But I thought your grandson had already surfed and drawn a blank.'

'For future reference,' said Tom, thinking here was an opportunity to save cash and save him further school yard lurking. 'I'll stick to the books for now.'

'Okay, but later, when our mission is complete.'

'Fair dos,' said Tom.

'And now, if you've quite finished messing about with that woman, I've found a whole shelf of Da Vinci stuff we should look at.'

'I was not messing about with any woman,' said Tom, indignantly.

'Doesn't surprise me,' said Brandy, under her breath.

'What was that?'

'I said, I've arranged them chronologically.' Brandy took Tom by the arm and led him to the Da Vinci shelf, but not straight to it.

'And this is his fourth novel, "Dovey Lovey",' said Brandy, shoving the copy under Tom's nose.

'We got time for this?' said Tom, beginning to think they were never going to get started on the mission.

'There's always time for Poppett,' said Brandy, brightly.

There's a song there somewhere, thought Tom, a bawdy one perhaps, but time was passing. 'I really think we should be looking at those Da Vinci books,' he said.

Brandy looked put out.

'Tell you what,' said Tom, who was finding he had had more than enough of the fairer sex for one day, 'you show me how to use a computer and I'll look at all the Poppett books with you. Wouldn't that be nice?'

Condescending little... 'Okay,' said Brandy. She put "Dovey Lovey" back on the shelf amongst its many brothers and sisters.

'Blimey,' said Tom, on noticing how many Poppett books there were, 'there are loads of them.' There goes retirement.

'Yes,' said Brandy, brightening up, 'He's written loads of biographies as well as novels you know. There's his toddler years, his university years, his first year writing year, his problem with his bowel movement years. It's all there.'

What about his, ripping off the public with endless biographies years, thought Tom. 'So where's the Da Vinci shelf then?' he said.

'Over there,' said Brandy.

At last they stood before the shelf they had come to sift through.

'There's loads of books here as well,' said Tom, wondering where to start.

'I took the liberty of stacking a few that might be the most useful on the table there,' said Brandy, wiggling over to a table. She pointed to a tome of gargantuan proportions. 'And I thought this one might be the best one to start with, it's got pictures.'

If she was trying to be funny it wasn't showing, thought Tom, but all was revealed when Brandy opened it. 'Ah,' said Tom, 'paintings! But shouldn't we be looking for dates and whatnot?'

'All in good time,' said Brandy, sounding most unBrandylike – serious almost, 'Look at this painting.'

Tom looked, and actually recognised it, sort of. 'It's that, what's it called? No, don't tell me. Got it, it's the last something or other. Am I right?'

'Yes, Tom, it's the Last Supper, but take a closer look and tell me what you see.'

The same as you I expect, thought Tom, puzzled, but he stuck his head closer to the picture anyway and studied it. And then noticed something that he couldn't remember seeing when last he had seen the painting, on the telly or somewhere. 'What are those?' he asked, pointing to something in the background.

'Hot air balloons,' said Brandy.

'Balloons?' said Tom. Even he knew they didn't have them in those days. 'They didn't have balloons in those days did they?' he asked, just to make sure.

'No,' said Brandy, 'and if by some quirk of fate they did, but their presence had somehow gone undocumented, I doubt that the fast food chain advertised on the basket beneath the right balloon would have been around.'

Tom gave the right balloon closer scrutiny. She was right. 'Good grief!' he suddenly spouted, as his close scrutiny moved to the balloon beside it. 'That one's advertising unmentionables. That's not right.' Tom closed the book to take another look at the cover, keeping his place with a finger. Surely the book was one of those humorous jobbies. 'Surely it's one of those humorous books?' said Tom.

'Afraid not,' said Brandy.

'Then what's going on?' said Tom, opening the book again.

'That is what we have to find out,' said Brandy, reminding Tom of their mission. 'I just thought it might be prudent to show you the consequences of whatever is happening back there. And remember, to the ordinary Joe public nothing is wrong – to them the painting has always had balloons in it.'

'Won't they wonder about the adverts though?'

'They'll just think that that's where the companies got their ideas from, Da Vinci had weird and wonderful ideas remember, apart from his paintings it's what he's remembered for.'

'And there's me thinking you're the pretty face around here,' said Tom.

'I am,' said Brandy, laughing softly.

'So how are we going to get all these books you've piled here home again? I can't see us getting through all these here without interruption and I don't think the gatekeeper will let us borrow all these at once.'

'Gatekeeper?' said Brandy.

'Private joke,' said Tom.

Brandy didn't ask. 'We'll borrow them last night,' she said.

Tom frowned at Brandy's suggestion. 'Then how can we be here looking at them now if we've already got them?'

'Because we'll put them back last night as well.'

'But won't I have… but… never mind.' Tom had tried and was giving it another go, but just couldn't get his head around this whole time travel malarkey. 'Let's go then,' he said, deciding this was something he could understand.

'Ouch!'

'Hang about I've got a torch,' said Brandy, delving into her apparently bottomless handbag.

'Aargh!'

'Sorry,' said Brandy, moving the torchlight from Tom's face.

As Tom now had trouble seeing, Brandy took point, Tom stumbling behind, dots before his eyes.

'Here,' said Brandy, stopping.

Tom, stumbling blindly behind, didn't.

'Oof!' said Brandy, tottering on her five inch heels.

'Sorry.'

Regaining her poise, Brandy shone the torch on a row of books. 'Hold out your arms.'

'Why?'

'You've been a naughty boy.'

'But you shone the tor...'

'I'm kidding, you idiot, I want to put the books on them.'

'Oh.' Tom stretched out his arms.

A couple of minutes later Tom was staggering back to the library toilet, arms laden, wondering why they needed so many.

'I know it's rude to ask a lady, but I don't suppose you could see your way to giving me a hand and carrying something?' said Tom, straining under the weight.

Brandy tut-tutted him. 'I am carrying something and yes, it is rude to ask a lady.' She showed Tom the book she was carrying, "Dovey Lovey" by Leslie Poppett.

'You've just bought that,' said Tom, struggling on.

'Silly, that was Lovey Dovey, this is the one before that one. I just wanted to read the last couple of chapters to refresh the mind before I started on the new one. Now come on, we haven't got all last night you know.'

Back at the cottage Tom rubbed his aching arms as Brandy arranged their haul on the kitchen table.

'Look,' said Brandy, leaning over the book of paintings they had been looking at later that day.

'Give me a mo,' said Tom, still rubbing, 'I still can't feel my little fingers.'

Brandy picked the book up and took it to Tom. 'Here,' she said, holding the book open at the Last Supper.

Tom stopped his rubbing and had a gander. 'Gawd,' he exclaimed, 'the balloons have gone.'

'Reverted back to how they should be.'

'Then they hadn't changed before we saw them later today.'

'No,' said Brandy, 'when I was told of our mission I checked ahead, they should still have the balloons in them.'

'So how have they changed?'

'I suspect it's because we've taken them into our time stream, where they're protected from outside influence. That's saves some worry.'

'Does it?'

'Yes, it means that the books we have, have the original text in them. I was a little worried that dates, places and so on, might have become corrupted, tampered with in some way or another.'

Tom stared at Brandy as she started flicking through further books. He couldn't make her out, one moment the composite professional, the next the ditzy blonde, two totally conflicting persona's. Which was the true Brandy? Was the ditzy Brandy just an act? Perhaps they were both Brandy, on and off duty, but whatever, he knew which one he preferred – the ditzy Brandy, you knew where you were with that version, providing it wasn't all just a show. The non-blonde version, the professional Brandy, was frankly unnerving, almost scary.

'So,' said Tom, grimacing as he flexed little fingers in the grips of pins and needles, 'what now?'

'I guess we start reading. The sooner we have dates etcetera, the sooner we can pay our painter friend a visit. You still got your notebook?'

'I have,' said Tom, pulling it from his jacket pocket. Such a shame he hadn't been able to get it out at the library and bamboozle nosey parkers with his Da Vinci code.

'Then get stuck in,' said Brandy.

Tom picked up the book nearest, read the title "Leonardo – the good years", wondered if there was one about the bad ones and was about to open it, when Brandy took it from him.

'You won't need that one,' said Brandy, who had been busy dividing the pile of books on the table into two. 'Now the books are back to normal it's only the reference books that need sifting through.'

'You mean I carried all those others back for nothing?'

'Not for nothing, Tom, at the time I didn't know we didn't need them, did I.' Brandy pointed to one of the piles she had made. 'I brought these with us because of the changes, we might have needed them to use as a cross reference should we have suspected a discrepancy in 'these.' She now pointed to the other pile. She placed the book she had taken from Tom back on the first pile.

'Okay,' said Tom, wishing he hadn't said anything. 'I'll start at the top.' He sat down at the table, licked the sharp end of his pencil, placed it beside his notebook, and took the first book from the top of the old pile.

'Good choice,' said Brandy, hovering by Tom's shoulder.

'Thank you,' said Tom, opening it, 'Which one are you going to start with?'

'This one of course, silly,' said Brandy, brandishing "Dovey Lovey". 'I thought I'd borrow your bedroom if that's okay and get started on those chapters while you're working, keep out of your way. Give me a shout when you're done, sweetie.' She gave a wriggled wave of her fingers then left, leaving behind a Tom so flabbergasted he hadn't noticed he had just snapped his newly licked pencil clean in two.

CHAPTER 31

A dishevelled, ruffled, tousled, book he didn't want under his arm, Smokowski, hurried across the square to the gents' toilets. He passed a furtive glance across to the tree where a small crowd was dispersing. Nothing to see there, he thought, as he maintained speed. He reached the top of the stairs, cast another furtive look, this time behind him, and raced down them. At the bottom, out of breath and having flashbacks of old dears dressed in leather and talking orang-utans, he pressed the hitchhiker and disappeared.

An instant later he was somewhere else. It took a second for Smokowski to gather his wits and hear the voices, voices that appeared to be all around him. Did he open his eyes? His earlier good work falling by the wayside. He knew he had too. A feeling of trepidation spread over him. What if he had materialised in the middle of a crowd? The temptation to press the hitchhiker was suddenly overwhelming. But he couldn't, what if he missed something important? What if? Smokowski opened his eyes and was overwhelmingly relieved to find he was in another cubicle. A cubicle that's door was standing slightly ajar. Heart thumping, he quickly closed it and slid the latch across. He could now listen to the voices in relative safety. He listened. The colour drained from his face. Sugar and spice, he thought, as he realised where he was. A school, and pound to a penny it was Marc and Katie's. Tom or not, he wasn't stopping there, shouldn't be there, he hurriedly pressed the hitchhiker.

An instant later he was standing in a small corridor, or at least that is what he thought it was when he first opened his eyes. He now saw that it wasn't a corridor, but two high racks of books, either side of him. He had landed facing the open end. He turned around, the other end was a wall. Had to be a library, he thought, noticing the thumbed look of some of the books. But why a library? Tom hadn't been in one for donkey's years as far as he could recall, but that is where the

121

hitchhiker had led him. Perhaps Marc hadn't been able to help this time.

After slowly edging to the open end, Smokowski cautiously peered beyond. No sign of Tom or anyone else for that matter, but he had to be careful, anyone, including Tom, could be browsing hidden from view. For the moment though it appeared all clear and he was about to step further than the one he had already taken when he noticed he wasn't alone after all, a rather stern looking lady was sat at a desk to his right, only visible when he had taken that step. Blimey, thought Smokowski, must be a Hell mouth needs guarding. He quickly ducked back to take stock of his situation, no point blundering about until he had an idea what he was going to do. If the entrance was anywhere near her, she might ask questions as to how he had got passed her without her noticing. He didn't need questions like that, could bring unwanted attention.

But he couldn't stay where he was, that was for sure. Tom could suddenly pop around the corner any moment and then what would he do? No, he had to try and spot Tom first and keep a discreet distance. But what if he wasn't in here, what then? He could have gone outside, be anywhere. Smokowski sagged against a wall of books. He was getting too old for this, but old or not, it had to be done. He gave himself a couple of seconds then, head down, went about his business. Less than ten minutes later he had covered most of the library, including the ladies' toilets, which he had had grave misgivings about. This left a room with a computer room sign fixed on its door as the last place to look. That and under the desk where the stern looking lady was still sitting. He had decided he wasn't going to look there whatever the repercussions for not doing so might be. So he sidled across to the computer room door and was about to carefully open it when…

'Can I help you?'

If Smokowski had been a cat he would have had kittens, but he wasn't, he was a man, so he had a very good attempt at jumping out of his skin. Luckily the seams, as old as they were, held firm. 'Agh!' he yelled. This yell was quickly pursued by a scream of pain. 'Ow!' he screamed.

'You're not thinking of stealing that book are you?' asked the same voice that had nearly sent Smokowski into orbit. It belonged to the stern looking lady from behind the desk, who had been watching Smokowski ever since he had crept from the bookshelves he had arrived between.

Smokowski, heart pounding, toe throbbing, bent down to pick up his copy of "Lovey Dovey" which, until a second ago, he had had secreted about his person. 'My toe,' said Smokowski, rising to face his accuser.

'The book please,' said the stern looking lady.

'It's mine,' said Smokowski.

'Prove it.'

Smokowski suddenly didn't look right. 'I don't want to,' he said.

But the stern looking lady wasn't having any of it and snatched the book away from Smokowski before he could react. The stern lady opened it and saw there was a hand written dedication on the first page; she read it. She raised an eyebrow. She then raised another.

'The notes got mixed up,' said Smokowski, desperate he should explain, throbbing toe forgotten about for the moment.

'None of my business, now that I know it's not property of the library,' said the stern lady, handing Smokowski his book back.

'But it was Madge's note. It's her leather and stockings he's on about. She was the one that wrote she wanted them filled with good things.' Smokowski looked as if he was going to sob.

'As I said, it's none of my business, I'm the librarian here and the library is what I care about. Now, how can I help you?'

She didn't believe him. Smokowski stuffed the book back out of sight, he didn't feel well. That's why he probably told the stern looking lady that he was looking for his friends. He couldn't think straight. She thinks I dress in stockings and leather, he thought, groaning inside.

'There's no one here but us,' said the stern looking lady librarian.

'They must have left,' said Smokowski, wishing he had too, aiming to do just that once he had escaped the librarian's clutches. 'I'll be off too then.'

But the stern looking lady librarian persisted, 'Perhaps I saw them. What do they look like?'

Drat, thought Smokowski, he didn't have time for this. He needed to find Tom. *She thought he dressed in leather and things.* He would make his excuse me's and barge past her. *She was imagining him in stockings and suspenders this very moment.* It might appear rude but… but there it was. He was a busy man. He needed to go. Instead, he heard himself describing Tom and Brandy to her. Why was he doing that?

'Oh them,' said the stern looking lady librarian, eyebrow arching, 'Mister noisy and Madam blonde bombshell. Not the sort I'd have thought to be interested in Da Vinci, but there you go.' The stern looking lady librarian crossed her arms. 'I suspect it's to do with the code, everyone's obsessed with it you know.'

Smokowski didn't want to, but had to ask, it might be important.

'Goes back years,' said the stern looking lady librarian, 'don't believe it myself, but you know what people are like, UFO's and whatnot.' She then started on about UFO's and the wherefore's of whatnots.

This was wasted on Smokowski as he knew all there was to know about UFO's and whatnots, but what she had said about a code had interested him. Was Tom really looking into that old poppycock? He should report it to Cat though, it might be important? That is, if he ever found where she was. 'What did they do then?' he asked.

'Well,' said the stern looking lady librarian putting the brakes on her whatnots, 'they must have left. I didn't actually see them leave, but as they're not here I assume that's what happened.'

'Then I'll take my leave as well,' said Smokowski, the pain in his toe reintroducing itself as he went to walk past the librarian. But the stern looking lady librarian didn't move, instead she hovered before him, barring his way. Smokowski's head instantly filled with dread, the sort associated with menacing grannies.

The stern looking lady librarian gave Smokowski a stern look and pointed. 'The exit's that way,' she said.

Ah, thought Smokowski, now also hovering, but without the menace. 'I need to use the toilet first,' he said, telling no lie, but wondering what she would make of his later non reappearance, because a woman like her would notice for sure. *Notice the non reappearance of the strange old man who likes wearing stockings and leather.* She was bound to mention it to someone when she raised the alarm and an investigation ensued. Woe was he.

'Take a left then right.' The stern looking lady librarian stepped out of Smokowski's way, 'But you'll have to let yourself out, I have work in the office before we shut for the day. Please close the door when you leave.'

Thank heavens, thought Smokowski breathing a rather large sigh. 'Thank you,' he said, trying to contain his relief, 'and I'll most definitely be sure to close the door behind me.' He hobbled off, eager to get away from the librarian's stare, which he was sure was burning into his back as he went. All he wanted to do now was get to a cubicle – he didn't think he should chance leaving from where he had arrived – squeeze the hitchhiker, and get the heck as far away from there as possible.

CHAPTER 32

'So you know him then?' said Invisible Bob, moving double time to keep pace with Cat.

'No,' said Cat.

'You know some of his merry men then?' Invisible Bob persisted.

'No,' said Cat.

'Then who do you know?'

'Here?'

'Yes.'

'No one.'

'Then who are you going to hook up with?'

Cat stopped dead.

Invisible Bob didn't, but didn't walk into her – instead he found a quite adequate sapling to provide the comic relief.

'We're here to survey the lie of the land,' said Cat, getting just a tad tetchy due to the constant dribble of questions Invisible Bob had aimed at her since they had arrived, 'and that is all, unless opportunity throws something our way.'

Twisting off his back onto his tummy, Invisible Bob raised himself up on his elbows and did some land surveying of his own. 'I'd say the lie of the land is trees, trees, and more trees,' he said, 'not unlike what we've been seeing the past quarter of an hour.' He stood up and brushed moss from his head. 'I've never seen so many trees. It's a good job old Robin isn't made of wood, we'd never see him.' Invisible Bob laughed alone at his little joke and brushed more moss from his knees. 'And talking of, when do you think that is likely, only I'm a tad thirsty and a little hungry and I don't see any of "ye old hostelries" about the place.'

'I didn't say the job would be easy, or quick,' said Cat, wondering if perhaps it would have been wiser to have left the little idiot behind after all. Too late now though.

'You haven't said a whole lot,' grumbled Invisible Bob, miffed at getting a whole line of negatives to his questioning. 'So until you tell me more about our plan, I'm not taking one step further.' Invisible Bob sat down.

'Good,' said Cat, moving off, 'I'll see you on the way back.'

'Wait!' said Invisible Bob, scrambling upright, 'You can't leave me here all alone, something might eat me.'

'Something won't be able to see you,' said Cat, stopping and looking back at the patches of moss stain that was all that could be seen of her companion.

'They could smell me.'

His point was valid, and Cat, ever the lady, kept any irreverent thoughts she may have just had to herself. 'You'll have to be careful then,' she said. She continued with her moving away.

'Okay, okay,' said Invisible Bob, taking after her on the hurry up, 'but just tell me one thing.'

'The sky's blue,' said Cat.

'Ha-ha,' said Invisible Bob, 'very droll I don't think.'

Cat called a halt to her moving. Perhaps she would get some peace to concentrate if she answered this one question. Personally she doubted it. 'Okay, but I thought I explained everything about the plan. We arrive, we search for whatever caused the ripple here, we retrieve it or stop it, whichever, then report back and move onto the next if it's not the cause of the true unfelt ripple, and ditto, stopping only to compare notes each time to see if we can establish a link. There, satisfied now?'

'I knew that,' said Invisible Bob.

'Then what?' asked Cat, the skin under her fur starting to turn purple. She counted to ten.

'I want to know how you did it.'

'Did what?' said Cat, exasperation moving into the red.

'Get us here, to Hoody land.'

Good grief, thought Cat, but if it will help us on our way in a modicum of silence. 'Magic,' said Cat, 'I used magic.' She shook her head and went to move off again. 'Can we get going now?'

'I know that,' said Invisible Bob, 'I'm not stupid, what I mean is how?'

Cat turned and glared at the moss patches floating in mid-air. Would anyone notice if he were to disappear she wondered? Perhaps – she slowly retracted her claws which had so dutifully made an appearance and forced her ire to follow suit. It was a reasonable question. She had chosen to bring him along. 'I imagine the past as being a huge book which I flick through until I find the page or time I'm looking for, then I step in and become one with it. Happy?'

'You don't need a Traveller or hitchhiker then?'

'No.'

Invisible Bob gave this some thought. He finished. 'So we have to travel to seven places in total then, unless we find the true unfelt ripple first?'

Cat's eyes widened. How did his mind work? Perhaps she would muse on it sometime, but not now, enough was enough. She lashed out. You can only push a cat so far.

Invisible Bob tumbled backwards as Cat's paw swept at him. Luckily for him, Cat was still of the mind someone might miss him so claws had been stayed. He rolled to a stop beside the sapling he had earlier been acquainted with. 'Something I said?' he wheezed.

'I was just saying,' said Invisible Bob, who had finally caught up with Cat after his tumbling.

'Just instinctive,' said Cat, 'don't take it personally, it's what we cats do.' She didn't add, "to small annoying creatures".

'Send harmless little people into orbit?'

'If the need be.'

'Not very friendly.'

'I didn't use my claws did I?'

Invisible Bob fell silent, a silence that stayed with him as they continued their way through the greenwood. A silence that after a while Cat found unnerving – unnerving in that she found herself actually missing his inane chatter. Strangely, Invisible Bob being quiet was worse than him making noise. So much so, she found she needed to say something. In a bizarre way perhaps she was missing Tom.

'England was once covered by forest you know,' said Cat, dragging forth small talk.

'You don't say,' said Invisible Bob, who had been dragging small invisible feet, but not as slow as to lose Cat.

'Acres and acres of it,' said Cat.

'A dog's paradise, eh?' said Invisible Bob, who then thought better of his remark, 'Pardon my French.'

'You're pardoned,' said Cat.

'Must...'

'Sssh!' hissed Cat suddenly, crouching low.

A noise split the air, a whooshing sound, followed by a thud and thwack.

Invisible Bob, wide eyed, near witless and so very nearly brainless, turned unsteadily and looked up to see an arrow, still swaying, embedded in the tree trunk behind him. Its goose feathered end not half an inch above his head. He suddenly felt very faint.

'Stay quiet,' whispered Cat, 'I don't want anyone to know you're here.'

'Wh...'

'Robin,' said Cat, paw held tight on Invisible Bob's mouth, head, neck and chest.

'Catranna?' said a surprised male voice, 'What are you doing here?'

I thought she said she didn't know him, thought Invisible Bob.

'There's a problem,' said Cat.

Cor, thought Invisible Bob, what's that pong?

'When isn't there?' laughed Robin Hood. He reached down and tousled Cat's head, something only a brave man would do. When he had finished taking his life in his hands he apologised for his errant arrow and explained he thought he had heard a stranger's voice and had fired on instinct. He and his men had just rescued Little John from the Sheriff's clutches, so he was a bit edgy. The smell, he explained was his reward for his trouble – he had fallen into a pigsty as they had hurried their escape. 'Anyone with you?'

'Just me,' said Cat. She exerted more pressure on Invisible Bob's mouth, head, neck and chest.

'Then you have to tell me what it is that brings you to my humble home. But first let me clean up and then we'll talk about our troubles over a hearty meal.'

Did he say something about food? Invisible Bob's mouth started watering at the thought, his imminent suffocation by toe fur and pong momentarily forgotten. He wondered if Robin had any chocolate.

'The usual place?' asked Cat.

Robin nodded, retrieved his arrow, and took his leave.

'Agh!' gasped Invisible Bob taking on air, as Cat finally felt sure it was safe to remove her paw. He quickly took another lungful – this one with only the faintest scent of *eau de pig*. 'Thank goodness he's gone, he smelt worse than a ferret.' He raised his head from the ground and stared up at Cat. 'I thought you said you didn't know him.'

'Did I?'

Invisible Bob frowned up at Cat then got up and started to brush dust from his butt. She had lied to him, but there were more important matters at hand than the whys of feline duplicity; food had been mentioned. 'Did I hear someone mention food?'

'Someone did, but you're not invited. As I said, I want your presence to remain a secret so you can have a poke about while I keep him busy.'

'Don't you trust him then?'

'Of course I do, but if he finds you snooping around I could lose his.'

'So you eat and I pry?' Invisible Bob was beginning to think their partnership was somewhat one sided.

'See what you can see.'

'Trees, trees and more trees at a guess.'

'I'll drop you off at Robin's camp as we pass. I'll pick you up when I return.'

'Will there be food?'

'Don't get caught!'

A grinning Invisible Bob took that as a green light for nosh snaffling. 'What should I look for?'

'Anything out of the ordinary,' said Cat, 'Now climb up.'

CHAPTER 33

Tom was fast becoming word blind. He looked at the clock. Good grief, he thought, I've been at it solid for over ten minutes. Tom decided he needed another cuppa.

With one book solidly skimmed and a second left open at page two, Tom put the kettle on. He needed a rest – it was hard work this researching lark. He thought about giving Brandy a shout to see if she wanted one, but decided against it; he needed to concentrate. Didn't need distractions. Needed to apply himself wholly to the task at hand. Tom went to the biscuit tin. He opened it and peered inside. One jammy one, of the dodging persuasion, two rich tea and half a cream bourbon. Rich pickings indeed. Tom reached inside and pulled out the remains of the bourbon.

Water boiled, cuppa made, kettle kicking its heels, Tom resumed his seat of learning. Only five more books to go, he thought, as he settled down to further mental exercise. He dipped his biscuit into his cuppa and moved onto page three. He picked up his pencil with his free hand – a quick note. No, perhaps not, not relevant. The pencil hovered. The notebook waited. Tom was sure he had already read what he was reading in the first book. Better move onto the third book.

The clock ticked on. Tom sipped at his cuppa and munched on his biscuit. The ticking was starting to get on his nerves. How was he supposed to work in these conditions? He finished his biscuit and started on book four. Four minutes later, and about to pick up book five, the door to the kitchen open and in flounced a flushed looking Brandy.

'Finished!' she announced, as she drifted in on a private cloud of satisfaction.

Tom wiped biscuit crumbs from his fingers. 'Have you?' he said, while trying to remember what it was she had started. It was no good, he would have to ask – must be all this learning clouding his mind.

'What?' He had noticed that she no longer had the beads in her hair; he wasn't keen on those.

'My book, silly.'

'*Your* book?'

'"Lovey Dovey".'

It all suddenly came back to him, but it still didn't make any sense. 'I thought you were going to read "Dovey Lovey"?'

'I did, but only the last couple of chapters. *Then* I read "Lovey Dovey". Easy-peasy.'

Tom's eyes roamed to the clock. She had only been away for about fifteen minutes, surely she couldn't have read it already. His gaze returned to the table and the books on it – the four he had "read". Maybe she had skimmed as well. 'All of it? Already?' he said.

'I'm a bit of a speed reader, comes with the job, but I have to admit I did slow done when I read it the second time. Oh Tom, it was so scrummy. So full of romance, love, horticultural tips and sex.' Brandy's eyes fairly twinkled with delight.

A spluttering Tom's, on the other hand, were now fairly full of tea.

Brandy brought him some kitchen towels and as he wiped his face she asked how he had been getting on. She went to pick up Tom's notebook.

'Ah-hem,' said Tom, just able to see what she was about to do and get there first, 'well, let's see. Ah... yes. He was born in fourteen fifty-two.' It was all that was written.

'Well done you,' said Brandy, still riding her high, 'Shall we go?'

'He'll be a little young don't you think?' said Tom, relieved his malingering had gone unnoticed.

'Strike while the iron's hot, I say,' said Brandy, 'Anyway who's to say things didn't start to go wrong from day one.'

As he looked to be off the hook, Tom couldn't agree more. 'Then lead on Macbeth,' he cried, getting into the Brandy spirit, but as usual getting his Macduff's and Macbeth's muddled up. And if it led to a dead end, he could always pick another date.

Brandy, who was now standing beside Tom, crouched down until her head was level with his. She whispered in his ear. 'It's Brandy.' She then patted Tom on the head and gave him a sad little smile. 'Sure you wouldn't rather have a little rest before we go after all your hard work? I shouldn't think a couple of hours will matter one way or the other.'

Lost for a second before he realised what she was going on about, he explained why he had said what he had said.

'Well I never,' said Brandy, all smiles as she stood up, 'you learn something new every day. I didn't realise they wrote stuff as well as made fishing tackle.'

Tom made a groaning noise.

Brandy gave him a look, but decided it must be his age. She became bright eyed and bouncy again. 'Right then, I'm ready when you are,' she said.

'I'll get my cap and jacket,' said Tom, secreting his notebook from sight.

'Then lead on MacTom,' she cried, 'You know, I might start calling you that, it's kinda cute.'

Tom hoped she wouldn't.

'But first the library.'

'The library?' said Tom, stopping mid rise.

'We need to take the books back,' said Brandy.

'Why?'

'We can't leave them just lying around willy-nilly, can we? So the best place for them is back where they live. Besides, by the looks of it you should have made enough notes to keep us going for a while.' Brandy started to pick up the books. 'We can always get them back if needs be.'

Tom's blood had run cold. What did he do? What could he do? And then, in a flash of inspiration brought forth by desperation, he had an idea. Like a bullet from a gun, like a greyhound from a trap, like a lazy desperate old sod from a kitchen chair, Tom ran from the kitchen, past a bewildered Brandy. He returned less than a minute later, carrying a digital camera. He headed to the table, past a still bewildered Brandy, and looked for one book in particular. When he found it he started to leaf through it, stopping here and there, taking pictures as he went.

'Ah,' said Brandy, nodding approval, 'like a spy.'

More like a lazy doddering old fool, thought Tom. 'Better safe than sorry,' he said, working like a mad man, 'If I lost my notebook and all my hard work with it, I don't know what we'd do?' He wondered if he should ditch the thing anyway. No, he decided; better to fill it in as he went, if he had time. Besides, the thing had cost money.

Less than five minutes later Tom was ready to place "Major Events in the Life of Leonardo Da Vinci" back on the shelf where it belonged. 'Finished,' said Tom, sweat beading on his forehead.

'Then lead on MacTom!'

'Ah, smell that,' exclaimed Brandy, embracing the romance of the moment, 'Florence, one of my favourite cities.'

Behind her Tom was once more busy rubbing life into his arms. The books had been safely transported without a hitch. Tom suddenly stopped his rubbing and patted his jacket pocket. It was all right, the camera was still there.

'Come on,' said Brandy, opening the loo door.

'Come on where?' queried Tom, under the impression they were already where they were supposed to be – the loo having deposited them in a loo in Florence, somewhere near where Da Vinci was born. All they had to do now was leap back in time to Da Vinci's birth.

'To see the sights.' Brandy stepped from the loo and started to take deep breaths. 'Smell that air, the romance lingering upon it.'

Tom took a breath. All he could smell was the faint odour of lemon and bleach. 'You do know we're still in the toilets?'

'Oh, Tom,' said Brandy, 'where's your soul, your poetry?'

'I only know one poem.' Tom started to recite, 'There was a young lady from Barry who...'

'I think that is quite enough of that,' said Brandy, cutting Tom off in mid ditty, 'Now, are you coming or do I have to drag you to the shops?'

'Shops?'

'Best ones in the world if you don't count Rome or Milan,' said Brandy.

'I thought we were going to find Da Vinci?'

'But Tom,' said Brandy, stopping, lashes a flutter, 'I thought you had planned this little surprise for moi?'

Surprise? thought Tom. 'What surprise?' said Tom.

'Why, you bringing me to Florence of course, one of my all time favourite places, without telling me. It's what I'd call a surprise.'

Tom had a sinking feeling building – if that's possible. 'But I thought that's where Da Vinci was born.' That is what he had thought he had read.

A shadow formed over Brandy's sunny disposition. She looked suddenly downcast. But it only lasted a moment. Smiling, she gave Tom a playful thump on the arm. 'You old devil Tom MacTom, you're playing with me, aren't you?'

'I am?' The shadow on Brandy returned. Tom touched the top of his arm – she hit like a boxer, he could feel a bruise. He didn't fancy another one. 'I mean, ha-ha, I am,' he said, forcing his laugh.

'I knew you were,' said Brandy, smiling, 'if you had his birthday you had to know he was born a couple of miles away from here in Anchiano, a village of Vinci town.'

You'd think so, thought Tom. He would have to study the photographs he'd taken when he got the chance. 'Anchovies it is then?' said Tom.

'Ha-ha,' laughed Brandy, 'you make me laugh, Tom MacTom. First you surprise me with Florence and now you want to feed me fishes.'

Tom, wishing she would stop calling him that, wondered what was he missing now? He decided to ask – which was a good thing as landing in the sea or a fisherman's catch in the fifteenth century, wasn't.

When Brandy had stopped laughing over Tom's mistake she decided perhaps it would be wiser to travel to Anchiano sooner than later, even though she could see he was upset about her missing out on his little surprise. Better to go now before Tom forgot the name again and got them into trouble. Florence wasn't going anywhere; plenty of other days to go shopping.

They went back to the loo and in a blink of an eye they arrived at the birth place of Leonardo Da Vinci. Another blink and they were just in time to see the great man plop into the world.

CHAPTER 34

Smokowski arrived in the same place he had just left – only this time it was darker. Puzzled, he left the toilet cubicle and crept towards the door that led to the small hall which led to the library proper. But halfway across the hall something caught his eye causing him to stop and duck.

The small hall had four walls, two of them solid; one had the door to the toilets in the centre of it, and the other one – the one Smokowski had been heading for, was solid at the base with the top half glazed. Smokowski was now crouched beneath the wall's windows. Beyond it, the torchlight he had caught in the peripherals of his vision played on shelves and walls.

Someone was out there? It had to be Tom, Smokowski figured, who else could it be? A chance to do a little detective work at last. But then doubts crept in. What if it was a burglar? But who would burgle a library? A book thief, that's who. And the chances are, if Smokowski had had the time, the debate would have gone on way into whatever small hours were left to him, but as time might be pressing, and he was getting nowhere crouched where he was, and he was starting to get cramp, he decided the only way to know for sure who was out there, was to look. Smokowski slowly raised his head until he was eyeball to reflected eyeball with the glass.

As the library was dark, but not pitch black, Smokowski began to gradually make out tables and shelves. He now saw the torch and the person holding it. But they were standing with their back to him, shining the torch's beam along a shelf of books. There was no sign of a swag bag – so was it Tom, and had he come back by himself? Smokowski couldn't see anyone else – not that that meant there wasn't others lurking out of sight. More reason to be careful. The person with the torch suddenly reached across and took a book from the shelf. They turned and faced Smokowski.

But Smokowski still couldn't quite see who it was out there. The light the torch cast on the book in front of them threw no light on their face. He shifted a little, trying to see from another angle, and that's when the cramp returned. Smokowski instinctively tried straightening his leg, but all that did was cause him to lean forward. He banged his forehead against the glass. Horrified, and glued to the spot, Smokowski could only stare as the person holding the torch, startled by the noise, fumbled with it, dropped the book they were holding and stared his way.

Uncertain whether he had been seen or not, and not wishing to find out, it was Smokowski's turn to fumble, as he frantically felt in his pocket for the hitchhiker. The position of the torch, held beam upwards because of the fumble, now illuminated the holder's face from under their chin. It was a face Smokowski recognised. It was the stern looking lady librarian.

The first thing the shaking Smokowski noticed, when he arrived wherever it was he was now, was that it was light. The second thing he noticed was that he was standing in Tom's hallway. The third thing that he noticed was the door to the bathroom standing open and the room empty. He went in. He was a relieved man.

Hands washed, heart beating regularly again, but still wondering why the librarian had been lurking about the library in the dead of night – something else to report to Cat perhaps – perhaps not – Smokowski left the bathroom and ventured back into the hall. Now what? He dithered. He was tired. He wanted to sit down. Hang it, he was going to make himself a cuppa and to heck with the consequences. But before he could take another step the kitchen door started to open.

Deciding it might be a wise move on his part if he took to hiding, Smokowski looked for somewhere to bolt. He opened the nearest door and prayed it wouldn't be a cupboard – it wasn't, it was Tom's bedroom. He slipped inside.

But now he was in there he realised he still wasn't safe. What if someone was to come in? Panic setting in and thoughts of using the hitchhiker not used, Smokowski looked to the room's window. He dithered. No, he decided – what if he got stuck? He now looked for somewhere to hide. There were only two places he could see; the wardrobe and under the bed. The door handle to the room started to turn. His fears bearing fruit he suddenly had to make a choice, he opted for the closest and dived under the bed, and not a moment too soon. The door to the room opened and someone walked in. Thank goodness for old fashion steel spring bedsteads!

He had of course been in worse situations. Trapped in the Alamo had been one. That close shave with the angry barber in Seville another. But none that Smokowski could recall had ever involved him being trapped under a sagging bed listening to a young woman constantly cooing and oohing. And trained as he was for situations that needed his full concentration, he couldn't help but wonder what was going on atop him. Thankfully that same training also helped him rein in his imagination every time it attempted to go awry. He was also thankful that at least whatever it was she was at – she was at it on her own.

Time crept on, but just as Smokowski was wondering if he was ever going to escape the domain of the dust bunnies, the cooing and oohing finally came to an end. The bed above him moved. Smokowski then watched as two tanned legs made contact with the floor. The legs then proceeded to take their mistress from the room. How long had she been at it? By the stiffness in his joints he guessed about fifteen minutes give or take. He waited until the door shut behind the legs, held fire for a couple of minutes more then, once he felt it was wise to, he crawled out from under the bed.

Bones creaking, Smokowski stretched as much as he dare and looked to the window. He was sure the hitchhiker would work from outside, but should he use it yet? Still outside was outside. Once safely out of harm's way he could think about what to do next. He went over to the window and quietly opened it. Drat! The windows had security restrictors. He wasn't going to squeeze through an inch gap. And the key was nowhere in sight. That left the door as his only escape option – that or stay put. He decided it might be safer to stay put for the moment, and was about to sit on the bed to wait the situation out when the sound of quick footsteps echoed from the hall. What now? The door handle turned. Smokowski was already under the bed.

Tom's legs appeared. They hurried across the room to a chest of drawers. Drawers were pulled open, each followed by the sound of rummaging. Smokowski heard Tom say he had got something, and then Tom was gone again.

Smokowski waited a couple of minutes, listened, and then crawled once more from under Tom's bed. Once on his feet he ventured to the door and listened, he could just about hear the murmurings of a conversation coming from the kitchen. What now? He was beginning to think hanging around wasn't such a good idea after all. Maybe he could make it to the front door. It was an idea. Smokowski very gently turned the handle on the door. He opened the door a smidgeon, the conversation got louder. So far so good, he thought. He opened it a bit more. There was a slight creak. Smokowski held his breath. He tried again. No creak this time. He pulled the door open all the way and cautiously peered round the door jamb. The kitchen door was ajar. There were flashing lights coming from within. Strange, thought Smokowski. The flashing stopped. Smokowski was now stuck again in two minds. But he didn't have time to use either of them. Grief, he thought, they're coming! Had Brandy called Tom MacTom?

Keeping the door open the slightest of slight, Smokowski listened as Tom and Brandy left the kitchen and went into the bathroom. As he did, a sudden thought sprang to mind. He had shut the bathroom door. When he had arrived it had been open. Would they notice? If they did he was a goner. They didn't, Smokowski had sweated cold for nothing. He listened. Apart from his own breathing, there was silence. It appeared he was alone again. Smokowski was on the move, but front or back door. With a little more time to think, he decided exiting from the front might not be a wise move, if inquisitive curtain twitchers saw him there could be questions, so he quickly headed for the open kitchen door, hoping the key to the back door was where it always was – in the lock. He was now determined; to have a cuppa, there was no way he was going off again without one. But not here – he was going to have this one at home.

Through the kitchen door, making sure he left this one as he found it, across the kitchen, backdoor and out; that was the plan. But halfway across the kitchen, something caught his eye; the lid was off the biscuit tin. This was such a rare occurrence in the Tom Tyme household that Smokowski couldn't help himself. He stopped, picked the biscuit tin up, and peered inside. Two rich tea and a jam one. No wonder he never offers, thought Smokowski, who found himself suddenly peckish. Pity there wasn't something chocolaty. Smokowski reached in and removed the jammy one; he would see Tom right later. He began munching on it and continued for the backdoor, where thankfully, the key was where he had hoped it would be.

Halfway out he heard voices coming from the hall. Surely they weren't back already. The cold sweat returned. Perhaps they hadn't really left. Perhaps it wasn't them. Whatever, there was no time to waste speculating. Smokowski shut the door behind him, scurried furtively for the back gate and once in the street, hoofed it for all he was worth.

CHAPTER 35

Cat's meeting with Robin Hood proved to be a fruitless one. Apart from the usual gossip concerning a certain maid, sheriff and prince, and a scurrilous rumour involving Will Scarlet, no clue had been thrown up about the unfelt ripple.

'I will see you again, no doubt,' said a cheery Robin, bowing, as he and Cat prepared to part.

'No doubt,' said Cat, returning his bow with a curtsey – always a complicated act for those with four legs.

'Until then, friend Catranna,' said Robin.

'Until then,' said Cat.

Cat left Robin and travelled a route that would take her to the outskirts of his camp, but not arouse her friend's suspicion as to her intended destination. As she travelled, she wondered if Invisible Bob had had any better luck.

'Burp!' belched Invisible Bob, as he lay amongst the grass and fungi of the greenwoods, waiting for Cat to return. He hadn't found any chocolate on his recce of Robin's camp, but he had come across a passable drink that although not beer managed to pack the same punch if one drank enough of it. Invisible Bob had. Luckily for him, as he smiled the smile of the inebriated who was about to drink that one too many, Cat arrived. He saw her and sat up, or at least tried to, spilling drink on his lap.

'Bob?' whispered Cat, on finding Invisible Bob wasn't where he was supposed to be.

'I's over 'ere,' whispered Invisible Bob. Then, putting a finger to his lips he told a blade of grass to hush. 'Yish yat yoo, Cat?'

'Bob?' Cat put her keen sense of smell to work. There were hundreds of scents in the air, but she homed in on the strongest. Not long later she located him. He was cosily ensconced in the centre of a tight ring of toadstools, one of which he had been using as a pillow.

'What happened?' said Cat, asking the sort of question usually associated with Tom.

Looking sideways at Cat from the lopsided angle he had managed to get himself in while trying to sit, Invisible Bob attempted to explain his current predicament, 'I wuz celibib-bob-no.' He tried again, 'I wuz cebralating,' he explained, his pickled brain trying its best.

She knew it; it was a mistake bringing him. Cat shook her head despondently. So what now? Sober him up, she supposed. She sniffed at the air again. There was water close by.

'Enough already!' yelled Invisible Bob, as he was dunked into the stream Cat had found for the umpteenth time.

'You sober yet?' said Cat.

'I said I was five minutes ago,' moaned the bedraggled Invisible Bob.

'No,' said Cat, 'what you said was, "yeth offither".'

'Well I am now, so you can stop with the water torture.'

'Once more for luck, I think,' said Cat.

'No! You ca...'

But she could. So she did. Invisible Bob's protestations ignored, Cat plopped him into the icy cold stream one more time. She waited a second then hooked him out again, landing him on the bank. 'Call it a lesson,' she said.

'I'll probably get pneumonia,' groaned Invisible Bob, as he lay there spread-eagled and shivering. 'This will be the death of me, mark my words.'

'No,' said Cat, scratching moss from a tree, 'I will, if you keep on whining. Here dry yourself with this.'

Begrudgingly, Invisible Bob took the moss offered and began to rub it over his body.

'So,' said Cat, watching the moss bobbing in mid air, 'what have you found out, if anything?' She wasn't holding out much hope.

'They don't wear tights,' said Invisible Bob, inviting another ducking.

'Sensible information I mean,' said Cat, ready to oblige him.

'Well *I* didn't know that,' said Invisible Bob, 'And they ain't that merry either.'

'Nor would you be, if you lived in the woods twenty-four seven and spent every day on the local most wanted list.'

'Bunch of savages if you ask me,' said Invisible Bob.

'Can we get back on track here?' said Cat.

'What track?'

Cat managed to count to seven. 'The one where we get back to the point of you being amongst those savages, as you put it, in the first place. A tad harsh calling them savages by the way, I think.'

'No,' said Invisible Bob, discarding the moss.

'What do you mean, no?' demanded Cat, hackles rising.

'Keep yer fur on, I mean, no, I didn't find anything out of the ordinary. Having said that, there was the naked dancing,' said Invisible Bob, cringing at the thought.

'No,' said Cat, 'that's a usual occurrence.' She was downcast. She had been so sure they would find something at the camp. Perhaps she had followed a red herring; so much for her feelings. The only thing to do now was travel back, tail between her legs, and look at the grid again. 'Okay, hop on, we're going back.'

Invisible Bob started to clamber aboard, but stopped mid straddle. 'Wait, my souvenir,' he said, looking at the ground.

'Souvenir?' said Cat.

'It's why I was celebrating, it's shiny. I like shiny.' Invisible Bob's face took on the look of the faraway.

'We haven't time.'

'But it's shiny!' said Invisible Bob, pleading, 'And it makes a great drinking vessel.'

'I don't know,' said Cat, eager to get back and share her misery, 'Where did you get it from?'

'The camp,' said Invisible Bob, slipping from Cat's back.

'The camp! You know you can't take things willy-nilly from the past. It might have repercussions,' said she, a pyramid crammed full of such items.

Invisible Bob stopped his search for a second to think about this. 'But it's shiny!' he decided.

And thinking about her pyramid Cat relented, 'Oh, okay, but I get to give it the once over first, okay?'

'Okay with bells on,' said Invisible Bob, scurrying back to where Cat had found him.

Cat followed – interest low, disappointment high. That was until Invisible Bob appeared, triumphantly carrying his shiny souvenir above his head.

'I think I'll get it engraved,' said Invisible Bob, all invisible smiles.

'Let me see it first?' said Cat, curiosity building.

Invisible Bob cheerfully handed over his find, confident Cat would be suitably impressed by it and thus, let him keep it.

As Cat held Invisible Bob's find in her paw, the day suddenly took a turn for the better. Cat instantly knew what the souvenir was and that it most definitely did not belong in the time of Robin Hood. 'Show me exactly where you found this,' she said, trying to keep her excitement from bubbling over.

Invisible Bob was all quizzical looks. 'Why?' he asked, as Cat handed his souvenir back to him.

'Because,' said Cat.

That was good enough for him, something was up. Invisible Bob led on.

When they arrived at the edge of Robin's camp Cat called a halt. 'Where?' she asked.

Invisible Bob pointed to a triangle of trees set aside from the rest of the camp. Wedged between them was a ramshackle hut.

'Show me.'

'Won't they see you?'

'I'm glamoured up.'

'This way then.' Invisible Bob went to take the lead again.

'Wait, leave that here,' said Cat, referring to the shiny object Invisible Bob appeared to have developed a death grip on, 'someone might notice it bobbing along.'

'*Someone* might find it,' argued Invisible Bob, loathe to let go of it. Cat's show of keen interest in it had him fearing the worst where his continued ownership was concerned.

'Not if you hide it well. There, in amongst that tuft of grass.'

Against his better judgement Invisible Bob placed his shiny object where Cat had suggested, but when Cat looked away, he quickly moved it to another tuft. It didn't help much, but it made him feel he was in control.

'You coming,' asked Cat, 'or are you going to move it again?'

Drat! thought Invisible Bob, his control in tatters. 'I'm coming,' he groaned.

With Cat following the gap made by Invisible Bob as he passed through the grass, they headed for the triangle of trees.

The grass eventually stopped parting at the foot of the largest of them. Two guards were loafing around a few feet away.

'We'll have to make like church mice,' said Invisible Bob, adding, 'pardon my French.'

'Pardoned,' said Cat, 'Where now?'

'Through here.'

The bottom corner of a piece of sackcloth masquerading as a door in the ramshackle hut, moved slightly aside. It moved slightly more so, as Cat tracked Invisible Bob in.

Inside the air was musty and stale. Two small windows were letting in meagre light. From this light Cat saw that the room was sparsely furnished, possessing only a rough wooden table, an equally rough chair beside it, and a bed. Beside the bed was a large irregular mass covered by sackcloth. None of this interested Cat as much as what was on the bed. It was Robin, dead to the world and snoring for his country.

'It's Robin's hut,' said Cat.

Invisible Bob meanwhile had wandered over to the irregular mass. 'This is where I found it,' he said.

'Under the sackcloth?' said Cat, homing in on Invisible Bob's voice.

'No, it was lying on the floor just here.'

'What's under the sackcloth?'

Invisible Bob didn't know. Maybe he should have been a little more thorough in his investigations. In his defence, to himself, he had already found and sampled the not beer stuff before coming into the hut, and then he had only come in looking for something he could use as a cup. 'Oh,' said Invisible Bob, feigning surprise, 'didn't see that before. Someone must have put it there when I left.'

''Course they did,' said Cat, running a paw across the thick dust lying on the sackcloth, before lifting a corner of it. She couldn't help but let out a low whistle when she saw what it was hiding.

'Blimey!' exclaimed Invisible Bob, all loud like.

Robin stirred on the bed.

Cat quickly slapped a paw across Invisible Bob's mouth, pinning him to the ground in the process; she held him there and waited. When she was sure Robin wasn't going to wake, she let him up, motioning for him to keep a tight zip on it.

'Must be a small fortune there,' whispered Invisible Bob, all saucer eyed.

'It's for the poor,' said Cat, dropping the sackcloth back in place.

'I'm poor,' said Invisible Bob, moving closer.

'And you'll also be seeing stars if you have any funny ideas,' warned Cat.

'So now what?' said Invisible Bob, backing away.

'I wait here and keep watch, while you clamber in amongst that lot and see if you can find anything that shouldn't be there. And do it quietly.'

'But it's dark in there.'

'Here, give me a finger.'

'Why?'

'Just do it.'

Once more against his better judgement, he did as Cat asked, and pointed a finger at her.

'You pointing?' Cat might be able to sense where Invisible Bob was, but not necessarily know what he was doing.

'I certainly am,' said Invisible Bob.

Cat whispered something under her breath and then gently blew. The tip of Invisible Bob's middle finger on his right hand burst into light, ending his little joke.

'Ya...'

But Cat was a head of him and clamped her paw. 'That's not a middle finger is it?'

Invisible Bob shook his head.

'It had better not be.' Cat removed her paw. 'Use it like a torch. Off you go now.'

Shocked at first, but now marvelling at his fifty candle finger, Invisible Bob wiggled and waved it in the air, making light shapes.

'How long will it last?'

'Long enough,' said Cat. She lifted the sackcloth for Invisible Bob to duck under. Invisible Bob and finger duly disappeared beneath.

While Invisible Bob was busy, Cat had a nose around. It didn't take long. There wasn't much to see. Robin Hood lived a frugal life. She returned to waiting beside the sackcloth and wondered about the object Invisible Bob had taken such a shine to. How had it got there? What did it mean? But those questions and any other she might have gone on to contemplate would have to wait because a glowing finger had just materialised from under the sackcloth.

'Find anything?' said Cat.

'Something,' said Invisible Bob, holding it up.

'It's a ring,' said Cat, sudden hopes that had risen against the odds just as quickly deflating.

'Yes,' said Invisible Bob.

'And?'

'Der-er,' said Invisible Bob, pointing to it with glowing finger, 'it's made of gold.'

'And?'

'It's gold.'

'And?'

Not knowing what else to say, or why Cat couldn't see the importance of his find, Invisible Bob repeated what he had said, hoping this time Cat's response would be different. 'It's gold,' he repeated, his voice this time though lacking a little of its previous enthusiasm.

'Bob,' said Cat.

'Yes?'

'Look behind you.'

Not sure what to expect Invisible Bob cautiously did an about turn. He was relieved to find there was nothing there. Which then begged the question – what was Cat on?

'What do you see?'

'Nothing,' said Invisible Bob, wondering if that was the right answer.

'Behind the nothing.'

All Invisible Bob could see was the sackcloth. It was worth a try,

'The sackcloth?'

'Underneath the sackcloth.' Cat decided to help by lifting it.

'The treasure?'

'And what is a lot of it made from?' Cat let the sackcloth fall in unison with the penny that was dropping.

'Gold?' said Invisible Bob.

'Give the invisible goblin a coconut,' said Cat, starting for the door. She aimed to retrieve the only piece of interest they had discovered before Invisible Bob could get his hands back on it. 'Let's go.'

'I'm not a goblin,' pouted Invisible Bob. He had only been trying to help. 'We won't be needing this then?'

'Nope.'

Invisible Bob looked at the ring in his hand. Perhaps he could... No, best not to ask. So, feeling reasonably dejected, he spat on the ring, threw it over his shoulder for luck, and went to follow Cat. At least he had his shiny. He cheered up a little.

Cat, who had been thinking perhaps she had been a little hard on the little fellow, glanced back, just in time to see the ring Invisible Bob had discarded bounce from the sackcloth and head for the sleeping Robin. She might have tried leaping for it. She might have used some magic, but that would have needed a split second more time than she had been presented with. She couldn't stop it.

The ring bounced through the air and struck Robin straight between closed eyes. He woke with a start and instantly reached for his sword. Eyes wide, but sense a tad behind, he leapt to his feet and swung his sword. Unbalanced by this he caught one of his feet on the sackcloth covering his loot, lost his balance and crashed to the floor, knocking himself senseless on the way down on the wooden frame of his bed.

Cat and Invisible Bob, held their respective breaths and stared expectantly at the sackcloth covering the doorway. After a long moment or two of not breathing, and no sign of guards running in swinging their swords, they relaxed.

'Is he dead?' said Invisible Bob.

'No, thank goodness,' said Cat, watching Robin's breast rise. But as good news as that was Cat wasn't for hanging around any longer than need be. The guards might be lax, but that didn't mean they were out of the woods yet – literally. She headed for the exit once more.

'Come on,' she said.

But Invisible Bob stood his ground. 'I think you should see this,' he said.

She doubted it, but Cat stopped anyway, if looking got the invisible lump moving.

'What?' said Cat.

'His arm,' said Invisible Bob, shining his finger on it.

'What about his arm?'

'Look.'

Shaking her head, she did as Invisible Bob wanted. What she saw instantly had her feeling foolish – very foolish indeed.

CHAPTER 36

'Well, that was a waste of time,' said Tom, opening the loo door. He wasn't choking for a change. He hadn't noticed.

'Depends how you look at it really,' said Brandy, philosophically, 'at least we know everything was as it should be on day one of his life. We just work our way from there.'

'That could take years, I could – oof!'

Brandy had grabbed Tom and pushed him against the wall, her hand pressing on his chest. She had an urgent look about her. 'Sssh,' she whispered, 'I thought I heard something.'

'Where?' wheezed Tom, having trouble breathing – the girl was stronger than she looked.

'The kitchen.'

Tom joined Brandy on high alert, senses heightening, muscles and sinew tensing, legs cramping. He would pay for it later, but he had some embrocating rub somewhere. He just wished Brandy would ease up a little on the rib crushing.

His wish came true as she edged forward, releasing him. She motioned for him to stay put. Trying not to gasp too noisily, Tom painfully adopted a defensive stance and tried to remember where he had last seen the rub. He suspected it was in the medicine cabinet.

Moving with the stealth of something you would never hear coming until the last minute, Brandy reached the kitchen door. It was ajar; she couldn't remember if they had closed it. She listened.

'Hear anything?' whispered Tom, from down the hall.

Eyes glaring Brandy turned and put a finger to her lips, her other hand on the kitchen door handle. If she was going to surprise any would be intruder she had better do it now before Tom gave them away. She threw the door open and burst into the kitchen, arms and legs all kicking and punching at once.

Tom was impressed. He wouldn't want to be in the intruder's

shoes if there was one. No sir, much better he had stayed where he was, defending the rear from… Tom went suddenly rigid as a worrying thought struck him. If there is an intruder, who was to say he was working alone? There could be any number of them right that moment, watching and waiting for their chance to pounce. He hadn't had any specialist training. He had a job to put his socks on some cold mornings. Cramps and crushed chest forgotten Tom moved, and moved swiftly towards the kitchen door, and when he got to it, he too entered the kitchen, his arms and legs striking out in all directions at once.

He had always meant to throw away that bloody doorstop. Cause an accident one day, he would often say to himself. Trip someone up. But he had never got round to it. He landed in a tangle on the kitchen floor. The next thing he knew was Brandy holding out a hand and asking him if he was okay.

'Has the bell gone?' asked a befuddled Tom, as Brandy hauled him up.

'I think you may have banged your noggin,' said Brandy, inspecting Tom's head for lumps. She helped him to a chair.

Further bump inspection drew a blank, but to be on the safe side, as Tom had a slight purple look about him, Brandy made Tom hold a pack of frozen peas to his right temple. 'You should see a doctor,' she advised, thinking high blood pressure.

Tom, who had recovered enough from his fall and embarrassment to regain near full crotchetiness, insisted there was nothing wrong with him. 'I'm okay I tell you,' he said, the right side of his head going numb.

'So you say.'

'You're beginning to sound like my dear departed ex-wife,' said Tom, moving the peas and prodding his head with a finger.

Brandy frowned at him. 'I thought she was…'

'Yeah, all right, she's still about, but the point is you're beginning to sound like her.'

'Okay, mister grouchy,' said Brandy, starting to fill the kettle, 'I was only trying to help.'

Tom put the frozen peas back to his head and was about to place elbows on the table and have a sulk when it suddenly dawned on him he had forgotten all about the intruder. 'The intruder,' he said, sitting straight, 'did you get him?'

Brandy set the kettle down and spread her arms. 'Does it look as if I did?' she said.

Tom's purple colour deepened. Dang silly question to ask; where did he think she was keeping one if she had, in her pocket? Maybe he had banged his head. He rested his elbows on the table. 'I mean was there one?'

'Of that I can't say,' said Brandy, moving over to the window, 'but I thought I saw the back gate close. I could be wrong, the heat of the moment and all that.'

'False alarm?'

'Looks like.'

'Back on the Da Vinci trail then?' But not right away Tom hoped, he needed a cuppa after all the excitement.

'A cuppa first though,' said Brandy.

'You read my mind,' said Tom, hoping there would also be time to have a quick glance at his camera. He also hoped Brandy couldn't really read minds – how stupid would he feel. He went to stand.

'Hey,' said Brandy, when she saw what he was about, 'I'll get it, you sit and rest.'

Tom thought she sounded a right little nursemaid; true, one that some men might have in their wildest dreams, but a nurse all the same. Tom sat.

'Biscuit?' asked Brandy.

'Please. In the tin,' said Tom, thinking he should really buy some more, especially as he had a guest. He'd make a mental note and put it with the one about the perfume. Not that he would remember either. Still, now was now, and if he remembered right, there was a jammy biscuit in the tin with his name on it. 'Do you mind if I have the jammy, I like the jam?'

Brandy made the tea, and having no idea what a jammy was, handed Tom what was at hand. She brought them over to him and placed plate and cup on the table.

'Thanks,' said Tom, the whole right side of his head now numb and the right shoulder of his jacket soggy.

'Shall I put those back for you?' asked Brandy, reaching for the peas.

'Good idea.' Tom handed the nearly defrosted vegetables over and dried the side of his head with his hanky. Job done he took his jacket off, wet seeping through, put it on the back of his chair and reached for his cuppa and jammy biscuit. ''Ere, where's me jammy' he exclaimed, when all he found on his plate was a rich tea.

'Is that not a jammy?' said Brandy.

'Jammy's have jam,' Tom explained.

'Sorry, but that was all there was, that one and another just like it.'

Funny, thought Tom, I was sure there was a jammy left. Must be the cold, he thought. Tom touched his frozen temple. That or his age. He plumped for both.

'You okay?' asked Brandy, noticing the frown on Tom's brow.

'Yeah, just thinking.' Tom dunked his biscuit in his tea.

'Good, in that case, I'm going to freshen up, see you in a mo.'

That's handy, thought Tom, it would give him a chance to have a look at his photos. By his reckoning he would have at least a good half hour before she returned; this judged on earlier freshening sessions she had had. 'No prob,' said Tom, lifting his cup to her, 'you take your time.'

Brandy smiled sweetly at him and headed into the hall.

CHAPTER 37

The recently repaired door to the dark room opened.

'Well?'

'She's found something.'

'Do we know what?'

'Not yet.'

'Where is she now?'

'Still there I believe.'

'Let me know when she moves.'

'There is something else.'

'There is?'

'The shopkeeper.'

'Smokowski?'

'I think Cat has got him tailing Tom and, well, he's not doing so well, he was nearly discovered, twice.'

'Where?'

'Tom's and outside a bookshop.'

'What was he doing at a bookshop?'

'It appears Tom and Brandy were there buying a book.'

'Which one?'

'It's called "Lovey Dovey" by someone called Poppett. I have one here.'

'Let me see.'

The book was passed across, and then suddenly snatched back. 'Sorry, that's my copy.'

'Does it matter?'

'It's got a personal message in it.' Another copy was handed over.

The light from a small pencil torch lit up the cover. It was opened.

'Why is the author's name different from the name on the cover? A tad suspicious if you ask me.'

'It's the done thing at the moment. All the B and C lister's are doing it.'

'Are they by gad. Damn odd.' A page was turned.

'About Smokowski?'

'Who?'

'The shopkeeper.'

'Oh yes, keep a close watch on him. If it looks like he's going to interfere, take him out.'

'Kill him?'

A book was dropped. 'Good grief, no. Pick him up.'

'Will do.'

A book was recovered from the floor. 'Oh, and tell everyone I'm not to be disturbed unless it's urgent or Catranna is back.'

'I'll be off then.'

'Yes – wait, are there any of those choccy eggs left?'

'I'll see what I can do.'

'Thank you.'

The door closed.

Another page turned.

CHAPTER 38

'How on earth did I miss that?' said Cat.

'Maybe he wasn't wearing it when you had your meeting,' suggested Invisible Bob, trying to be helpful for once.

Cat tried to recall if he had, but she drew a blank. 'We'll have to take it back with us.'

'Do you think it's got something to do with the unfelt ripple?'

'I strongly suspect it might,' said Cat, 'but even if it isn't, we can't let him roam around this century with a wristwatch on his arm. If you could do the honours?'

Invisible Bob climbed onto Robin's arm and undid the wristwatch. 'What do we do now?' he asked, handing the watch to Cat.

'We take it back to the Chief,' said Cat, placing it on the ground and examining it. She turned it over with her paw. The back of it was grimy, but she thought she could make out what looked like a letter; something important she wondered. And while she was thinking of important things, it might be wise if she took charge of Invisible Bob's little souvenir; that she thought, might be even more important. Wouldn't do any harm keeping it a secret for now.

'But it's mine,' protested Bob, who had flung his body across his souvenir as Cat had attempted to pick it up.

'You'll get it back,' said Cat.

Invisible Bob gave this some careful consideration. 'Promise?'

'On my honour as a familiar,' pledged Cat, her little toes crossed behind her back – she couldn't be a hundred percent certain she would.

It did make sort of sense, thought Invisible Bob, as he clung tight. He couldn't carry it and hold on to Cat. And he most definitely couldn't put it where he usually kept things – it was too big. Why, even the thought of it brought a tear to his eye. 'Okay,' said Invisible Bob, wiping away a tear, 'as long as you promise.'

Toes still crossed. 'I do.'

He handed it over.

'Oh,' said Cat, taking it, 'and for the moment, let's keep it our little secret, shall we?'

'Why?' said Invisible Bob, smelling something fishy.

Canny little fellow aren't you thought Cat, but she could be just as canny. 'Because even though I promised to give it back, and I will,' toes still crossed, 'I can't vouch for anyone else who might see it. Anyone who might see your souvenir as evidence and you know what happens to evidence.'

A mortified Invisible Bob suddenly lost his sense of smell, commonsense replacing it. 'What souvenir?' he said.

'Good man,' said Cat.

CHAPTER 39

Darren was as happy as a lark, one that had mastered the ways of the mechanical. This newly obtained skill of the till would alas go uncelebrated by a number of disgruntled customers who had earlier that day left the premises unable to pay or obtain wares, but this did not cast a shadow on Darren's achievement, far from it.

Ker-ching, went the till as Darren pretended to serve yet another satisfied customer. Of course it didn't come anywhere near being a king, but it did have a certain satisfaction to it.

'Good morrow good sir,' said Darren, as another imaginary customer turned up to pay, 'that will be four shillings, twelve new pennies and a groat, thank you.' Darren opened the till and closed it again. 'Have a good day now, you all.' Darren most certainly needed to get out more, and we are not talking cinema.

Darren played on, his shop keeping fantasies gearing up to that magic hundredth customer, but little did he realise, as he did, he was being watched.

From the other side of the storeroom's keyhole an eyeball looked on with interest. Perfect, thought its owner, the man's a simpleton; this is going to be easy.

Sadly for Darren his next customer wasn't there to buy.

CHAPTER 40

As soon as Tom heard the bathroom door close, he set about viewing the photos he had taken. It wasn't easy, but with help from the zoom facility and the notes he had made as to what picture was of what, he succeeded in gaining a little more knowledge of Da Vinci's life.

When satisfied he had enough to be going on with, he put notes and camera into his jacket pocket, got up, and moseyed on over to the biscuit tin to relieve it of its last occupant. Biscuit grasped, he heard Brandy in the hall. Just in time, he thought, glancing at the clock and noting she hadn't been as long as usual.

Brandy waltzed in looking freshened up to the hilt and a smile across her face that would have lit up the darkest corner. 'All done,' she said, 'ready to go when you are. How's the head?'

'Thawed,' said Tom, 'but the shoulder on my jacket is still wet.' Wet from where the pack of peas had dripped.

'Haven't you got another one?'

Tom looked aghast. Did he look the sort of man that swanned through life with more than one jacket? Did she think he was made of money? The millions in the off shore savings account left to him by Great-Uncle Rufus were for a rainy day. 'No,' said Tom. 'Would you like a biscuit?'

'Do you have more?' asked Brandy, remembering the biscuit tin's meagre offerings.

'Ah,' said Tom, peering into the tin, 'perhaps not. Here have half of this one.' He broke his biscuit in two and offered Brandy the smaller half. He was unselfish like that. He knew how a lady liked to look after her figure.

'That's okay,' said Brandy, declining Tom's offer, 'a girl has to watch her figure you know.' She giggled.

Bingo! thought Tom, do I know women or what?

'Second thoughts,' said Brandy, grabbing the larger piece, 'a girl does have to keep up her strength.' She smiled at Tom and took a bite. 'What's that?' she said, looking over his shoulder at the table.

Tom, still dazed by the unforeseen biscuit snatch, turned to see what it was Brandy was talking about. 'That's my cap,' said Tom, 'I've been wearing it since I met you.' Had she overdosed on the freshening? 'It's my universal translator,' Tom explained.

'I see you more of a fedora man myself, but I meant this.'

Blimey, thought Tom, as Brandy picked up his saver, I must have taken it out when I was looking for the camera. And as Cat had told him to keep its existence a secret from anyone outside of their immediate circle, and she meant anyone, warning him that if it fell into the wrong hands there wouldn't be room in the world for all the problems it could cause, this wasn't good. Brandy seemed trustworthy enough to Tom, but as Cat hadn't included her in their circle before she'd left, he thought it best to keep with the program.

'It's my lucky charm,' said Tom, not entirely lying.

'Looks like a penknife to me,' said Brandy, tipping it one way then the other. 'Ooh!' she said, 'So rude.' Brandy giggled. 'It's not me is it?'

A puzzled Tom soon became a flustered Tom, when he realised what Brandy was seeing. He had been experimenting with the saver, seeing how close he could think it to what he wanted. Savers did what it said on the tin – saved you when in the direst of situations, but what was in the tin wasn't always what you expected; some say tomatoes some contain creosote, hence Tom's practise. His latest try had been very successful – if what you wanted was a penknife. Tom had wanted a pen, but what was on the side of the pen, what Brandy was giggling over that moment, Tom had also wanted; call it nostalgia; some people would say it was something else.

Whatever, Brandy was having fun. 'She's dressed, now she's undressed, she's dressed, now she's un...'

'Yeah, all right,' said Tom, putting out his hand, 'it's a bit of fun, that's all.' He wanted it back all the more now.

'There are magazines you know,' teased Brandy, handing it over.

'It was my dad's,' said Tom, telling another lie that had a small element of truth behind it. His dad had had a pen with a strip teasing lady on the side of it, and it was this that Tom had tried to get the saver

160

to imitate. He quickly stuffed the saver into his pocket.

'I think I would have liked your dad,' said Brandy, purring.

'Oh look,' said Tom, attempting to steer Brandy's attention away from the saver and anything to do with it, 'I think my jacket's dry.'

It worked; Brandy went over to the jacket and felt it. 'It's still a little damp.'

'It'll do,' said Tom, taking his jacket from the back of the chair he had been sitting at and donned it. He did the same with his cap. 'Shall we go?'

'So which period of Da Vinci's life are we heading to this time?' said Brandy.

'When he was living in Milan,' said Tom, hoping that he had read that right. 'In a castle called Sforza Castel or something like. He did most of his scientific stuff there.'

Brandy's eyes had lit up. 'Did I ever tell you Milan is just about my fave place in all this world?'

'You might have done,' said Tom, letting the "this world" comment slip by.

'Milano! Milano! Milano!' shrilled Brandy, all excited like.

'I take it we've arrived in the right place,' said Tom, dodging Brandy's elbows as she clapped enthusiastically. They had ventured a little further this time and were standing in a street.

'It's Milan,' said Brandy, her grin threatening to split her head in two.

'I gathered that,' said Tom, hoping Brandy's antics weren't drawing too much attention their way. They weren't. Tom suspected the locals must see the likes of Brandy quite a lot.

'Did I ever tell you what I think of Milan?' said Brandy, grabbing hold of Tom's hand.

'A little,' said Tom, trying to break free; afraid to be associated with the excitable woman.

'Come on,' said Brandy, starting to tow Tom along, 'there's so much to do.'

Tom dug his heels in. 'But shouldn't we head back to the cubicle so we can head back to Da Vinci's time, now we know we're in Milan?'

'Don't worry,' said Brandy, 'plenty of time for that and we can shop on the way.'

'Way? Shop!'

But it was too late for questions. Brandy was on a mission, and like it or not Tom was going along for the ride.

Five minutes later, as Milan whizzed on past him, Tom decided to try and dig his heels in again. 'That's it, I'm not going another step until you tell me exactly where it is we are heading?' he said, nearly tripping over as Brandy suddenly came to a halt. But it was none of Tom's doing.

'Oooh,' look at that,' said Brandy, nose almost pressed against the glass of a shop front window.

Tom looked. All he could see was a single handbag, positioned in the centre of the window, and held in place by four rusty old chains that ran away into the four corners. He didn't comprehend. He shaded his eyes and tried to peer into the shop. 'They ain't got much stock, have they?' he said, minimalism lost on him – which was a surprise when one considered his attitude to biscuits.

'Memo to self,' said Brandy, 'treat oneself to new handbag.'

Memo to self, thought Tom, as soon as this mission is over, lock oneself in shed.

'Right,' said Brandy, mental note filed, 'let's get to that museum.'

'What museum?' said Tom.

'You need clothes,' said Brandy, gripping Tom's hand again.

'Do I?'

'This way.' With Tom again in tow Brandy headed for a side street.

'It's closed,' said Tom, as they climbed a couple of steps to the museum's main entrance.

'No problem,' said Brandy, 'I know another way in.'

'Been here before then have you?'

'Many times,' said Brandy, winking, 'come on.' Brandy led Tom down another side street that led to the back of the museum.

'This is locked as well,' said Tom, trying the door handle.

'That's okay,' said Brandy, delving into her handbag, 'we won't be using it yet.'

'What do you mean?' said Tom, fearing he wasn't going to like

Brandy's answer – especially with what she was now holding. 'Whoa,' said Tom, backing away, 'I ain't using that.'

'Calm down, it's for me,' said Brandy, 'You just stay out of sight until I get back?'

Tom liked the sound of that. He had had a fish hook caught in his ear when he was a kid, hurt like heck and that was only a small one. He stepped back as Brandy started to swing the grappling hook she had taken from her handbag.

'In the doorway,' said Brandy.

Again Tom was happy to oblige. He wondered what else she had in her bag. He wondered how the hook had fitted as it looked bigger than the bag, and there was the rope. Perhaps it was bigger on the inside, like that… that… dormer bungalow his mate Elvis lived in. Looked hardly enough room to swing a cat from outside, but inside…

'You listening?' said Brandy, who had been trying to tell Tom something.

'Sorry?' said Tom, leaving the bungalow.

'I said, if someone comes along, whistle and go on your merry way. I'll find you later, understand?'

'Whistle and wander,' said Tom, nodding.

'Good, I won't be long.' Brandy tugged on the rope to make sure the hook was secured and then started to shin up it. 'See you in a minute if all goes well.'

Tom stepped from the doorway. Sooner her than me, he thought, as he watched Brandy heading for the museum's roof. Then vertigo took hold sending Tom back into the doorway. When he got there another thought struck him. What did she mean, if it all goes well?

Ten minutes of nervous waiting and watching ended when the back door suddenly opened. Tom, all set to whistle and run should anyone come, hadn't expected that. With a squeak of surprise he started for the street.

'It's me,' said Brandy, emerging from the doorway, her arms full of clothes.

It took a moment to register – Tom having spent the last ten minutes envisaging all sorts from police to irate curators, had worked himself up into quite a little frenzy.

'You,' said Tom, 'but I was expecting…' He looked for the rope, it was gone. 'I thought you were coming back the way you left. Where's the rope?'

'Fine lookout you are,' said Brandy. 'I pulled it up after me.' She pushed the clothes into Tom's arms, who stared dumbly at them.

'What's all this?'

'I told you,' said Brandy, shaking her head, 'they're your clothes.'

A deeply frowning Tom looked at them with a certain amount of disdain. 'And I need them why? I don't remember you telling me that.' He had taken a serious dislike to what appeared to be a pair of tights. 'And what are these?'

'Hose,' said Brandy. 'Now, if I might suggest, I think we should make ourselves scarce before someone discovers one of their manikins has taken up naturism.

'They're itchy,' complained Tom, struggling with his hose.

''They're silk,' said Brandy, 'it's all in your mind.'

'Tell that to the back of my knees.'

'It's what they wore.'

'You sure?' said Tom, not believing any man, whatever era they lived in, would ponce about in the gear Brandy had foisted on him.

'Said so on the little plaque,' said Brandy.

'Believe everything you read do you?' said Tom.

'Here,' said Brandy, handing something to Tom, 'the final bit of your ensemble.'

'What is it?' said Tom, sniffing at it.

'It's your codpiece,' said Brandy.

'Certainly smells like some sort of fish,' said Tom, wondering if it was some sort of hat, 'where do you put it?'

Brandy told him.

Tom threw it to the floor. 'You let me sniff it.'

'It's clean,' laughed Brandy, retrieving it. 'Here, do you want me to fix it on?'

'Give me it here,' said Tom, grabbing it, 'I'm quite able to do that myself, thank you.' He wedged it in place.

'It's upside down.'

Tom re-wedged it.

'Voila!' said Brandy, 'Quite the fifteenth century man about town.'

Tom thought he looked more like a clown, but he was wrong – he looked more your common or garden jester. 'More like a clown,' said Tom, not happy, not happy one little bit. Especially as it appeared Brandy was going to give the fancy dress party a miss. He looked her up and down. She was dressed in a figure hugging, smoky-grey cat suit, her hair worn in a bun. 'Tell me again, why you aren't joining in with the dressing up?'

'I told you, it's how I work. I merge into the shadows. Besides, it's a man's world where we are going, I won't be able to move about as freely as you.'

'What am I going to merge with, a kaleidoscope?'

'You are funny, Tom,' laughed Brandy, 'no, you will merge with the people. No one will notice you.'

Tom wasn't so sure. 'So why aren't you wearing black, if you're going to disappear into the shadows?'

'Because shadows aren't that dark.'

'Ah,' said Tom, still in his own version of the dark. 'You going to black… sorry, grey your face?'

'*What*? Do you know how much this foundation costs?' Brandy produced something from her handbag of plenty. 'I'll be wearing this.' She pulled on a grey ski mask. Menacing only went halfway to describing how she now looked.

'Blimey,' said Tom, 'I'm glad you're on my side.'

Brandy laughed. 'So you should be. Now, are you ready?'

'Just about,' said Tom, reaching for his cap.

'You can't wear that,' said Brandy.

'But I have to,' protested Tom, 'how else am I going to know what's being said.'

'It'll stick out like a sore thumb.'

But Tom was adamant.

'All right,' said Brandy, finally agreeing, but with reservations aplenty, 'but we'll have to try and disguise it.' She started rummaging in her bag again and pulled out a purple glitter covered cowboy hat with pink feathers stuck in its band. It read *I love Brighton* on the front.

'I'm not wearing that on top of my cap,' said Tom, trying to catch a glimpse of the inside of Brandy's handbag. Perhaps if he had the chance he might dare a look inside, must be like a cavern in there. Second thoughts, he might fall in and never be seen again. He returned to protesting, 'Not in a million years.'

'Keep your thermals on, Tom, I'm just going to use a couple of the feathers. Might get away with it – call it a new fashion if anyone asks.'

'I don't wear thermals,' said Tom, 'and I'm not wearing pink feathers.'

'If I have to carry you, you will.'

As Brandy was still wearing her mask, the threat was all the more sinister. Tom decided that perhaps he *was* open to a *little* compromise, he could always get rid of them later and claim he had lost them. 'Okay, as it's you.' Tom handed over his cap.

Feathers fitted, Brandy handed it back. 'Give us a twirl then,' she said.

But Tom stood his ground. He felt stupid enough thank you very much. All the way from the pink feathers at the top to the shoe things that curled over on his feet. What was that all about; curly shoes?

Brandy, laughing again, didn't push it. Tom looked a picture without giving a show. A true Renaissance Man. 'Right, we had better be off.'

'Hang about a tick.' Tom started to fiddle with the small man bag that had come with the clothes. At least he had somewhere to put the camera and his notes. He took out one of those notes. It had written on it the dates Da Vinci had lived at castle Sforza. 'Just want to check the dates first,' he said. He ran his finger down the paper. 'Got a choice, but I don't think we'll be far wrong if we head for fourteen ninety, it seems that's when he started to jot things down in earnest.'

'Fourteen ninety-nine it is then,' said Brandy.

'Ninety,' said Tom.

'Oh, thought you said ninety-nine, silly me.' Brandy held out an arm. 'Shall we go?'

CHAPTER 41

As Smokowski arrived back at the shop two things immediately struck him – a thought that the shop looked dark and empty, and the end of a walking stick brandished by a little old lady. He decided to deal with the little old lady first.

'Please,' Smokowski begged, 'stop hitting me.'

'Pushed me out she did,' said the old lady, staying her weapon to speak.

'Who did?' Smokowski asked, preparing to parry any further blows.

'Why that Tom Tyme's daughter, that's who,' said the little old lady, taking another swing. 'Manhandled me she did. Then locked the door and turned off all the lights.'

'Lucy?' puzzled Smokowski, dodging.

'Said, she and her husband needed to take an urgent stock take, canoodling more like. And that husband of hers, a strange one that, kept smiling at the till.'

'Tom's daughter you say?' said Smokowski, having trouble getting his head around what he was being told. Why would Lucy want to stock take? 'When?'

'You deaf?' The old lady aimed her stick.

'Oof! Will you please stop hitting me!' Smokowski rubbed his ear.

'I only wanted milk. You'd think they'd have time to sell me a pint.'

Smokowski was mortified. 'Darren wouldn't sell it you?'

'You're flipping daft as well as deaf,' said the old lady, preparing another swing at Smokowski.

'Wait... look,' said Smokowski, dodging it while going for the shop door, 'I'll open up and as a gesture of...' He pulled his keys from his pocket and opened it. He went in, closely followed by the stick wielding old lady.

'As a gesture of what?' said the old lady.

But Smokowski wasn't listening, he was wondering why the storeroom light was also off. You couldn't stock take if you couldn't see to do it. He then noticed, with horror that the fridges were also off. The power had been cut. Something wasn't right, he could feel it. He also felt a tug on his sleeve.

'You said something about a gesture,' growled the little old lady, persistent to the point of being menacing.

'Sorry?' said Smokowski, still wondering and horrified.

'You said...'

'Ah yes,' said Smokowski, thoughts clearing as he caught sight of the old lady's stick being raised out of the corner of his eye. 'The milk.'

'You said something about a gesture.'

'Did I?'

'You know you did,' said the old lady, giving Smokowski her best stony glare.

'Oh yes,' said Smokowski, knowing when he was beaten. 'As a gesture of good will, you can have a fr... half price one for your trouble.' Proving that although he was down, he wasn't necessarily out.

'You were going to say free,' growled the old lady, her eyes now piercing. She tugged on his sleeve again. It was the grip of a tenacious terrier.

Realising he wasn't going to rid himself of the old lady's attention unless he gave in, he relented. 'I did,' said Smokowski, trying to free his arm from her grip. 'A free half price one.'

The old lady looked puzzled for a moment, but then released Smokowski. 'Semi-skimmed,' she said, 'got to watch my figure.'

Smokowski went to the upright chiller and breathed a sigh of relief when he looked inside, he had semi-skimmed. He was also relieved to find it was still fairly cold within. The old lady had been right. Whatever was going on had not long gone on.

He returned to the old lady and gave her, her milk. As she took it, she grabbed his arm with her other hand. It gripped like a vice. Suddenly Smokowski was gripped by something else; fear. Oh grief, he thought, as the old lady held on, staring up at him, she's a robot.

Smokowski had a thing about robots. What did he do? All this felt and thought in a split second. There was only one thing he could do. 'Are you a robot?' he stammered.

The old lady looked at him, steely cold blue eyes burning into Smokowski's. Her grip tightened even more. She spoke. 'You're as bloody daft as that lad that works for you, you are. Here take it back.' She handed Smokowski his milk back. 'I'll get it somewhere else. Somewhere where there's normal folk.' The old lady backed away, gave Smokowski another icy stare, and then, with a final wave of her stick, left the shop. Mumbling as she did about how the world had gone crazy and to pot.

Smokowski didn't know what to be most relieved about – the old lady leaving, her not being a robot, or not having had to give groceries away. But that was bye the bye. There were other fish to fry. Smokowski quickly locked the shop door and headed for the storeroom. He hoped the old lady was wrong about the canoodling.

When he got there he reached in an arm and flicked the switch; the storeroom the only place not reached by daylight. 'Darren?' Neither switch nor assistant responded. Smokowski didn't like it. What could they be doing in there? He decided not to give the thought too much rope, but whatever, he would have to go in; the fuse box was in there. The food in the freezers wouldn't stay frozen for ever. Smokowski went to the counter and took the torch he kept for such emergencies from under it. He returned to the storeroom and, steeling himself for whatever he might find or see inside, Smokowski went in.

'Just thrown,' said Eddie Albright, the local electrician, when he had finished inspecting the fuse box.

When Smokowski had found the storeroom and toilet empty, and he couldn't see anything wrong with the fuses, he had panicked. Something most definitely strange was going on, but who could he call? He didn't know where Cat was. He couldn't tell Tom, and there was no way he was going to contact the travellers; what would he say? Then it had come to him; Eddie Albright, at least the lighting problem would be fixed. He could then put the kettle on and have a cuppa as he tried to figure out what to do next. 'Thrown?' said Smokowski, electrics not his strong point.

'The switch,' said Eddie, putting it back into the on position. The lights came on. The hum of the freezers started. He handed Smokowski an envelope.

'The bill already?' said Smokowski, taking it. 'But how could you possibly know what the problem was before coming out?' New fears started to rise in Smokowski's mind.

Eddie knew that Smokowski could be a tight old buzzard at times – peas in a pod him and that pal of his, but he had never seen the old man in such a tizzy before. He thought he had better put him out of his misery. 'It's not a bill,' said Eddie, 'it was on top of the fuse box.'

'Oh,' said Smokowski, wondering how he had missed it. He looked at it; it had his name typed on the front.

Eddie picked up his bag. 'I'll pop the bill in the post, it won't be much.' He went to step past Smokowski who was staring at the envelope, but stopped, he patted Smokowski on the shoulder. 'Perhaps a few early nights,' he said helpfully, 'Helps me.' Eddie Albright said his goodbyes and left.

Smokowski, envelope gripped tightly, followed Eddie out and locked the door behind him. What was all this about? he thought, looking at the envelope. Perhaps it had been there a while – he may have left it there and had forgotten all about it? But there wasn't any dust on it. Smokowski didn't have a good feeling. What did he do about it? Only one thing really he supposed; open it. No, a cuppa first; no, that was Tom not him. Better to treat it like a plaster you needed to pull off – a quick rip and get it over with. Smokowski tore the top from the envelope and peered inside. But it wasn't empty as he had been secretly hoping it would be. He stuck a couple of fingers inside and pulled out the contents. It was a piece of card. It had something written on it; he read what it said. 'Oh dear,' he said, when he had finished, 'oh dearie, dearie me.'

CHAPTER 42

'A wristwatch?' said the Chief Traveller, clearly astounded, as Cat handed it to him. She had just finished telling him *almost* all of what had happened on her trip to see Robin Hood. The Chief in turn handed the watch to Beatrice. 'Give it a thorough going over and see if you can find out what is written on the back. Make it a priority Beatrice.' Beatrice nodded and left the operations room. 'So Catranna, tell me your thoughts?'

'I don't think this unfelt ripple is the one we're looking for, but I do think my hunch was right and all seven unfelt ripples are linked.' Cat looked thoughtful. 'I also believe the watch is a bit obvious.'

'A red herring?' said the Chief.

'A distraction or a clue should they be noticed,' said Cat, 'but which one I don't know.'

'But why would anyone go to all the trouble of concealing a ripple and then help us find it?'

'If that is what they are doing,' said Cat, 'they could be giving us the run around to buy time if the alarm was raised. Having to investigate seven instead of one could do that.'

'Buy time for what?'

'To finish what they're planning maybe?'

'But Hood's time could have easily been the right one?'

'But it wasn't,' said Cat, looking grim, 'If it had been, I doubt the welcome would have been so welcoming. Perhaps none of the seven are the unfelt ripple we are looking for.'

'Perhaps it's one big practical joke.'

The Chief jumped. 'Who said that?'

'I did,' said Invisible Bob, 'Bob.'

'Oh yes,' said the Chief, regaining composure, 'I forgot you were here.'

'Thanks,' said Invisible Bob.

'He could be right,' said Cat, happy to throw any suggestions into the hat.

'But why would anyone want to do that?' puzzled the Chief.

'Perhaps they like chocolate,' said Invisible Bob.

'What? Beatrice!' yelled the Chief.

Beatrice appeared from nowhere. 'Yes Sir?'

'Can you take Invisible Bob here...'

'Here,' said Invisible Bob.

'There... wherever, and sort him out?'

'A pleasure, Sir. I'll just get a pair of rubber gloves.'

On the operations table, for there is where he was sat, a large invisible smile was spreading across Invisible Bob's face.

Less than a blink of the eye and Beatrice was back.

'Thank you, Beatrice,' said the Chief.

'Ooh,' said Invisible Bob, as Beatrice reached for him, 'blue ones and so cold!'

'I had them in the fridge especially,' said Beatrice, lifting Invisible Bob, 'extra grip.'

'See you all later,' said Invisible Bob, grinning for all not to see.

Two disturbed faces watched as Beatrice apparently carried nothing away; a nothing that apparently could giggle most disturbingly.

'Er... hum, as I was saying,' said the Chief, who himself seemed disturbed and distracted, 'Now, I... what was it I was saying?'

'You know,' said Cat, thinking perhaps they had enough on their plates without adding the practical joke line to it, 'I can't remember.'

'Nothing out of the ordinary in itself,' said Beatrice, who had managed to give the wristwatch a thorough examination as well as tend to Invisible Bob. She handed it to the Chief. 'But I thought you might find this interesting.' Beatrice pointed to something on the back of the watchcase. 'It's as Cat thought, there's a letter engraved on it.'

The Chief showed the watch to Cat. 'It's a U,' he said, 'mean anything?'

'And an arrow,' said Beatrice. 'My investigations lean towards both the letter and arrow having been engraved outside of Robin Hood's timeline.'

172

'A clue, Catranna?' said the Chief, tipping the watchcase this way and that, 'Looks like some sort of code to me.'

A tad convenient if you ask me, thought Cat, a U with a convenient arrow pointing to it. It appeared too obvious – or was it? 'Maybe,' said Cat, non-committal.

The Chief though was more inclined to believe what he was seeing. 'Here,' he handed it back to Beatrice, 'take it along to the boys in decipher and see what they think.'

But Beatrice was less optimistic about anything of use being found at this time. 'I think they will need more than this to go on before any conclusions could be drawn.'

Enthusiasm slightly tempered, the Chief nevertheless persisted. 'But if there is something, better to be one step ahead, eh, what?' he said.

'Straight away, Sir,' said Beatrice. She had been his number two long enough to know arguing wasn't an option once he had the bit between his teeth.

'Well Catranna, it looks to me like we may be on our way to discovering something,' said the Chief, as he watched Beatrice heading off to the decipher room.

'It's early days yet,' cautioned Cat, siding with Beatrice's misgivings.

'True... true,' agreed the Chief, but his mind had already moved on. 'So Catranna, where next?' He was facing the operations wall. The bulb signifying a ripple in Robin Hood's time, now dark. 'Six left to choose from.'

Cat stared at the six remaining bulbs. It was all so random – but was it? Again Cat couldn't shake the feeling that everything was staged – but why? 'You choose,' she said.

The Chief studied the wall for a moment. 'How about that one?' he said, pointing to a bulb.

'Why not,' said Cat, deeming it as good as any.

'Good, I'll get Invisible Bob and you can set off.'

CHAPTER 43

Darren was hanging around and feeling pretty darned sorry for himself. He was also more than a tad puzzled by the goings on of the last… actually, he didn't know how long the goings on had been going on for, so that was beside the point. He was puzzled though, and had every right to be so. It wasn't everyday one was kidnapped by their own wife, who then disappeared without so much as a cheery bye; hence the puzzlement. He also had every right to be feeling sorry for himself. The hanging about, you see, wasn't his fault either, and it wasn't your common or garden variety of hanging about either. There were chains involved. Darren rattled them; the chains that were fixed to the shackles that held his wrists, which were fixed to the wall at the other end, somewhere high up and beyond him – hence the hanging. Having said that, he could just about touch the floor with his tippy-toes – so ergo, technically not completely hanging.

So, not completely hanging around, Darren, his eyes only just grown accustomed to the meagre light let in from somewhere on high, completed his first worthwhile sweep of his place of incarceration.

He observed that there were four walls; he was taking it on faith that there was one behind him, the one furthest away with a door set in the centre of it. In the door was set a barred window, about three quarters of the way up; man height he guessed. He didn't bother with a floor and ceiling count, feeling that if there should be more than the norm for a room it didn't need thinking about, mainly as he was now realising, the light now registering perhaps the catalyst, that his head was hurting like… a hot place men and women of good moral standing felt ill thinking about. So Darren, as he thought of himself as a man of good morals, didn't – think that is – of the hot place that is. So, head now registering pain, Darren took to looking at the floor, but not to count it you understand.

The floor was a hard and cruel looking floor, a mass of cold grey unfriendly looking, rough hewn, flagstones. A floor that cried out, *come and try if you think you're hard enough!* Darren averted his eyes, he didn't like the look of some of the dark stains that were spread here and there on its surface. Stains that suggested some poor souls had thought they were hard enough and had regretted it.

With headache just manageable, averted eyeballs strayed onto something the gloom had earlier hidden from him. It appeared Darren was not alone.

In a far corner hung the dishevelled shape of what Darren took to be a man. A man, whom it was certain, had been there a very long time. The man's clothes were grubby and ripped in places, his hair shaggy long and unkempt, the colour of… Darren plumped for dirt. This wasn't good, Darren decided, but at least there may now be the chance he could find out where he was and perhaps why. Darren spoke.

'Hello!' said Darren, in his best trying to attract someone voice. 'I say, can you hear me?' The dishevelled shape said nothing, did nothing. Darren tried again, 'Yoo-hoo!' Again there was nothing. Then Darren had a horrible thought – what if he was… no, that didn't bear thinking about. The man was asleep, that's all. He would just have to shout a little louder. 'HELLO!' shouted Darren, politely.

Again there was no response. But then it struck Darren what he was doing wrong. He had to forget his twenty-first century persona. This wasn't a job for Darren the polite yet industrious shopkeeper cum househusband – this was a job for Arthur, King of the Brits. Darren-Arthur, tried again.

'You man, come, speak up, you are in the presence of royalty!' ordered Arthur. There, that's better, thought Darren.

In the far corner, the dishevelled shape of a man at last stirred, slowly raising his head to face him that had spoken to him. He appeared to study Darren. He spoke. 'Sod off!' he said.

'What?' said Darren, forgetting for the moment he had been speaking Arthur, 'What did you say?'

The dishevelled shape of a man became more animated. 'Sod off you fool dolt of a boy,' he wailed, 'and leave me to my misery.'

Couldn't understand a word of that, thought Darren, knowing a foreign language when he heard it – for the second time. It sounded Roman to him, but Darren wasn't daunted.

'Do… you… speak… English?' asked Darren. 'Or Saxon?' In what light there was Darren saw that the dishevelled man's eyes had grown wide.

The wide eyed dishevelled man stared in despair at Darren. A blooming foreigner, he was thinking, that's all he flipping needed. Perhaps if he went back to ignoring the foreign fool of a boy, he might shut up and leave him alone. The man dropped his head.

But Darren didn't. 'My… name… is… Darren,' said Darren, far from giving up.

The dishevelled man raised his weary head again, looked at Darren, shook it, and began to shout at the top of his voice. 'Guard!' he cried. 'GUARD!!'

CHAPTER 44

'Come in.'

The door to the dark room opened and Beatrice entered. 'All done,' she said.

'What is?'

'Smokowski.'

'Didn't hurt him did you?'

'No, just doubled the watch on him, and told them to bring him in if he starts getting in the way.'

'Well done, keep me informed.'

Beatrice hesitated a moment. Should she say something?

'Is there anything else Beatrice?'

'I was just wondering if you were having any problems with your new night vision goggles.'

'Good grief Beatrice, how did you know? I'm having a deuce of a time trying to read this bally book.'

'You've got them on back to front.'

'Have I?' There was a twanging as rubber was removed. 'Well I never. Well done Beatrice.'

Beatrice smiled and went on her way.

The Chief finished adjusting his goggles and returned to his copy of "Lovey Dovey".

CHAPTER 45

The flusher was flushed – old habits die hard. The mental image was thought. The time travelling loo did its job. And it, Tom and Brandy, arrived just after eight o'clock in the evening, in the year fourteen ninety, somewhere in the confines of Sforza Castel, Milan.

'Coo,' said Tom, peering from the loo, 'it's dark out there.'

'The sun's gone down,' said Brandy, sliding past him, into the dark. 'Come on.'

Tom took no more than two steps to find he could no longer see where Brandy was. 'Brandy?' he said, talking to the nearest shadow.

'Yes?' said Brandy, stepping from a different one, no more than a foot from where Tom stood.

'Grief woman,' said Tom, holding hand to chest, 'give a man a warning before you do that.'

'Do what?' said Brandy, the whites of her eyes just visible behind the hazy gauze covering her eye slits.

'Creep up on someone like that.'

'I never moved,' she said, frowning behind her mask.

Tom decided not to argue. 'Where now?' he said, screwing his eyes up so to see better, which didn't help one iota.

'Your guess is as good as mine,' said Brandy, 'So I'd guess straight on.'

A cup of tea is as good as a cup of coffee to a thirsty man, thought Tom, who then wondered why he had thought it. 'So be it,' he said. He closed the loo door and did something he always did when he had done it; he stood and marvelled for a moment, because now the door was closed there was nothing there – just empty space.

'Keep close.'

'Right behind you,' said Tom, scratching at his codpiece, and hefting the small backpack he had in his hand onto his shoulder. A backpack Brandy didn't know he had.

Ten minutes later they had travelled more or less some distance, yet they still found themselves in the dark – in both senses of the word. They decided to stop and see if they could get some sort of bearings as to their whereabouts. While they did, Tom thought he would ask Brandy something that had been nagging at him since their visit to watch the birth of Da Vinci.

'Brandy?'

'Yes.'

'Why didn't I wear clothes like these the first time we went back?'

'Never thought,' said Brandy. 'Look, a light.'

Fair dos, thought Tom, neither had he. He looked for the light.

'Come on,' said Brandy.

As obedient as a faithful hound, Tom tagged along behind.

'Candles,' said Brandy, coming to a halt.

Tom peered around her. They had reached a T junction. Sconces with burning candles were dotted intermittently along the walls of the corridor leading off and along the walls of the rest of the corridor they were in. Tom and Brandy's route the only one in darkness.

'That's typical,' said Tom.

'What is?'

'Us picking the only corridor without lighting is what.'

'Lucky perhaps.'

'If you say so.'

'Look a light.'

'I thought we'd gone through that?' said Tom.

'There, in the wall, a crack.'

Tom looked. She was right, there was a crack of light coming from the far side of the corridor leading off, which could only mean...

'What's it mean?' asked Tom.

'A doorway. Someone's left a door ajar.'

'A door a jar? Oh, right, I get you.'

'Stay close.' Brandy started forward, her body tight to the shadows left untouched by the candlelight – training.

Tom ambled behind in his own time – reservations.

Brandy reached the door; Tom was still ambling. She cautiously peeped through the gap. Tom caught up.

'We're not going in are we?' he asked on arriving.

'You've got to go in and check it out,' said Brandy, carefully edging the door open so she could see more.

'But we might be seen. And we don't know if it's his room or not,' said Tom, reservations building to worries. 'What do you mean *I've* got to go in?'

'I can't be seen,' said Brandy, stepping back from the door, 'if you get caught, you're going to need back up.'

'Hold up,' said Tom, backing away, 'I can't do this on my own, I don't know what I'm at.'

'Find, observe and investigate,' said Brandy, all authority, 'And if you are still alive when you're done, we put it right.'

Tom was aghast, flabbergasted, shocked, all three. He suddenly wanted to do something that rhymed with three.

'Only joking,' said Brandy. She giggled. 'You should have seen your face.'

'Bu... bu...'

'Right, we both go in, but I'll be keeping out of sight. If you're seen, we deal with it. But when we discover what is going on, leave it to me to deal with, okay?'

Tom nodded. He wasn't in a fit state to say anything. The girl's got a sadistic streak running through her as wide as a road, he thought, as he watched Brandy return to pushing open the door. Cat wouldn't have treated him like that. But on the bright side, he wasn't going to have to go it alone. Small compensation though, he thought, for nearly wetting himself.

'You coming?' Brandy was disappearing through the doorway.

He didn't want to, but he was a Traveller, like it or not, and he had responsibilities, like them or not, so he straightened his cap, threw back his shoulders – nearly throwing one out because of the backpack – girded his codpiece, and stoutly ambled behind.

But there wasn't a room on the other side of the door, just another corridor; the junction had been a crossroads. This one was lighter than the others as the sconces here were closer together.

'That's weird,' said Tom.

'What is?' said Brandy.

'This corridor having a door.'

'Could lead to the living quarters.'

'Not many shadows,' Tom observed.

'I'll make my own if needs be,' said Brandy, who was tight up against the wall.

Whatever that means, thought Tom. 'What now?'

'Proceed with caution.'

Tom cautiously proceeded.

'Tom.'

'Yes?'

'Without the whistling please.'

'Sorry,' said Tom, 'nervous.'

Without further ado they continued down the corridor, fifty paces later further ado decided to rejoin them. Noises, a menagerie of them, were coming from just ahead. Brandy inched forward. Tom, who wasn't a great fan of the metric system decided, on this occasion, to give it a go and centimetred forward.

'We must be getting close,' whispered Tom, believing the talking, swearing, shouts, bangs and clangs he could hear, was the endeavour behind invention. 'Sounds like a workshop.'

'That, or a kitchen, or a torture chamber, or any number of other things,' said Brandy, dampening Tom's hopes with reason.

'Or them,' said Tom, scowling.

As it happened, when they reached another door, this too ajar, the noises proved to be coming from a kitchen. They tiptoed past and continued on their way.

'Long isn't it,' said Tom, after a while.

And Brandy would have undoubtedly answered him with some witty retort or other if something more important hadn't just grabbed her attention. She pushed Tom and herself against the wall.

'What's wrong?' said Tom, whispering as low as possible so even he had a job to hear.

'Can you hear that?' said Brandy.

Even with ears straining Tom couldn't hear anything. 'Hear what?' he said.

'That flapping sound.'

Tom inspected his codpiece – it was still in place. 'No.'

Still as tight to the wall as she could get, Brandy edged along the corridor. 'There, hear it now?'

Tom, who had also edged on, couldn't at first, but after turning to his good ear – the wax-less one – he found he too could hear flapping. 'Bats?' ventured Tom.

'Canvas,' said Brandy.

'Tents?' said Tom.

'Wings,' said Brandy.

'Bats?' said Tom.

'Come on,' said Brandy.

Together they moved on – Brandy, determined, as quiet as the night – Tom, lethargic, dragging his feet. An archway loomed, set in the side of the corridor they were following. Archway reached, Brandy stood one side, Tom the other. They listened.

'Flapping,' said Tom.

'Somewhere through here,' said Brandy, indicating past the archway.

'Surely down there,' said Tom, feeling the flapping sound had come from further down the corridor they were already in.

'Definitely through here,' said Brandy, moving beneath the arch.

And as Tom had no inclination to go any other way on his own, he decided perhaps he was wrong, and did like the faithful hound again, but without any playful bounding.

The corridor they entered was smaller and shorter than the one they had just left and the end of it was already nigh. When they reached the nigh end they found two even shorter corridors, one either side – another T junction. There was a stout looking door at the end of each of them.

'This way,' said Brandy, turning right before Tom had had a chance to even think about which way next. The door Brandy was heading for had a small barred window about three quarters of the way up it.

Tom didn't like the look of it. 'I don't like the look of it,' said Tom, as Brandy stopped before the door. He listened; he could no longer hear the sound of flapping. 'And I can't hear the flapping noise either.' He was sure they had come the wrong way.

'I'm sure it came from behind here,' said Brandy, trying to peer through the window, but finding her view obstructed by something. She reached for the door's handle.

But before she had a chance to turn it, the door started to open, pushed from the other side. As quick as a flash – one that was trained for just this kind of situation, Brandy slipped behind it.

Tom on the other hand stood as transfixed as a rabbit caught in the headlights of a combine harvester. The door opened wide. Tom stood his ground, mouth open. A man, dressed not dissimilar to Tom, stepped into the corridor. He looked startled for a moment on seeing Tom standing there, but then relaxed almost immediately and spoke.

'Da Vinci?' said the man, shaking his head and looking downright perplexed.

Tom closed his mouth. Then opened it again when he found it made talking difficult. 'Er... no,' said Tom, 'it's Tom.'

The man looked puzzled then smiled. 'No,' he said, 'I meant, are you looking for him?'

'Oh,' said Tom, wondering how he should answer, but as his brain was recovering from the glare of the headlights, no useful wonderings were at hand, so he said he was. Behind the door Brandy engaged in some eyeball rolling.

'In there,' said the man, holding the door open for Tom, 'but don't hold your breath if it's ideas you want, the man's crazy.' The man put a finger to his temple, twirled it and sighed. 'And as for being thirty odd, well, my arse is he, more like seventy.'

'Thank you,' said Tom, grabbing hold of the door while making sure he was positioned in front of Brandy.

'You're welcome.' The man wandered off without giving Tom a second look and disappeared through the archway.

'Phew,' said Tom, brushing a hand across his brow, 'that was a close one.'

'Let's go,' said Brandy, squeezing between Tom and the wall.

'But we don't know what's in there,' Tom protested.

'Da Vinci,' said Brandy, 'you heard the man.'

'But how do we know he's telling the truth?'

'We won't unless we go in, will we?' Brandy grabbed Tom by the arm and glanced towards the archway, 'And let's make it snappy before our helpful friend out there chats to someone with a curiosity gene.' She pushed a still protesting Tom through the doorway and closed the door behind them.

CHAPTER 46

'That was weird,' said a panting Invisible Bob, bobbing up and down on Cat's back.

'Tell me about it,' said Cat, 'who'd have thought William the Conqueror would talk like that.'

'Sounded like he'd breathed in a whole canister of helium,' said Invisible Bob, panting and bobbing some more.

'Will you cut that out,' snapped Cat, 'and get off me, I stopped running ten minutes ago.' Cat was flat on her tummy – the position she had adopted after outrunning the company of Norman soldiers that had been chasing them – although it was doubtful they knew they were also chasing an invisible man. She should have used a glamour on them, but as it was a nice day and she felt she needed the exercise she had decided the run might do her good.

'Sorry,' said Invisible Bob, who wasn't in the slightest as he slid down from her back.

Afraid to ask, but doing so anyway, Cat asked him what he had been playing at. She was more than a little relieved by his reply.

'Riding the range, yahoo!' yahooed Invisible Bob, waving an imaginary invisible Stetson in the air, 'Was weird though wasn't it?'

'You or the Duke?'

'And we found another watch.'

'Yeah,' said Cat, standing and stretching, 'but I can't help thinking that we were expected this time.'

'You think?'

'They were saddled and waiting and came after us as soon as they saw me.'

'Maybe they just like chasing cats.'

'Perhaps,' said Cat, but she thought it was something more than coincidence.

'Well whatever, I make that…'Invisible Bob started to count on his fingers – which wasn't easy as he couldn't see them, 'four. Four watches so far.'

'Three,' Cat corrected, 'and each with a letter engraved on the back.'

'Oh yeah, I was counting two S's. Still don't make much sense though,' said Invisible Bob, trying to form, in his head, the letters they had gathered so far into a word. 'Nope,' he said, failing miserably, 'can't do much with two U's and an S. Do you think it is some sort of code?'

'I don't know what to think,' admitted Cat, 'but I don't think we should try to guess what the letters or watches mean until we collect the other ones.'

'You think there may be more in the other ripples?'

'Call it an educated hunch, but yes, it does seem likely given what we've found so far.'

''Spose so,' said Invisible Bob, looking invisibly thoughtful. He voiced a concern, 'Are you sure we shouldn't tell the Chief about the other watches we've found?' He wasn't really that bothered about it one way or the other, but he was about getting into trouble because of it.

'We will, but if I'm right about there being more watches, I can't see the point in keep going back. Better to wait until we've got them all. Besides, after that near escape with the Normans, I don't want anyone to know where we're going next.'

'You think there might be a spy back at the ops room?' Invisible Bob was shocked. 'But no one surprised us before, and no one knew where we were going this time.'

'No, that's true, but when we didn't go back, we may have worried someone and I'm not talking concern for our health. It wouldn't be hard to set traps in each timeline so safety first I think. I could be wrong, but better safe than sorry.'

Not one to argue when there was an issue with his safety, Invisible Bob felt it wise to bow to Cat's superior knowledge and nous. 'Where next then?' he asked.

'Vicky, I think,' said Cat.

'Blimey,' said Invisible Bob, 'That narrows it down. Any Vicky in particular you got in mind?'

'Queen Vicky.'

'Cor, luv a duck,' said Invisible Bob, incredibly impressed. 'I ain't never seen royalty up close before I ain't, apples an' pears an' wotnot. London ain't it?' For some reason, only known to Invisible Bob, he had come over all cockney.

'In this instance, yes,' said Cat, raising cat eyebrows at Invisible Bob's antics.

Invisible Bob started to giggle.

'What now?' said Cat, starting to worry.

'Nothing really,' said Invisible Bob, tittering, 'it's just that I had a vision of you chasing a mouse from under her chair.'

Cat said nothing, she just flicked a paw in the direction of Invisible Bob's tittering, smiled when it made contact, felt the chill of him landing on her back, and enjoyed a nostalgic moment as she recalled one of those good old days people were always going on about. It was never a mouse. It had been a blooming great black rat, the size of a spaniel. Happy days!

CHAPTER 47

A worried Chief Traveller prowled the operations room; things were not going well. He stopped prowling for a moment and stared at the wall that led to his room. Where was that girl? He went to start his prowling again, but he was stayed as the wall started to revolve.

Beatrice hurried in. The look on her face was far from encouraging.

'Well?' asked the Chief, almost pouncing on her.

'Nothing, Sir.'

'Nothing at all?'

'No, Sir. I've been through all the normal channels, but not a glimpse of Cat has been seen.'

'What about the abnormal channels?'

'Checked and same there too, Sir, no sight of fur or nothing.'

'They couldn't have just vanished.'

'Excuse me for saying so, Sir, but Bob has made a career of it and Cat, well she...'

'Yes... yes,' said the Chief, getting huffy, 'not quite what I meant, but I get your point.' He leaned forward and rested his hands on the operations table. Could his day get any worse? Yes it could.

'There's something else,' said Beatrice, not sure how the Chief was going to take the news.

'There is?' said the Chief.

'Yes, Sir, Darren has been kidnapped.'

'Darren?' The name didn't register.

'King Arthur, Sir.'

'Oh,' said the Chief, 'that Darren.' The day had definitely got worse. 'Anyone know why?'

'Not as yet, but we believe there's a note.'

'Have you got it?'

'No, Sir, Smokowski has.'

The Chief didn't like the sound of this; didn't like the sound of it one little bit. 'Pick him up straight away. We don't want him running amok and getting in the way, we've got enough on our plate, he's bound to try and contact Tom or Catranna. Could jeopardise everything.'

'There is one other thing.'

'More? Should I be sitting down?' said the Chief, looking as if he should.

'It appears that Lucy, Tom's daughter, was the kidnapper.' Beatrice quickly moved a chair behind the Chief.

CHAPTER 48

Safely on the other side of the door, Brandy continued with her dragging of Tom, and pulled him into the shadows of a large shelving unit. From there they could see someone working at a bench.

'Da Vinci?' whispered Tom. The room they were in certainly smacked of workshop, somewhere where Leonardo Da Vinci might feel at home.

'That's me,' said the man at the bench, who evidently had hearing of the highest standard.

Brandy, who had been in the process of shrugging, now glared at Tom before pushing him out of the shadows.

'Sugar,' said Tom.

'Sugar?' said Da Vinci.

'Drat!' said Tom.

'Drat?' said Da Vinci, cocking his head to one side.

'What do I do?' whispered Tom, as low as he could get his voice.

'Go?' mouthed Brandy, shooing Tom away. She now saw the backpack for the first time, but it was too late to ask questions.

Tom made a desperate face at her, but he knew he was on his own. Feet dragging, he headed away from where Brandy was hiding and stepped closer to the bench Da Vinci was working at. What did he do now, make small talk? Tom took another couple of steps forward; Da Vinci still had his back to him. Tom coughed.

'Ah-ha! Finished,' said Da Vinci, all of a sudden. Tom took one of his steps back. Da Vinci put down whatever it was he had been working on and finally turned round, whereupon he immediately clapped his hands together in delight when he saw Tom. 'What fun,' he said, grinning like a madman behind his wild and whiskery grey lip and chin covering, 'a jester!'

If Tom hadn't seen with his own eyes the get ups of Italian Renaissance men he would have thought Brandy had pulled a fast one on him. Instead, Tom wondered what the old fool was going on about. And yes, the arse of the man he had met at the door had been right – Da Vinci certainly didn't look thirty-eight – more seventy-eight. Da Vinci stood before Tom dressed in a nightshirt of sorts that hung from his old frame. He had a hard used look about him. He also looked as mad as a March hare. But if that's what he thinks, thought Tom, seeing a chance to avoid any unnecessary questions. 'At your service,' said Tom, bowing ever so slightly. Thank goodness for swashbucklers like Errol Flynn, thought Tom, who had been a fan in his youth.

'Aba-dabba-dab!' shouted Da Vinci.

Frowning at the old man's outburst, Tom discreetly tapped at his cap. That's all he needed, his universal translator going on the blink.

'That's what they say isn't it?' said Da Vinci.

'Who does?' said Tom, breathing a sigh of relief that his cap was all right after all.

'Magicians, fakirs,' said Da Vinci, waving his hands about.

Tom could now see why the man at the door had wished him good luck. Da Vinci was gaga. He cast a quick glance in the direction of the shelves and its shadows, but if Brandy was there he couldn't see her. What had she said? Find, observe and investigate. He tried not to think about the, *if he was still alive* bit. Okay, find first then. But hadn't he found what he was supposed to find. Observe it was then. Tom cast his eye around the room. Nothing looked out of the ordinary – then again he had never been in a fifteenth century workshop before. Right, thought Tom, now looking at Da Vinci, who had returned to his bench, perhaps I should start with him. Who's to say he is Da Vinci. He could be just a mad old man who happened to wonder in. Or an assistant – didn't all great men have at least one crazy in tow. Or he could be an imposter, he didn't look thirty-eight for a start. Tom decided he would start by finding out if the man at the bench really was who he said he was. From there his next question would have to be one of three. How did you get to look so old? What have you done with the real Da Vinci? Or, and this to himself, how did I get the timeline so wrong. He suddenly had the feeling the latter might be the one he ended up asking. But hang about, surely that was investigating, or was it back to finding? Tom was getting confused, but hey-ho. Tom took a deep breath.

'Leonardo Da Vinci,' said Tom.

The man at the bench suddenly whipped round to face Tom, a deeply puzzled look on his face. 'I thought I was Leonardo Da Vinci,' he said, scratching his head.

'You are,' said Tom, confusing himself, 'aren't you?'

'How can I be Leonardo Da Vinci if you are?' asked the old man.

'But I'm not, I'm called Tom,' said Tom.

'Are you, well nice to meet you, I'm Leonardo Da Vinci, you can call me Leo.' Leo held out a hand.

Fair dos, thought Tom, shaking Leo's hand. At last Tom felt he was getting somewhere. Where that might be was next on the agenda, but he hadn't discovered anything yet, apart from Da Vinci being gaga, if that was who this was, and preferring to be called Leo; couldn't construct a case for evil-doings on that. So, no closer to finding out what was going on and why. Tom decided a different approach was needed; something that would perhaps open things up a tad and throw some light on things.

'I've come to inspect...' But Tom's new approach shuddered to a halt as the smile on Leo's face dropped and was instantly replaced by a glowering stare. Leo's top lip started to quiver. 'Perhaps that's not what I meant. What I meant to say was… was…' Leo had reached for and wrapped a gnarled fist around a rather nasty looking mallet. Quickly now Tom old boy, thought Tom, eyeing up the instrument with horror. 'What I meant to say was…' Quickly! Got it! Tom hoped. 'Admire,' Ha-ha-ha! 'I've come to admire… your work.' Tom crossed sweaty fingers.

Leo's face twitched. A battle was going on somewhere in his head. His grip on the mallet loosened. 'Admire?'

'Yes,' said Tom, holding back the relief for a moment or two.

'My work?' The corners of Leo's mouth began to twitch.

'I certainly have,' said Tom, praying what he was saying was the right thing to say.

Leo's lips stopped their quivering and accepted, for now, an uneasy narrow set. 'Which one?' he asked.

Which one? thought Tom. A good question that, which one indeed. Tom plumped for a blanket answer, 'Why, all of them of course.'

'Ah-ha!' yelled Leo, causing Tom to jump. He threw the mallet behind him over his shoulder and the smile was back, only bigger this time. 'Come with me then young fellow.' He stepped forward and placed an arm round Tom's shoulders. 'This way.'

Tom, allowing a little relief in for now, was gently bundled through an archway and into another room. Tom's eyes widened. The room was filled with... crammed with... packed from floor to ceiling with... the most amazing amount of craziness and rubbish Tom had ever seen. Nothing of it smacked of Leonardo Da Vinci – at least not from what he had seen in the books and pictures on his camera it didn't. Something was most definitely wrong here.

Leo beamed with joy as he showed Tom about, pointing out one moment of lunacy after another, until at last they came to the last object. This one was the only one covered over. Leo left Tom's side and approached it with reverence.

'This,' said Leo, a tear glistening in the corner of his eye, 'is the crowning glory.' He lifted the cover and stepped back so Tom could see it clearly.

Tom stared. And then he stared some more. It was... he took a step back. It was... he took two steps closer. Wherever he stood it was the same, it was... it was... it was just plain awful, that's what it was, but there was something about it that nagged at him – something that made him think he had seen something like it before, but where?

'So,' said Leo, stepping beside Tom again, 'what do you think of my masterpiece?'

What do I think? thought Tom, it's awful, that's what, but I can't tell him that. Tom was thinking of the mallet. 'It's...' Tom tilted his head to one side, 'It's...'

'Yes?'

'Lovely?'

'LOVELY!' roared Leo, looking fit to burst, 'You think my masterpiece is lovely?'

'Well,' said Tom, meekly, looking set to run, 'when I said lovely...'

'LOVELY!' Leo went over to the wall where his masterpiece was hanging, removed it, and stared at it. His face was the colour of a lighter shade of a purple plum. He looked at Tom. 'Lovely? You... think it is lovely?' His eyes were filling up. Leo gave his masterpiece another look then hung it back on the wall. He turned to Tom. 'It is isn't it?' he said, tears starting to fall.

A passing feather could have knocked Tom over. 'Very,' said Tom, now remembering where he thought he had seen it before. He needed a private moment. 'I couldn't use your loo, could I?'

'Loo?' said Leo, dabbing his cheeks with the sleeve of his nightshirt thingy.

'Toilet.'

'Through there.' Leo pointed to a curtain in the corner of the room.

'That'll do.'

'And please wipe your feet afterwards.'

Fair enough, thought Tom, not daring to ask why. He reached the curtain. 'Through here?'

'Yes.'

'I won't be a moment.'

'Enjoy.'

'Er… thanks.' Tom lifted the curtain and went in. He had expected at least a seat, but the loo was still in the style of the, hole in the floor, garderobe. It reminded Tom of the toilet on an around the island boat trip he had been on once while visiting Greece – now that was a feat, he remembered – but as he wasn't there to use it, it didn't really matter. Then again, as he was there, and he had had that cuppa not long ago.

Tom finished, cleaned his hands with the cleansing gel he had in his pouch, something he discovered he needed after his other trip into the past, not a lot in the way of soap in some era's, and settled down to deal with the real reason of why he had wanted to use the loo. He slipped the camera from his pouch, turned it on, and started thumbing through the pictures he had taken. Some of the text had had photographs alongside. He soon found what he was looking for. He zoomed in on the picture, hardly believing he had been right. Blimey, thought Tom, no wonder they called her a moaner, she don't look very happy. He then looked for a picture of Da Vinci.

'Hello?'

Leo's tentative call brought Tom back to the here and now. He quickly put the camera away and checked his codpiece; all was in order. Tom left the toilet.

Leo was standing in the archway. 'I thought you might be stuck or something… sorry, what did you say your name was again?' he said.

'Tom,' said Tom, emerging from the blanket.

'Tom,' said Leo.

'Tom,' confirmed Tom, nodding.

'Tom Tom?' said Leo, thinking this over, 'I like it.'

Oh good grief, thought Tom, first Brandy, now this old fool, but whatever. 'You wanted me?' said Tom.

'Did I?'

'You called.'

'Oh yes,' said Leo, brightening as he remembered, 'I did this while you were a doing and thought you might like it.' He handed Tom what looked like a rolled up newspaper.

'What's this?' said Tom, taking what was offered.

'It's a copy. Open it,' a grinning Leo encouraged.

Holding it at arm's length, because one never knew what might happen, Tom unrolled it.

Leo was thrilled and clapped his hands. 'Do you like it Tom-Tom? Is it… is it as lovely?'

'It is,' said Tom, trying not to show what he really thought. 'Thank you.' He gave it a closer look; was that numbers he could see in the eyes? The great Da Vinci crayoned by numbers? Tom, after seeing what he had seen on the camera had decided that Leo was the real Da Vinci, only not as everyone knew him. Who's to say the historians hadn't got his age wrong by thirty odd years. And art was in the eye of the beholder wasn't it? thought Tom, thinking of the shambles surrounding them.

'I used the same crayons as I used on my masterpiece,' said Leo, shaking with delight, 'only took a minute.'

Not doubting that for a moment, Tom rolled his small masterpiece back up. He had a question for Leo. 'What do you call it?' he said.

'A picture,' said Leo.

Ask a silly, a silly question, thought Tom. 'I meant, what do you call the picture?'

This question gave Leo pause for thought. 'Ah!' he said, after a couple of seconds, 'you want to know what the lady is called.'

It'll do, thought Tom. 'Yes.'

'I call her the moaning lady,' said Leo.

'Not the Mona Lisa then?' said Tom, now in investigating mode.

A simple yes or no would have sufficed, but Tom wasn't about to get that. As soon as Leo heard the name two things happened, his face darkened and he began to pull at his hair. He also started to cry – more a wail really, which was technically three things if anyone was counting. Tom wasn't.

Tom was mortified by Leo's response. Rule one when dealing with crazy, don't upset. Tom went into action. 'Leo old fellow,' he said, back in Errol's shoes. 'What did I say?'

'That name,' sobbed Leo, tugging harder on his wispy grey locks, 'it haunts me. So beautiful she is, yet so mean. It is she that keeps me here.'

'What, Mo-doe's it-she?' said Tom, just managing to keep his foot out of his mouth, while not having the faintest idea what Leo was going on about.

Leo had dropped to his knees. 'In my sleep,' he sobbed, 'at my wakening. All day it follows me. Alack and alas, woe is me! Oh bitter woe!'

'And that's what she calls herself is it?'

'Oh bitter woe!'

Oh bitter balls, thought Tom, thinking perhaps his work was done here. Where was Brandy? 'Now listen here old chap,' said Tom, 'it can't be all that bad now can it? You wouldn't have painted her otherwise.'

With red and raw beseeching eyes Leo looked up at Tom and spoke. 'With hopeful alacrity I sow the seed of my beginning day and pray mayhap it grow different than the last, but lo then weave with doubt and sorrow and awe as it does compound and crowd me in with each passing moment as it did before. Yet still I search for peace maiden fair on which I may seek succour, and yet come to know restful night, for my soul to slip within.'

Yeah, well, right, okay, thought Tom, all well and good, but this is one sucker you are about to see the last of, once I get the chance to skedaddle. 'Is there anything I can do?' asked Tom, too late remembering his old dad's advice, don't volunteer for nothing – something to do with his army days.

'Why,' said Leo, face suddenly full of sunshine again, 'why not? I'll have one too.' Leo promptly stood up. 'Red or white?'

'What?'

'Won't be a moment,' said Leo, heading for the arch.

'Red or white what?' Tom called after him – Tom not being a wine man.

'Why wine my dear Tom-Tom,' Leo shouted back. 'Wine!' He stopped and turned round, 'And do you know, I think this little chat of ours has cured me of my fears.' Leo tousled his wispy wayward locks, 'and from this day on I shall bury myself in my work. Cut my hair. Wear day clothes. Throw away my crayons. Yes Tom-Tom today is a good day for such things. Today is the beginning of a new me. I'll get us that wine.' Laughing, Leo went to get it.

Tom on the other hand wasn't laughing. He was worrying. What if Da Vinci had always been rubbish? What if his meeting him had changed all that, got him to pull his socks up to become the man everyone knew him as? What if he repainted his moaning lady in the future and called it the Mona Lisa? What if he only looked old? What if he goes mad again later in life? What if that's why the pictures start changing? What if Tom realised how stupid he was being? But Tom was in too much of a panic to do that. Gawd, he thought, it's only me that's gone and changed the future.

CHAPTER 49

A guard arrived, conversed with the old man in chains, left, and then returned with another man – this one with an officious looking plume of feathers attached to his helmet.

After he too had spoken to the old man, he walked across the cell to where Darren was hanging around. 'I am captain of the castle guard and am here because I have the misfortune to speak your language. It is English you speak?'

'And Saxon,' said Darren.

'Sack son?' said the captain, 'I know nothing of sack son, so I will ask you my question in English. Why are you tormenting your fellow prisoner? Who in turn is tormenting my guard with his wailing, who has been put in the unfortunate position of gaoler and torturer because the stupid man whose place he took dropped a red hot iron on his foot and died of the shock. This guard is one of my best men; I do not want him upset. He is also my sister's husband. Tell me?'

'I'm not,' said Darren.'

'He said you were.'

'I was only trying to tell him my name,' said Darren.

'Ah,' said the captain, 'that is something we too would like to know.'

'It's Darren,' said Darren, wondering why they didn't know.

'Ah, so the mystery man left unconscious on our doorstep with not so much as a note, but trussed like a pig has a name. Darren? I have not heard of such a one before.'

'It's Arthur really, but everyone calls me Darren,' confided Darren.

The captain gave Darren a look that said he had just found out why Darren had been left and bound on the castle steps; the man was obviously mad. Why would anyone call someone by a name that is not the right one? 'And that fellow over there,' poking a finger in the old man's direction, 'says he is Leonardo Da Vinci.'

'Wow,' said Darren, remembering the film the man had been in, the one about the seaside. 'I'm a big fan, but he looks a lot older than I thought he was.'

'Ha!' exclaimed the captain, 'That is what we said. He says he is Leonardo, but Leonardo is above us right now in his workshop, with the features that befits a man in his late thirties.'

'He's an imposter?' said Darren, clearly disappointed by the news, but in turn excited about the real one being so close at hand and running a film workshop to boot. 'Do you think you could get me his autograph? I'd go myself but…' Darren rattled his chains.

'Eh?' said the captain, backing away. He turned to his brother-in-law. 'Mad,' he said, 'Mad and dangerous, both mad and dangerous. We were a prison now we wet nurse lunatics.'

'Eh?' said the guard, who couldn't speak English.

The captain apologised and repeated what he had said in his mother tongue.

'Ah,' said the guard, nodding his head in agreement.

'But now I must leave,' said the captain. 'The duke is due to arrive back within the hour and I need to make sure all is ready for his return.' He turned to the old man. 'And you can wail all you want because no one will be here to hear you; I'll not be wasting good soldiers guarding the likes of you. Vincenzo, you are with me.'

Smiling, the guard saluted and held the cell door open for the captain.

'Wait!' yelled Darren, suddenly remembering something, 'What about me, I shouldn't be here?'

'That is what they all say,' said the captain, as the door closed behind him.

'But I should be in the shop. What will Mister Smokowski say?'

The key turned in the lock.

'Wait!'

But Darren's plea was in vain. The captain and the guard had gone.

CHAPTER 50

After much deliberation and general dithering and reading and rereading of the card, Smokowski finally came to a decision, he would…

But could he do that? Smokowski returned to his dithering. He needed to tell Cat what had happened, but he doubted he could. He suspected there would be some serious security surrounding her and her whereabouts, a security blanket imposed that was so thick it would be more of a duvet – a forty tog.

Tom then? But what could Tom do? And besides, he wasn't supposed to contact him, just tail him. But this was an emergency. Perhaps Tom would be able to contact Cat. No, how could he? 'Oh dear,' said Smokowski, looking at the card again. He had to do something.

Card in envelope, envelope gripped tightly in hand, Smokowski, figuring there would be less chance of bumping into further irate customers going via the back door, made for it. He was going to head over to Tom's. He didn't know what he was going to do when he got there, but it would buy him time to think.

He would never get there.

'That him?' whispered a voice from the depths of a shadowy gateway as Smokowski passed by.

'Yes,' said a companion shadow hugger.

'I'll signal the others.' A signal was sent and a trap was set.

Smokowski, collar up, head down, oblivious to all around, mind set on only one thing, getting to Tom's cottage, passed the shadowy gateway where the shadow huggers were, without a glance. If he had, he wouldn't have seen anything – the shadow huggers were too highly trained to be seen.

On Smokowski went. On for another twenty paces without incident. It was as he took the twenty-first that things changed – when the lights went out for Smokowski. He would have struggled. He had been trained for such incidents, but his assailants knew this – were ready for it. A speedy jab with a hypodermic needle was administered. It was over. As Smokowski slumped to the ground an unmarked black van pulled up beside him.

'Quickly now,' said someone. 'Elsie.'

'Hold your horses,' said Elsie, who had been one of the shadow huggers, 'I'm not as young as I used to be.' Elsie climbed from the van and, ably assisted by her walking stick, helped push Smokowski into the back of it.

CHAPTER 51

Queen Vicky couldn't have been more helpful. She knew of the Travellers and their work, and had met Cat on a number of occasions – the rat affair being one of them. She also knew not to ask too many questions, and not to engage Cat in idle chit-chat concerning the Victorian age, because of Cat's dislike of the meddling of the time. And she was more than happy to hand over the wristwatch, as Albert said the strap chaffed his wrist something horrible.

'Well, well, well, me ol' cock sparrow,' said Invisible Bob, as they left the royal residence, 'can you Adam 'n Eve it? Luv a duck. She was a good ol' stick, weren't she?' Invisible Bob was giving his elbows the old in and out – thumbs in invisible braces.

'One of the very best,' agreed Cat, 'Bob?'

'Yes cobber?'

'That's Australian.'

'Is it?'

'Can you please stop now?'

'Stop what, me ol' apples and pears?'

'Your inane gibbering, and I am not a staircase.'

'Didn't say you were,' said a mystified Invisible Bob, 'did I?'

'Yes, so stop with the cockney chat. Wouldn't be so bad if you knew what you were saying.'

'Oh, okay,' said a pouting, miffed Invisible Bob, 'So where's our next port of call then?'

'Funny you should say that. Can you breathe under water?' asked Cat.

'No,' said Invisible Bob, suspicious of what was coming next.

'Then keep close.'

Their fifth quest proved to be a success. And what a place! One of the most beautiful and best kept secrets in the universe, as anyone who had ever visited Atlantis would not have been privy to tell you. As for the sixth though, albeit also successful, the less that was said the better.

'I didn't like that,' said Invisible Bob, wiping disgusting goo from his invisible body.

'Me neither,' said Cat, wondering who in their right mind would. She shook a paw and watched with revulsion as the gloop that was clinging to it splattered on the ground.

'Lest said, I say,' said Invisible Bob.

'Ditto,' said Cat, shaking goo from another paw.

'But what I want to know is...'

'Don't,' said Cat, 'best not to know.'

'Lest said,' said Invisible Bob, nodding. But there was something else he wanted to know. Where was it they would be heading on their final quest? He asked.

He was told.

CHAPTER 52

As Leo went for drinks, a panicking Tom decided it might be a good time to make with the feet – the moving of. He quickly headed for the door hoping Brandy was watching from somewhere and would appear. She did, from the shadows whence he had left her.

'Grief!' said Tom, as she suddenly appeared, 'Were you there all the time?'

'Not all the time,' said Brandy, 'what's the hurry?'

'I think I know why things changed,' said Tom, meaning his suspected future changing gaff.

'You do?'

'Yes, and we've got to tell someone before it's too late.' Tom went to grab the door handle.

'In good time,' said Brandy, barring Tom's exit, 'first though, tell me what you know.'

'Tom-Tom!' shouted Leo, from somewhere behind them.

'We've got to go,' said Tom, urgently.

'Okay,' said Brandy, opening the door, 'quick now.'

Tom didn't need telling twice and dashed out into the hall, straight into an unwelcome surprise.

'Hello,' said a voice Darren would have recognised, 'what have we here?'

'Brandy!' yelled Tom.

But Brandy had seen what was outside the door and had hurriedly closed it. There was no point in the both of them getting caught.

'Ha!' said the captain of the castle guard not recognising Tom as someone, who should be in the castle, 'perhaps we have another madman running loose Vincenzo?' His attention was drawn to the rolled up picture in Tom's hand. 'And what does Brandy have in his hand?'

Tom instinctively put his hand behind his back.

'Come now,' said the captain, 'don't be shy, share it with us.'

'It's mine,' said Tom, stepping back and into the door. 'Brandy!' he hissed.

The captain took a wary step forward and held out his hand. 'In that case, you won't mind if I have a look.'

Tom weighed up his options. It didn't take long, he handed over his picture.

The captain unrolled it and smiled. 'You did this?' he asked.

'No,' said Tom, disturbed that the man should think so, 'Leo did.'

'Leo?'

'Da Vinci.'

'Da Vinci did this for you?'

Tom nodded.

'Perhaps we should ask him to verify what you say,' said the captain, maintaining his smile.

Drat, thought Tom, not relishing the idea of seeing Leo again, but as his current options hadn't shown any sign of increasing in the last few seconds he could do nothing but agree.

As soon as Brandy had closed the door behind Tom she darted into the shadows. She wondered what Tom had discovered. She needed to find out, but first she had to make herself scarce. Brandy watched as Leo, bottle in hand, wandered across the workshop, looking here and there and calling for Tom. He went into the adjoining room. She took her chance, glancing furtively after him, she made a break for a door on the far side of the workshop, but when she reached it, it was locked. There was another way out though – there were high arched windows in the room where Leo had wandered. Treading warily, Brandy peeped within just as Leo wandered back again. Brandy disappeared into a handy shadow and waited for him to pass. His back to her, she slipped through the archway.

'Tom-Tom?'

Brandy whirled round to find Leo staring her. He must have heard her.

'Who are you?' asked the puzzled Leo, 'Where's Tom-Tom?' He stepped closer to Brandy and fixed her with a watery stare, 'Why are you wearing a mask?'

Brandy didn't have time for this. 'So you can't see who I am,' she said, moving closer.

'Your voice sounds familiar, do I know you?'

'I don't think so,' said Brandy. Swift as a snake, her arm shot out, the edge of her hand connecting with Leo's neck.

Eyes rolling back to show the whites, Leo crumpled and fell to the floor. The bottle in his hand didn't.

'Waste not, want not,' said Brandy catching it. Seconds later, she was gone.

The captain opened the door and called to Leonardo.

'He likes to be called Leo,' said Tom, not sure why he said it.

'Leonardo!' called the captain, again, ignoring Tom's advice.

Someone answered in a voice that sounded like Leo, but didn't. Tom reasoned it must be down to Leo's new beginnings.

'Ah, Leonardo,' said the captain, as a man Tom didn't recognise approached, 'the duke has returned early and wishes to see you.'

'I shall get my coat,' said the man Tom didn't recognise.

'There is one other thing,' said the captain, grabbing Tom's arm.

'Yes.'

'Do you know this man?' The captain thrust forward a confused Tom.

'Never seen him before, why?'

'He says he knows you, and calls you Leo.'

'The man is obviously a madman.'

Ah-ha, thought the captain. 'Just one more thing, did you do this?' He unrolled the crayoned version of the Mona Lisa.

The man Tom didn't recognise looked at it. 'Is this a joke, Captain? Do you think to belittle my talents? I have never seen such a thing. What is it?'

'The Mona Lisa,' said Tom.

'Never heard of it,' said Leonardo.

The captain apologised, 'Sorry, of course not, I am only doing my job. This man,' he jostled Tom, 'said you gave it to him.'

'I didn't,' said Tom.

'You did,' said the captain, no longer smiling.

'I didn't,' argued Tom, 'I said Da Vinci gave it to me.'

'Leonardo Da Vinci?'

'If you like,' said Tom, deciding to leave off with the Leo for the moment.

'But this *is* Leonardo Da Vinci,' said the Captain.

And in that split second between *is* and the captain finishing what he was saying, Tom developed the horrible feeling that the captain might be telling the truth. That the man standing before them who was young, in his late thirties, as Tom had expected to first find him, was indeed Leonardo Da Vinci. Which beggared the question – what the heck was going on? Tom suddenly burst forward escaping the captain's grip, he ran into the room to the archway that led to the room that had been filled with Leo's nonsense. He stared into it, disbelief etched on his face. The nonsense, all the craziness, had gone. Order now reigned over the chaos.

At the door the captain had had enough of madmen for one day. 'Vincenzo.'

'Sir?'

'Take that madman to the cells and throw this in with him.' He slapped Tom's copy of the Mona Lisa into the guard's hand. 'I'll deal with him later.'

CHAPTER 53

'They've got him.'

'Good. Tell them to bring him straight to the ops room as soon as they arrive.'

'Will do.'

'Oh, and Beatrice.'

'Yes?'

'Jolly good book this what?'

'I'm glad you're enjoying it.'

The revolving wall in the dark room revolved and Smokowski, wedged in a wheelchair, was wheeled into the operations room. He had two guards with him.

'Is he all right?' asked the Chief Traveller, crouching to look at Smokowski.

'As well as can be expected,' said one of the guards.

'Anyone see you?'

'In and out, clean as a whistle,' said the other guard, the one with the walking stick.

'Good... good. Beatrice.'

'Here, Sir.'

'Wheel him into a debriefing room will you. We'll keep him there until he comes round.'

Beatrice claimed the wheelchair's handles from the guard and wheeled Smokowski away.

The Chief watched Smokowski go then, looking extremely grave, he spoke to the guards. 'So,' he said, 'it appears Lucy has gone rogue.' He was one for the dramatic.

'Not herself maybe,' said Elsie, leaning on her stick, 'but rogue, that's a bit strong, Chief.'

'Not herself then. Do we know that for certain?'

'Mildred is on it as we speak, Chief.'

'Good work,' said the Chief, nodding thoughtfully. 'Keep me informed as things develop.'

'Will do, Chief,' said the guards, speaking and saluting in unison.

Thankfully the Chief was quicker on his pins than it looked and caught Elsie as she toppled over. 'You okay Elsie?' he asked, supporting her.

'Sorry Chief, forgot and put all my weight on my gammy leg.'

'Field injury?'

'Jam pot.'

'Full?'

'Yes, Sir.'

The Chief had heard of such things happening – grim stuff. 'But you're on the mend?'

'A jam pot won't stop me.'

'Well done that woman, well done.' The Chief saluted her, 'and keep up the good work.'

'You can rely on the LISPS,' said Elsie.

CHAPTER 54

'Blimey,' exclaimed Invisible Bob, as something whooshed an inch from his head, 'not again.' But this arrow wasn't from the quiver of Robin Hood.

'Keep quiet, and keep down or you'll be enjoying a parting where you don't want one,' said Cat, laying low.

Invisible Bob, who had been standing on tiptoes, took Cat's advice and crouched down beside her. He wasn't a parting sort of fellow. 'Which one do you think is his?' said Invisible Bob.

'The largest one I suppose,' said Cat, 'warily raising her head to see if the coast was clear or not. It wasn't. She ducked low again as a tomahawk flew overhead. It came to rest embedded in a tree a couple of feet away.

'Why are we still here?' enquired Invisible Bob, taking fright and clambering aboard Cat.

'Get off me,' said Cat, shaking her back.

'Not until we're safely out of harm's way,' said Invisible Bob, clinging on for dear life.

Cat didn't have time for more of Invisible Bob's shenanigans but decided to leave him where he was for the time being; she didn't like him sitting on her any longer than need be, but at least she knew where the little menace was. 'Sit still then,' she said, rising. The encampment they were heading for was still a quarter of a mile away. She crept closer.

'It's your fault anyway,' whispered Invisible Bob.

'What is?' Cat whispered back.

'Couldn't just glamour near, oh no, you have to land us, out in the open, smack in the middle of where they weapon practice. Crazy is what I call-yah!' Invisible Bob ducked low as a lance landed less than a foot away.

'I told you, glamouring doesn't work on Native Americans, never has and no one knows why. And how was I to know where they practised? We arrive close to where the ops wall indicates.'

'Convenient I say,' ventured Invisible Bob, now convinced someone was out to get them. 'My guess,' he said, 'is that whoever caused the ripples knew you would be involved. All these quests are part of a trap and as we haven't found the unfelt ripple yet, reason says this one is it. The trap was set and now it's going to spring.'

'You finished?' said Cat, who was secretly thinking along the same lines, but wouldn't admit so to Invisible Bob for a very good reason; if he thought that she thought the same, the little idiot was apt to panic and do something stupid. Cat was also thinking that this last quest, the most dangerous one, because of the restrictions on her use of magic, and as such, a perfect place to set a trap, could so easily have been the first or third one chosen. What did that mean? Was someone hoping to get her out of the way early if she had chosen it earlier? Or did they know she would pick this one as her last quest. If so, then the others were just there to delay. Delay to what end? Was it a ploy to keep her out of the way while something else was going on? Or time needed to prepare the perfect trap? Was this about her? Answers on a postcard... Cat crept on; she would soon find out.

She stopped on the outskirts of the encampment. This wasn't going to be easy. They had six watches now and on each occasion it had been attached to the wrist of the most important male in the vicinity. And the male in question now was Chief Sitting Bull. To make matters worse the encampment was on edge as it was soon to be Custer's last stand. Worse still, she was going to have to rely on Invisible Bob to get it – *if* there was one this time. *Worse still,* she hadn't told him yet.

'Whoa-ah!' said Invisible Bob, as Cat suddenly dropped.

'Quiet!' hissed Cat, as she hid behind what cover was at hand – it wasn't much. 'To your right,' she whispered. Invisible Bob chanced a peek. 'Your other right,' sighed Cat.

'Oh,' said Invisible Bob, ducking down. Two Sioux braves appeared to be looking straight at them. 'Do you think they've seen us?'

'Me perhaps,' said Cat.

'What're we going to do?'

'Wait and see if they start this way.'

'What if they do?'

'Hold on tight.'

Being the scared out of his wits chap that he was at moments like this, Invisible Bob took heed and grasped clumps of fur as tight as he could.

Away to the right the two braves were deep in conversation – an occasional look thrown Cat and Invisible Bob's way. It seemed to Cat they were in two minds about something. She hoped it was nothing more than what to have for tea that evening. Then one of them suddenly started to walk their way. Cat tensed. Invisible Bob wished he was somewhere else. Someone shouted. The approaching brave stopped and turned. The shout had come from the encampment; he was wanted. With one final glance and a shrug of his shoulders, he rejoined his companion and they headed away.

'Phew,' sighed Invisible Bob, 'that was close.'

'Too close,' said Cat, 'and that is why I can't go any further.' It was time to tell Invisible Bob her plan. He wasn't going to like it.

'No way,' said Invisible Bob, who didn't like Cat's plan one iota.

'Sorry, Bob, but there's no other way,' said Cat.

'There must be,' he wailed, 'What if they see me?'

'I can't see you, and I'm looking straight at you,' said Cat.

'You're not,' said Invisible Bob, his heart then slumping in his chest as he realised the very words he spoke vouched for Cat's plan. 'Okay,' he said, his voice subdued, 'but you keep an eye out for me.'

Cat said she would, as far as she could.

With Cat's reassurance, failing to reassure him, Invisible Bob set off for Sitting Bull's lodge. He dodged. He rolled. He fell into pony poo. He quickly found some water in a bowl and washed it off. He figured a little man seemingly made of poo might draw attention. He continued. He paused to watch a rather attractive squaw go past. He wished he was taller. He just managed to stop from wolf whistling. He moved on again. He arrived. He waved to Cat – then remembered she couldn't see him. He went to go inside, stopped, had a cautious look about, realised it was the wrong tepee and scooted off again for the one Cat had pointed out. At last he arrived at the right one; he knew this because as he had eyed up yet another comely squaw, he had tripped over, and landed on the foot of the very man whose lodge he had been looking for.

Sitting Bull, halfway out of his tepee, looked down, frowned, and shook his foot.

Invisible Bob, unbalanced by the shaking moccasin, fell backwards and stared skyward, looking straight up into the frowning face of Sitting Bull. He knew it was Sitting Bull from a photograph Cat had shown him when they deposited the latest watch in the safety of her pyramid. He also noticed he wasn't wearing a watch. Sitting Bull went on his way. Invisible Bob rolled out of harm's way and then quickly scuttled inside.

Once inside the tepee, Invisible Bob had a quick scout round to make sure he was alone. It appeared he was. His next job, find the wristwatch. Here, he was of the same mind as Cat – *if* there was one. If there wasn't... well, he didn't want to think about that right then. Fact was, he didn't want to think at all at the moment – too many things, horrible things, were ready to spring into the imagination. Instead he made himself busy.

But five minutes of searching later Invisible Bob was still empty handed. It wasn't looking good. He rubbed his tiny invisible eyes with his tiny invisible hands and rested his tiny invisible back against a handy wooden pole with furry things hanging from it. What did he do now? Surely he had looked everywhere possible. Dejected, Invisible Bob tilted his head back and closed his eyes – seeking inspiration perhaps, but he really didn't have time for such fancies. He would have another look around, and then, and only then, would he go back and give Cat the bad news.

Invisible Bob opened his eyes and set off for his final search. But he had only gone a couple of paces when he suddenly stopped. He turned round. Had he... no, surely not. There was only one way to find out. Invisible Bob returned to the pole he had been leaning against and looked up. He had! Invisible Bob slapped an invisible thigh. Way above him, attached to the end of the pole, which he now saw was a lance, was a wristwatch – hidden away from any view but from beneath, by a multitude of feathers. Invisible Bob kissed the lance with joy. Only problem now, was how did he get it down?

Guessing the distance was six feet high from ground to wristwatch, Invisible Bob calculated, given that he was only just over three inches tall, that to him the distance equated to, *a flipping long way up*. He grabbed the pole, there seemed to be decent grip. But first, you never knew, Invisible Bob tried to shake the pole. It didn't move, but at least he had tried. He started to climb.

All went well for the first three feet, but then he had to negotiate the first of the furry things. No problem for an athlete such as me, thought Invisible Bob, as he reached it. Sadly, as it is with the delusional, things don't always work out as they imagine. With all the agility of a dead two legged mountain goat, Invisible Bob slipped and started to fall. Luckily for him he fell the right way and just managed to grab onto the furry thing with a flailing hand. Shaking, but in one piece, Invisible Bob took a moment then continued on his way – only three more furry things to negotiate.

It took a little longer to get past the second furry thing, but the third, now Invisible Bob had learned his lesson, was traversed slightly quicker. One furry thing left. He reached it. He passed it. The route to the watch was clear.

Chest heaving, Invisible Bob shimmied up beside it. He surveyed the knot holding it. It didn't look as if it would be too much trouble. It wasn't; Invisible Bob let the watch drop to the ground. If only it were that easy for me, he thought, then, realising it could be, he wished he hadn't; it was a long way down for someone so small.

Invisible Bob started the long climb down again. Halfway, just as he reached the last of the furry things, a thought occurred to him – how was he going to get the watch to Cat without it being seen, the place crawling with trigger happy braves as it was? This stopped him in his tracks. His plan had been quite simple up until then – climb down, collect watch, run like the wind. What now? Then it hit him. A gust of wind, blowing in through the door of the tepee, caught the last furry thing, sending it into Invisible Bob's face as he hung there thinking. He furiously started untying the knot holding the furry thing to the lance. He would use it as cover; surely no one would take any notice of a mole scurrying past.

On the ground again, Invisible Bob grabbed the watch, pulled the furry thing he had let fall to the floor over his head, and made for the door. Happy as Larry with his idea – a Larry who had not given much thought to what a passing mutt might make of his disguise – he headed to find Cat.

*

'Aargh! Yuk!' said Cat, as Invisible Bob sidled up in his disguise and revealed himself – figuratively speaking. Cat had been keeping a wary eye on the furry thing that had left Sitting Bull's lodge more than twenty minutes ago. Had watched and wondered at its erratic course as it had wandered and weaved, stuttered and stopped, had scared the living daylights out of a rather attractive squaw and various other native Americans, had fought off the attentions of a curious dog, before arriving there, by her side. She had guessed it was Invisible Bob within the furry thing, so hadn't been surprised by that. No, her surprise and exclamation was upon realising *what* the furry thing *was* that Invisible Bob had been using as cover.

'It's me,' declared Invisible Bob, throwing aside his disguise, 'and I've got a watch. What?'

Cat's expression was all horror and disgust. 'Where did you get that from?' she exclaimed.

'Sitting Bull's tepee,' said Invisible Bob, wondering why Cat was acting so. 'It's moleskin… I think. And he won't miss it if that's what you're worried about – he's got loads of them. Strange thing to collect mind, but I think I know why.'

'You do?' said Cat, gingerly flicking the moleskin aside.

'Oi!' said Invisible Bob, going off to retrieve it, 'I'm going to make a coat out of that.' He dragged it back. 'As I was saying,' he said, when he had, 'I reckon it's a token of bravery, or something, and as I've been brave, I think I deserve one too. You should have seen those so called braves run when I went past them – run like mice they did.' Invisible Bob had himself a good titter.

'I did,' said Cat, not laughing.

'Yeah,' said Invisible Bob, basking in his glory, 'thought I was a goner a couple of times when they crowded round, but nope, afraid of moles you see. I reckon I should get a medal or something.'

'Something,' muttered Cat, shaking her head in disbelief. 'You have no idea have you?'

'About what?' said Invisible Bob.

'What your moleskin really is.'

A look of alarm suddenly pervaded Invisible Bob's features. 'It… it's not a fake is it?'

Cat leaned forward and whispered in his ear.

'A what?' said Invisible Bob.

Cat repeated what she had said.

'*Noo*,' said Invisible Bob, dropping the moleskin.

'Yes,' said Cat.

'A… a… I think I'm going to be sick,' said Invisible Bob, reeling from the truth – that the furry thing wasn't so much furry as hairy, that it was a scalp!

'Look sharp about it then,' said Cat, sounding not in the least bit sympathetic, but with a small smile on her lips. She picked the wristwatch up from where Invisible Bob had dropped it and grimaced as the sound of retching reached her ears. 'You finished?' she said after a moment or two.

'Yeah,' said Invisible Bob, who was feeling every bit the funny shade of green, he would have been if he had been visible.

'Then hop on and hold tight, we've an ops room to get to.'

CHAPTER 55

He was not dragged screaming, or complaining, along corridor after corridor, stairway after stairway to the cells. Instead, he was led away by Vincenzo the guard as quiet as, well, a rodent that dwells within the walls of a certain religious building. Tom you see was bemused, bewildered, and downright confused. What had just happened? He was wondering. He was thinking, but not sure what to think. He knew it would have something to do with time somehow, doesn't it always? But that didn't make it any clearer. Was the room gone forever? He wondered about Brandy. Was she all right? Had she disappeared forever? One minute she was right behind him, the next... who knows where. Not in Da Vinci's workshop, that was plain. Or perhaps she was, with Leo, wondering where he, Tom, had gone. And what about the chap he had met in the corridor before going in, surely a witness? But where would he find him? Perhaps he had disappeared as well? Tom sighed. A dead end there, no doubt, he thought.

Along another corridor they went, down another stairway. At the bottom of which they came to a small chamber with a table and two empty chairs. Someone was moaning.

'It's not fair,' moaned Darren, as he hung listlessly from his chains, 'I haven't done anything.' But no one was listening. He glanced over to the old man; he appeared to be asleep, or ignoring. 'Good thing too!' shouted Darren. Anyone in their right mind could see he was too old to be that actor chappie – silly old fool. Darren shifted his gaze to the chains holding him. What would Arthur do in a situation like this? Wait a moment, I am Arthur, thought Darren, thus answering his own question. He would be hanging about listlessly from these chains wondering why he was there and what he could do about it. Darren/Arthur shook the chains. 'Aargh!' groaned Darren aloud, as it achieved nothing more than the removal of a few flakes of rust, a few

216

flakes of skin, and a jingling noise. But wait a minute, thought Darren, the jingly sound hadn't come from the chains.

The keys Vincenzo had dropped onto the stone floor had made a jingly noise. 'Goodness gracious me!' snarled an unhappy Vincenzo, as he retrieved them. He put a key in the door's keyhole, then tried another. Third time he was lucky, the key turned and the door opened. Tom was shoved inside, the picture of the Mona Lisa thrown after him.

'Have a nice stay,' said Vincenzo, as he went to pull the door shut.

Suddenly it dawned on Tom what was happening to him. His cloak of confusion dropping from his mind he quickly decided this wasn't for him; there was no way he was going to be locked up, not while there was breath in his body, life in the old dog yet. He darted forward. Just in time to collide with the solid oak door Vincenzo had just closed.

Looking through the small barred window, Vincenzo winced. That has got to hurt, he thought. He locked the door and headed for the stairs.

On the other side of the door, Tom, breath knocked out of him, was apt to agree, and did. 'Ow!' groaned Tom, as he fell to the floor.

'Ooh!' said a certain chain dangler, 'You okay mister?' asked Darren.

Tom rolled onto his back, gasping for a decent breath.

'*Tom*?' said Darren, hardly believing what he saw.

Tom, still groaning, with bells ringing in his head, now rolled onto his stomach.

'Tom! It's me!' shouted Darren.

Tom rolled back onto his back.

'Tom?'

Tom, determined not to try and count the multitude of stars that were spinning before his eyes, groaned again and rolled onto his side.

'Tom! It's me, Darren,' shouted Darren, straining on his chains, 'You okay?'

Tom, not as senseless as he was knocked a minute or so ago, managed to give the words that were assaulting his lugholes some semblance of thought. Was he okay? The mist started to clear a little more. He decided he might well be if some idiot didn't keep shouting at him. Hang about – did someone say Darren? Tom rolled back onto his back. Couldn't be, I must be dreaming, thought Tom. How could Darren be here? Tom decided he couldn't be and rolled onto his side again. But there it was again, someone shouting, shouting about Darren.

'Tom!' shouted Darren, again, 'It's me Darren. Can you hear me?'

He could. Tom could hear. Blimey, thought Tom, it's not a dream, it's a bloody nightmare. What the heck was he doing here? Tom rolled on to his back again and tentatively opened an eye.

'Tom,' said Darren, when he saw Tom open his eye. He waved, causing his chains to rattle. 'It's me.'

Bally budgies! thought Tom, as the mist in his head cleared some more, it *is* him. Tom managed to raise his head a little to get a better look. 'Darren? Is that really you?'

'Hi Tom,' said Darren, smiling weakly, 'how was the trip? Did you all have to dress as clowns?'

It really was him. Tom went to raise his head further, but it was having none of it. 'Ooh,' groaned Tom, returning it to its previous position. 'How… what trip?'

'You know,' said Darren, 'the one with turkey and tinkle.'

Good grief, thought Tom, as he lay there, it's a good job we keep his true identity out of the public eye; King Arthur being a solid dumb arse at times would not go down well. 'It went great,' said Tom, attempting to sit up, 'and this isn't a clown suit.' Pain or no pain, he had things to do, and the first thing, as it appeared there were no char making facilities at hand, was to find out how his daft lump of a son-in-law Darren had managed to end up chained to a wall in a castle in Milan in the fifteenth century. He could hardly wait. Tom, now sitting, standing not an option just yet, gave Darren his full attention.

First thing Tom noted was that Darren wasn't dressed like he was – a clown. He also noted he was wearing an apron like Smokowski's. Then he remembered. 'Why aren't you at the shop?' In hindsight Tom thought it a daft question, but he had to start somewhere.

'I was kidnapped,' said Darren.

Did he hear that right? 'Did you say kidnapped?' said Tom, who was still suffering from the odd bell ringing in his belfry.

'Yes,' said Darren, 'while I was in the shop.'

Tom still wasn't sure he had heard right. 'Someone kidnapped you from Smokowski's?'

'Yes.'

'Who?'

There followed a momentary pause before Darren answered, 'Lucy.'

Now he most definitely *wasn't* hearing right. 'Sorry,' said Tom, blinking at Darren, 'I thought you said Lucy.'

'I did,' said Darren.

'Lucy?' said Tom.

'Your daughter.'

'My Lucy!'

'Yes.'

Well... well, thought Tom, she's come to her senses at last. But chuckling in his head as he was, levity time it wasn't, this sounded serious and however much it was going to hurt, he was going to have to get to his feet and get his thinking cap on. Lucy... a kidnapper? And how would she have got Darren here, in the past? It just didn't ring right. Not unlike that bell in his head.

'Ow-ooh-ow,' groaned Tom, as he slowly edged into an upright position. The head wasn't so bad now; he hadn't actually bumped it, more shaken it. But what did hurt, now the head was clearing, was his backside, where he had landed on the floor. 'For the love of do-dah,' he moaned, 'how did that get there?' He had sat on his pouch. He checked the camera, it appeared to be still in one piece. He now hobbled over to where Darren was hanging.

'You sure it was Lucy?' said Tom.

'She looked like Lucy.'

'And you, King Arthur and big muscular lad that you are, just let her?'

'She jabbed me with something,' said Darren, jiggling a shoulder, 'on the shoulder. Next thing I knew was waking up here.'

Tom was certain it couldn't have been Lucy; why? Unless she had been got at, or... 'A doppelganger!' he said, 'has to be.'

'I don't think she was German,' said Darren.

Tom rolled his eyes. This was no good, he was getting nowhere. So he decided to deal with what was at hand first, he'd grill Darren further later. 'We've got to get out of here,' he said, looking at the chains holding Darren; he didn't fancy ending up like that. 'But first we have to get you out of those.'

'How?' said Darren.

'Never fear, Tom is here!' Tom took off the backpack no one had so far noticed – apart from Brandy that is, but who was too late to ask questions, and whipped out his saver.

Darren's eyes widened. 'I don't think you'll be able to cut the chains with a knife,' he said. His eyes then widened even further. 'Is that a naked lady?'

Tom quickly turned the penknife the other way up. 'Stand back!'

'I can't,' said Darren.

'Oh yeah, close your eyes then.'

It took but a second to free Darren from his chains, but not quite in the way Tom had envisaged. He had thought *key*, but what he had got was bolt cutters.

'What about these?' said Darren, shaking the shackles that were still attached to his wrists and ankles.

'Least of our problems,' said Tom, eyeing the locked door. He went over to it and peered through the small barred window to check all was quiet, it was - the room beyond empty. Perhaps he should have done that earlier, before cutting Darren's chains, but hey-ho. Time to make their escape. Tom looked at the saver in his hand and wondered what it might come up with this time. To be on the safe side he placed it on the floor – he didn't want to be holding it if it changed into a battering ram. Eyes firmly shut Tom concentrated all the harder on a key. When he opened them he was to be disappointed. Tom picked the saver up.

'What is it?' said Darren.

'A screwdriver,' said Tom. He took it over to the door and examined the plate where the keyhole was, but there were no screws, just iron rivets. 'Well,' he said, scratching his head, 'fat lot of good this is going to do.' He was perplexed; the saver had never let him down before.

'Here, let me try,' said Darren, grabbing it.

'Here,' said Tom, holding tight, 'get off.'

A tugging match ensued which ended with the saver flying through the air.

'Oh no!' yelled a horrified Tom, trying to catch it.

'I've got it,' said Darren, diving for it.

But neither managed to grab hold and it fell to the floor, landing in a flash of brilliant light.

Tom, who was first to recover his wits, scurried over to where the saver had landed. Please don't be broken, thought Tom, as he picked it up.

'Look,' said Darren.

Tom was looking, and thankfully the saver appeared to still be in one piece. 'That's lucky,' he said, 'no thanks to you.'

'Not at that, that,' said Darren, pointing behind Tom.

Tom turned to see what the fool boy was going on about and starred in disbelief. Where the lock had been, there was now a hole the size of a football. 'Wow,' said Tom, giving the screwdriver closer scrutiny and noticing for the first time a small button on its handle. Without thinking he brushed a finger against it. Another flash of light pulsed from the screwdriver towards the ceiling, where another football sized hole materialised. How Tom had kept his nose he would never know.

'Was that sonic?' said Darren.

'More like laser,' said Tom, blinking.

'Cor, a laser screwdriver,' enthused Darren, not totally sure what one of those was.

'And with a hair trigger,' said Tom, quickly thinking the saver back into a penknife.

'Marc would love that.'

'Marc will never know about it,' said Tom, sternly.

'Oh yes, course, sorry,' said Darren, 'forgot.'

'We had better make tracks,' said Tom. He went over to where he had dropped the rucksack and started to empty it.

'What's that?'

'My clothes,' said Tom, 'I hid them in here while Brandy wasn't looking. I was going to change as soon as it was possible and now seems as good a time as any.'

'Brandy?'

'My temp familiar, didn't Smokowski say?'

'Oh yeah, Brandy.'

When he was back in his civvies, Tom stuffed the contents of the pouch and the saver into a jacket pocket and retrieved the picture of the Mona Lisa from the floor. He was ready to leave. 'Right,' he said, 'let's be off.'

'What about him?' said Darren.

'Who?'

'The bloke that reckons he's an actor.'

Tom was lost again. 'What bloke?'

'Over there.'

'Well I never… how long has he been there?' said Tom, noticing the other man for the first time.

'He was there when I woke up,' said Darren. 'He reckons he's Leonardo Da Vinci, the actor, but he's way too old.'

Tom's ears pricked up at the mention of Da Vinci. He went over for a closer look. It couldn't be, thought Tom, as he saw the man's face. He got closer. He was a lot dirtier, but the same hair, same bed clothes. 'Leo?' whispered Tom. But then again, he thought, on closer inspection, though the man did look like Leo, there was something about him that wasn't Leo. Tom tried to put a finger on it. Yes, that was it – this man didn't look half as crazy as the one he had met upstairs. This man was a Da Vinci, but was no way a Leo. Which meant – and this was weird, very weird – that this Da Vinci made three.

CHAPTER 56

'Where am I?' demanded Smokowski, to no one but the four walls that surrounded him. Not long awake, disorientated, in a wheelchair, and feeling numb all over, Smokowski feared the worst.

Beatrice suddenly and silently appeared beside the Chief Traveller – something that occasionally unnerved him. 'I wish you wouldn't do that,' he said, heart pumping a little quicker than it had been.

'Sorry, Sir,' said Beatrice, 'but I thought you would want to know instantly we had word of Cat.

'News you say?' said the Chief, gathering his wits.

'She is on her way here.'

'Here? Good, 'bout time. Bring her to the ops room as soon as she arrives.'

'Will do, Sir.'

'What's that?' asked Invisible Bob.

'A feather,' said Cat, 'I found it when you were on your hair-raising adventure.'

'That's not fair,' said Invisible Bob, 'I told you I hadn't realised what it was.'

Cat smiled.

One of the walls Smokowski had been shouting at had a door in it. This door now swung open. A figure filled the space.

'Who are you?' demanded Smokowski, ready to defend himself, but having to admit he hadn't been doing such a good job of that lately.

The figure removed a pair of night vision goggles. 'Sorry, still trying to get used to them, how are you old chap?'

'Eric?' exclaimed a surprised Smokowski.

'Chief Traveller now my old friend.'

'Chief Traveller eh?' said Smokowski, who might have been slightly more impressed if he wasn't so angry. 'When did that happen?'

'A couple of years ago, want a humbug?'

'What I want, Eric,' said Smokowski, 'is to know where I am, why I'm here, why I can't feel my legs and why I'm in this wheelchair?'

'Sorry old chap, sent the LISPS after you, needed you in HQ. Wheelchair belongs to them – needed something to transport you in after they drugged you.'

Ah, thought Smokowski that explains the numbness, I was drugged. 'But why?' he asked.

'Couldn't have you running loose when you discovered Darren was missing, what?' said the Chief, still holding out the humbugs – he knew Smokowski couldn't resist a humbug.

He was right – Smokowski gave in and took one. 'But why didn't you just call me in? You know I'd have come.'

'Didn't want to be obvious, didn't want anyone to know. That's why we called in the LISPS. Secretly see.'

'Has this got anything to do with Cat?'

'She told you?' The Chief didn't appear too surprised.

'She trusts me.'

'As do we old chap, as do we, but after reading the note you were carrying, warning you off or else, we figured for sure you would try and contact Tom about Darren, who would then have tried to contact Catranna. The whole thing would have started to get messy. Need them with eyes only on *their* missions. You of all people surely understand that?'

Smokowski did, but that didn't mean he was happy about it. 'You read the note?'

'Yes, sorry about that, but it fell out of your hand when the LISPS went in. It looked suspicious.'

'What about Lucy?'

'She's in the clear, nowhere near the shop,' said the Chief, features clouding.

'Which means?' said Smokowski, knowing that look.

'Which means, Smokowski dear friend, we may have a spy in our midst.'

224

*

Beatrice led Cat and Invisible Bob into the ops room.

'Where's the Chief?' asked Cat, noting he wasn't there.

'He'll be along in a moment; he's with an old friend. Can I get you something while you wait, chicken, chocolate, something to drink?'

'I'm fine thanks,' said Cat, leaping onto the ops table.

'Ooh,' said Invisible Bob, 'a nice piece of chocolate wouldn't go amiss.' He slipped from Cat's back and onto the gloved hand Beatrice was holding out. 'Oh I say,' said Invisible Bob as he landed, 'polka dot grips.'

'I thought they might appeal,' said Beatrice, lifting him.

'When you've deposited him Beatrice,' said Cat, feeling slightly nauseous, 'I've more watches for you to take a look at.'

'I'll be back in a trice.'

'Smokowski?' said a puzzled Cat, as the Chief led him into the ops room.

'Cat,' said Smokowski.

'What's going on? I thought...' Cat pulled up short.

'It's okay, the Chief knows what I've been doing.'

'It's Darren, Catranna, he's been kidnapped.' The Chief then filled her in on what had happened.

'Any idea who's behind it and why?' said Cat when he had finished.

'A total mystery,' the Chief admitted, 'but it has to be connected to the ripples.'

'We found more watches,' said Cat, 'perhaps they'll throw a bit of light on what is going on.'

'That's something I was meaning to ask you about,' said the Chief sternly.

'Yes, sorry about not calling in Chief, but I also had suspicions. A couple of times it seemed as if we were expected. Coincidence maybe, but I didn't want to take any chances by coming back and showing my cards each time.'

'That's fair enough,' said the Chief, happy with the explanation, 'would have done the same under the circumstances. Where are the watches?'

'Beatrice has them.' Cat wondered whether she should say something about the other objects she had found, the feather and the small lid Invisible Bob had been using as a drinking vessel. She decided not to – for the moment.

'Watches?' said Smokowski.

'Oh yes, sorry Smokowski, didn't I say?' The Chief explained.

'Any idea what those letters mean?' asked Smokowski, his natural bent for espionage aroused, 'Is it a code?'

'Catranna?' said the Chief.

'Could be?' said Cat, doubtfully.

'What were the letters?' said Smokowski.

'Here,' said the Chief, producing a pen and notepad, 'tell us what they were Cat and we'll see if we can work it out before Enigma.'

'Enigma?' said Cat, 'what's that?'

'Not a that, Catranna, a him, head of our Decipher department. He has the brain of a computer. Now Catranna, those letters if you please,' said the Chief, ready to jot.

'U-U-R-P-O-S-Y,' read Cat.

'Well,' said Smokowski, when the Chief had finished jotting, 'nothing jumps out. Something to do with flowers perhaps?'

'How so?' said the Chief.

'U-U-R POSY,' said Smokowski, speculatively.

'See what you mean,' said the Chief, rubbing his chin thoughtfully. 'Something-something-something flowery. What do think Catranna, right track you think? A code based on flowers perhaps? What sort of flower starts with a U or an R?'

Cat took to frowning. 'I think you may be taking them too literally,' she said, 'that's just how I remembered them, not the order I found them in.'

'Well, I'm stumped then,' said the Chief.

'Already?' said Cat.

'Me too,' said Smokowski, his espionage bent obviously not what it was.

So much for that then, thought Cat. She hoped the Enigma chap would have better luck – he couldn't be any worse. She crossed her toes anyway.

'Have to wait on Enigma then,' said the Chief. 'Ah!' Beatrice had appeared just like that.

'Sir?' said Beatrice, placing a tray on the ops table.

A sudden burp sounded from amongst the watches on the tray, startling the eager to know faces that were looking at them.

'Sorry,' said Invisible Bob, 'the chocolate I think. Do you know it comes in liquid form as well? Shakes they call it.'

'Beatrice?' said the Chief, who clearly wasn't impressed.

'Sorry, Sir, I didn't see him get on. Shall I remove him?'

'Yes... no, wait, I know it's early days, but has Enigma had any luck with the code yet?'

'He told me to give you this, Sir.' Beatrice handed the Chief a folded note.

'Already?' The Chief took the note and read it. 'What!' he blustered, when he had finished. 'Is this some sort of joke? Because if it is, I am not amused.' He then threw the note onto the table, narrowly giving Invisible Bob a nasty paper cut.

Cor, thought Invisible Bob as the note whizzed past, he sounded just like Queen Vicky.

'I don't think so, Sir,' said Beatrice, as Cat and Smokowski rounded on the discarded note, 'I don't think Enigma has a sense of humour.'

'Let me see,' said Invisible Bob, as Smokowski picked up the note.

'Oh,' said Smokowski, when he read it.

'Oh,' said Cat.

Smokowski showed it to Invisible Bob.

'Blimey,' said Invisible Bob, 'I think someone's been yanking your chain, Boss.'

The thunder cleared a little from the Chief's face. 'What do you mean?' he said, 'What chain?'

'The one attached to your...'

'I think he's right,' said Cat, quickly, 'it looks as if someone has been leading us up the garden path.'

'What I think Cat and Bob are trying to say Chief is that someone has been leading you a merry dance,' said Smokowski.

'Okay... okay, enough with the idioms, I get it, someone's been leading us on a wild goose chase.'

'Yes,' said Cat, exchanging a look with Smokowski.

'So, we're back to square one again. No clues, no code, no nothing.'

'Not quite,' said Cat, thinking it was perhaps time to divulge what she had found beside the watches, 'I found something else while we were away.'

'You did?' said the Chief, bucking up a little.

From the tray Invisible Bob gave Cat a look, but as she couldn't see it, she ignored him.

'Yes,' said Cat, 'but I think we should find somewhere a little more private.'

The Chief was about to say something about being among friends when he realised the room had fallen ominously quiet. The usual noise and bustle heard from the travellers and familiars that worked there as they went about their business had disappeared. He of course trusted every one of them implicitly and no one was actually acting suspiciously, but… 'This way,' he said.

As Beatrice held out her hand for Invisible Bob to climb on, she cast a glance at the note. She smiled as she quietly read out loud what was written on it, '"UP YOURS".'

CHAPTER 57

'But we can't just leave him,' Darren protested.

'He'll slow us down,' said Tom, who reckoned he'd had more than his fair share of Da Vinci's for one lifetime.

'But what if they take our escape out on him,' argued Darren.

As arguments went, Tom could see that this one was going to get him nowhere fast if he didn't agree. 'Okay... okay,' said Tom relenting, 'but you look after him, right? Da Vinci's aren't just for Christmas you know.'

'Aren't they?'

'Never mind,' said Tom, pulling the saver from his pocket. 'Stand back.' Tom gave it some thought and the saver changed instantly – into a chainsaw.

'Will that work?' said Darren.

'Not a chainsaw,' groaned Tom, 'a *chain saw*. Oh never mind.' Tom thought again and a pair of bolt cutters appeared. He picked them up and cut through the chain holding Da Vinci up – which was different to Darren's, in that Darren had a chain for each wrist and Da Vinci had only one for both. Da Vinci fell flat on his face. 'Oops,' said Tom.

Darren went over to the stricken Da Vinci and felt his pulse. 'He's alive you'll be glad to hear,' he said, 'but I don't think he'll be waking up any time soon.' He gently turned Da Vinci's head so Tom could see the growing lump on his forehead.

'It was an accident,' said Tom, shrugging – and a dang handy one if you ask me, he thought. He cut through the chains holding Da Vinci's ankles. 'There, all done. Can we go now?' Tom put the changed again saver back in his pocket.

'I suppose so,' said Darren. He grabbed Da Vinci, hauled him upright and threw him over one of his massive shoulders.

Tom led the way from the cell, through the guards' chambers, and to the foot of the steps; there he stopped. The way above was cast in shadow – anyone might be lurking, but as the only way out appeared to be up, Tom had little choice and moved onto the first step.

The stairs were steep and narrow, but surprisingly easy enough to climb and soon they were at the top. Here Tom called another stop. 'Which way?' he asked, as Darren joined him.

'Drugged remember?' said Darren.

'Oh... yeah, right, let me see.' Tom had a choice, left, right, or straight ahead. He chose left, then changed his mind and opted for right, then beckoned for Darren to follow him – straight ahead it was.

They soon came to another staircase.

'Up is it?' said Darren.

Tom held his tongue – the sarcastic part of it. 'Aye,' he said, stepping onto it. He remembered – a miracle in itself, that along with what had seemed an endless amount of corridors, he had also walked down at least two staircases – or was that three? At the top of the stairs was another corridor.

'Tom?' said Darren, as they crept along it.

'Yes?'

'Where are we going?'

'Along here.'

'Where are we heading?'

'To the end.'

'Tom!'

'The loo.'

'Tom?'

'Yes?'

'Do you know where it is?'

Tom stopped so quickly, Darren nearly dropped Da Vinci. 'Yes,' said Tom.

'Where?'

'Along here somewhere.' Tom waved his hand vaguely in front of him and set off again.

At the end of the corridor was another junction. They paused as Tom gave their next move some thought.

'Which way now?' said Darren, taking the weight off his feet by propping Da Vinci into a sitting position against a wall.

'I'm thinking,' said Tom.

'You don't know, do you?'

'I wouldn't say that,' said Tom.

'What would you say then?' asked Darren rubbing an aching shoulder; the old boy was heavier than he looked.

'Proceed with caution, is what I say,' said Tom, starting off again – with caution.

Darren hoisted Da Vinci back onto his shoulder and followed. Another junction later, he had had enough.

'Wait,' said Darren, unloading Da Vinci again.

'What?' said Tom, who was quite a few paces further on.

'I'm knackered,' said Darren, leaning against the wall.

Tom ambled back. 'A big strong lad like you,' he said.

'He's heavier than he looks,' said Darren.

'We'll have a rest then,' said Tom, thinking perhaps he had been a tad harsh with the lad, 'but not for long.'

'Tom?'

Here we go again, thought Tom. '*Yes*?'

'You don't know where we're going, do you?'

Tom wondered should he come clean. 'No,' said Tom, deciding on the full douche.

Great, thought Darren, the new shiny *ooh-ah* world he had recently been introduced to, losing a bit of its edge under the influence of the shadier past he now dwelt in, allowing a touch of Arthur back in. This touch had an idea. 'Why don't you use the saver,' said Darren – or was that Arthur?

It was a good idea. A brilliant one in fact. So much so, Tom would have pretended not to have heard if he thought he could have got away with it. Why hadn't he thought of it? But credit due where credit earned. 'Not a bad idea,' said Tom, 'was just going to suggest it myself.' Thinking it was a good job his nose wasn't made from wood, he took the saver from his pocket and thought, *directions*. The saver sprang from his hand and landed on the floor, Tom only just managing to get out of the way. Tom shielded his eyes. In the middle of the corridor stood a huge arrow on a stand, lit by a multitude of glowing bulbs. It pointed right.

'Handy,' said Darren.

Was that irony from young Darren? thought Tom, there might be hope for him yet. Tom tried again and added *compact* to his thought. The saver changed again and Tom picked up a small object the size of a pocket watch.

'What is it now?' asked Darren.

'Looks like a sort of compass,' said Tom.

'For drawing circles?' asked Darren.

And normality returns, thought Tom. 'No, for finding north, south and such, but this one has got only one direction written on it.'

'Which is?'

'HOPE END,' read Tom, aloud.

'Oh, I don't like the sound of that,' said Darren.

'I do,' said Tom, 'it's the name of my cottage.'

Darren's face brightened. 'So it is. Shall we go?'

'Let's,' said Tom.

And off they went, to the right, with a lighter step and new hope in their hearts, and as they did Tom looked at the compass in his hand and turned it over. There was something written on the back, it read: TOM PENDING. Huh, thought Tom, everyone's a comedian.

CHAPTER 58

'Well, Catranna,' said the Chief, when they were safely out of earshot, sight, and anything in between, 'what is it you've found?'

Cat divulged.

'New evidence,' said the Chief, who looked at Beatrice, who looked at Smokowski, who looked at Cat, and continued with each of them looking at each other. They would have looked at Invisible Bob as well if they could have seen him. As for Invisible Bob, he was looking at Cat in a most disgruntled glaring way.

The new evidence was laid on the table.

'A *pink* feather,' the Chief observed.

'It doesn't look much like a drinking vessel,' said Smokowski, attention on the other piece of evidence.

'It does to me,' said Invisible Bob, aiming to make a grab for it before the Chief, who was reaching for it, could pick it up, but only succeeding in stumbling into the Chiefs outstretched fingers. 'Ow!' He sat back down again and rubbed at a shin.

'He found it,' said Cat, explaining Invisible Bob's eagerness to possess it. Was she feeling a tad guilty?

'And he can have it back once this mess is sorted out,' said the Chief, 'but for the moment it might be important. Please go on, Catranna.' He picked the lid up and inspected it.

'I'll start with the vessel. As you can see, it's really a top from a container.'

'Is not,' said Invisible Bob.

'Be quiet, Bob,' snapped the Chief, 'or your next assignment will involve cold, damp and smelly.'

Invisible Bob frowned and pursed his lips, but said nothing.

'Go on, Catranna.'

'As I was saying, the vessel is really the top from a lipstick, a special lipstick.'

'A lipstick top? Special you say?' said the Chief.

'Bespoke. And most definitely not belonging in Hood's time where Bob found it.'

'An anomaly? And you didn't think of telling me?' said the Chief.

'Sorry, Chief, but the less that knew,' said Cat.

The Chief nodded. 'And the feather?'

'On the outskirts of Sitting Bull's camp.'

'Which leads us to…?'

'If I'm not mistaken Chief, the culprit.'

Three expectant faces turned towards Cat.

'Well?' said the Chief.

Cat told them her thoughts.

'Blimey,' said Smokowski.

'Impossible,' said the Chief.

'Impossible,' said Beatrice, 'there are checks.'

'Chocolate,' droned Invisible Bob, who was too depressed to join in.

'That's what I thought,' agreed Cat, 'but the evidence.'

'Can we be sure?' asked the Chief.

'There are tests.' said Beatrice, 'Fingerprints, DNA, which, if present, can be checked against our database.'

'What about the feather, can't see you having much luck finding prints on that?' said Smokowski.

'Maybe not, but as Beatrice said, there could be traces of DNA,' said Cat, 'If there is, the traces, along with the bespoke lipstick and any telltale prints should be enough to prove guilt.'

'But if they're more red herrings?' said the Chief.

'A path we will have to carefully cross, but questions will have to be asked,' said Cat.

'What about Tom?' said Smokowski, suddenly fearing the worst for his old mucker.

'Beatrice, as quick as you can.'

'On my way.'

'Chocolaaaate,' groaned Invisible Bob.

'And could you *please* take Bob with you Beatrice.'

'Yes Sir.'

CHAPTER 59

'So,' said Darren, shifting Da Vinci from one shoulder to another, 'how did you know where to find me?'

'Find you?' said Tom, watching the compass needle.

'To rescue me.'

'I didn't,' said Tom.

'Then why were you there?'

'Long story,' said Tom, turning right into another corridor.

'Part of your mission?'

'Yes,' said Tom.

'Tom?'

'Yes?'

'Why were you dressed as a clown again?'

Tom, by his own admission, wasn't exactly lightening on his pins these days, but he didn't need to be – Darren had his hands full.

'Ow,' said Darren, rubbing a rapidly reddening ear, 'What did you do that for?'

'Let's just say you had to learn a life lesson,' said Tom.

'What...'

'Whoa,' said Tom.

'What?' asked Darren, covering his exposed ear just in case there was another lesson he didn't know he needed learning.

'A little flashing light has just come on.'

'It probably means we're close to the loo,' said Darren.

Tom looked at Darren. 'What makes you say that?'

'It's behind you,' said Darren.

Tom now looked behind him, and sure enough, there in the middle of nowhere, and the corridor, was the loo, its door standing wide open. 'Well I'll be...'

'Good job the door was open otherwise we wouldn't have seen it,' said Darren, wandering around the back of the loo to wonder at the lack of anything there. He waved at Tom with his free hand, but all Tom could see was the waiting portable loo interior.

Grief, thought Tom, where's he gone now? 'Darren?'

'Here,' said Darren, appearing from round back. 'Amazing isn't it?'

'You've been in it before,' said Tom, growing a little impatient now that they had found what they were looking for.

'Yeah, but it's amazing.'

'Yeah amazing, now come on before someone discovers we've escaped.'

Darren went to go in.

'Whoa,' said Tom, 'we can't take *him* with us.'

'But we can't just leave him.'

We could, thought Tom, but he supposed they had better not. Though what he was going to do with him when they got home was another thing entirely – and there was that rule about not bringing things back from the past, just in case it changed something. Tom dreaded to think what would be said about a souvenir Da Vinci. 'All right, but you put a card on Smokowski's lost and found notice board when we get back.'

'What?'

'Never mind, wedge him on the toilet.'

'Home then, Janes,' said Darren, when Da Vinci was safely wedged.

'What? Oh, James,' said Tom.

'Who is?'

Ignoring his royal highness the son-in-law, Tom took a last quick peep outside and then shut the door.

CHAPTER 60

Beatrice was soon back.

'Well?' said the Chief, who had never been able to read Beatrice's face.

'It's as Cat thought,' said Beatrice, handing the Chief a printout, 'fingerprints are a match, as is the taste in scent.'

'We have our culprit then,' said the Chief, 'You ready, Catranna?'

'All set, Chief.'

'Smokowski?'

'Ready,' said Smokowski.

'Here,' said the Chief, handing Smokowski Invisible Bob's hitchhiker, 'we confiscated it while you were drugged.'

'That's mine,' said Invisible Bob, back on the table and holding a square of chocolate.

'And you can have it back when this is all over with.'

Yeah... yeah, thought Invisible Bob, where have I heard that before?

'What are we doing about Darren?' said Cat.

'I've already set things in motion on that score, Catranna, you just concentrate on getting Tom back in one piece.'

'What about Brandy?'

'What *about* Brandy?'

Heads turned. Eyes narrowed.

'Good gad!' exclaimed the Chief, 'Get security!'

'Security?' said Brandy, who had just emerged from the revolving wall, 'what do you need security for?' She took up a stance that spelt trouble.

'As if you don't know,' said Smokowski, taking up a stance that would see him needing the use of Tom's rub.

'Where is he?' snarled Cat, tail swishing like a windsock in a force nine gale.

On the floor nothing visible moved with lightening speed towards Brandy.

'Hold it right there, nothing boy,' said Brandy, grabbing something from her handbag and throwing it in the direction of Invisible Bob, at twice the speed of lightening. On the floor, the special strength hair net did its job – tangling its target to a standstill. 'Now, before anyone else gets a silly idea, perhaps you'll tell me what is going on?'

'How did she know Bob was going for her?' whispered Smokowski, watching the hairnet wriggle.

'She must be wearing thermal disturbance contacts,' whispered Beatrice, back.

'Oh,' whispered Smokowski.

'Where is he?' Cat demanded for a second time.

'I take it you mean Tom?' said Brandy.

'Who else, unless you thought I meant Darren?'

Brandy shifted her weight.

'I wouldn't,' warned Cat, ears flat to her head.

'It's why I've come back,' said Brandy, 'Think before you take another step Beatrice.'

Beatrice became a statue.

'Because of Darren?' said the Chief.

'I don't know what you're talking about,' said Brandy, 'I'm here because Tom's in trouble.'

'If you've hurt him,' snarled Cat.

'We know,' said the Chief.

'Know what?' said Brandy, not liking what she was hearing one little bit.

'That you are behind the ripples.'

'What ripples?'

'Come on now,' said the Chief, 'let's not make this harder than it already is.'

Cat rolled the top towards Brandy. 'Perhaps this will jog your memory?' said Cat.

Brandy watched with the intensity of a hawk as it rolled towards her. It came to a stop by her feet. With one eye on her surroundings Brandy stooped and picked it up. 'A lipstick top,' said Brandy, 'is it supposed to mean something?'

'Read what it says on the end,' said Cat. Brandy turned the top in her hand, and when she saw what was written on it her eyes become like cold steel. 'Recognise it? Bespoke I believe, cherry cola with a twist. Perhaps you'll also recognise this?' Beatrice held out the feather. 'Your DNA all over it says you should.'

Brandy recognised them all right. Moving her hand so it was nothing but a blur, she went for her hitchhiker, but security had already been called, and security in the ops room was the best.

'Well done, Beatrice,' said the Chief, wringing his hands.

'Just doing my job,' said Beatrice, the head of security, as she put her blowpipe back whence it had come.

'Large enough dose I hope,' said the Chief, warily stepping closer to Brandy's prostrate body.

'A double,' said Beatrice.

The Chief ordered Brandy to be taken to the securest unit they had. He then picked the lipstick top up from where Brandy had dropped it and read what was written on the top of it. 'Cherry cola with a twist, dashed strange that, eh what? Sounds like a drink.'

'Unbelievable,' said Smokowski, rubbing his back as Brandy was taken away, 'Never thought I'd see the day when a BIMBO went rogue.'

'Yes,' agreed the Chief, 'but thanks to Catranna we now have our culprit under lock and key. Well done, there'll be something in this for you no doubt.'

'I don't need rewards,' said Cat, ears still tight to her head, 'just my Traveller back in one piece.'

'Good grief, of course,' said the Chief, 'go... go, we'll find out what we can when she comes round. Good luck.'

Smokowski went to squeeze the hitchhiker.

'Wait,' said Cat.

Smokowski's thumb hovered. 'Why?'

'We're forgetting someone.'

'Are we?'

There came a pitiful groaning from the floor, Invisible Bob had given up the fight and was lying, flat on his back, entangled in the net.

'So we are.'

'There,' said Cat, arriving back at the table with Invisible Bob still in the hairnet, 'ready when you are.' She rested a paw on Smokowski's arm.

Smokowski took his cue and squeezed the hitchhiker.

CHAPTER 61

Darren heaved, the still out to the world, Da Vinci from off the toilet and onto his shoulder.

'Cuppa first I think,' said Tom, a tad cheerier now he was home, 'and then we find Cat.' As always, Tom was hot on priorities. Tom opened the loo door, took a step forward, and then quickly took it back. 'Blistering biscuits!' he stammered.

'What's up?' said Darren, who had nearly dropped Da Vinci when Tom moved back.

'Can't be,' said Tom, sticking his head outside the door.

'What can't?' said Darren.

'We're back in the blooming castle.'

'How?'

The inclination was there one hundred percent, but luckily for Darren the effort just couldn't be raised, otherwise he would have had another flicked ear. 'How the flipping heck do I know?' said Tom.

'Perhaps you got your homes and castles mixed up?' suggested Darren.

'I'm old, not decrepit,' snapped Tom, who had been thinking along those very same lines, 'I'll just try again.'

'Second time best time,' said Darren, who had heard Marc say it.

'Right, give us some hush, I'll have another go.' Tom put fingers to temples and concentrated.

The loo flushed.

Darren, who had backed onto it, apologised.

'Right,' said Tom, as he opened the door for a second time, 'anyone for a cuppa?'

'Please,' said Darren, 'got any...'

'Blooming heck!' said Tom, 'we're back *again*.'

Darren craned his neck best he could to have a look see.

'What the heck is going on?' said Tom, at a total loss. Then a thought struck him – what if they weren't returning to the same spot at all, what if they hadn't even moved? Something odd was at hand – or was that a foot? Whichever, Tom didn't like it.

'Perhaps you should try again?' said Darren.

'No,' said Tom, 'something tells me we're not meant to be going home just yet.'

'What now then?' asked Darren.

'Brandy,' said Tom, a feeling forming.

'Brandy?'

'I don't know why, but I've a feeling she might have something to do with this. We have to find her.' Tom had suddenly developed a sick feeling deep inside his belly. He didn't want to spend the rest of his years hanging from rusting chains.

'But why would she do?'

'A good question,' said Tom. One he hadn't the remotest idea of an answer to.

Darren asked another good question, 'How are we going to find her?' He was on a roll.

So was Tom. He didn't have an answer to that either. Unless… the saver was still in the form of a compass, he took it from his pocket, and gave it some thought. The saver changed slightly – the words Hope End changing to Leo Da Vinci's workshop. They needed to start somewhere so why not the place he had last seen her? Who's a clever clogs then? he thought, giving himself a pat on the back. Though perhaps if he had given it more thought and changed Hope End to Brandy the BIMBO, it might have seen him nearer the top of the class. But, before a certain genius could go a wandering, there was a problem that needed dealing with first.

'Are you sure he'll be okay in there on his own?' said Darren, as Tom closed the loo door on Da Vinci.

Tom didn't answer, there was no way he was going to tempt fate any more than needs be.

CHAPTER 62

'What happened there?' asked the astounded Chief Traveller, as he took in his surroundings with growing bewilderment.

'Breached containment field, I'd say,' said Beatrice, taking the hitchhiker from Smokowski. 'There must be a fault with its integrity parameter.'

Four blank faces stared at Beatrice. One of them was double blank.

'Where are we?' asked the double blank face that was Invisible Bob.

'Tom's kitchen,' said Smokowski, giving the biscuit tin a guilty glance.

'Isn't that where we're supposed to be?' said Invisible Bob.

'You, me and Smokowski, yes,' said Cat.

'Ah,' said Invisible Bob, no longer wondering why the Chief was looking so surprised.

'So, what do we do now?' said Smokowski.

'That depends on the state of the hitchhiker?' said Cat, watching Beatrice fiddling with it.

'Nearly there… done,' said Beatrice, 'good as new.' She handed it back to Smokowski.

'Good,' said Cat, 'we'll drop you and Beatrice back to ops Chief, and then set off after Tom. Can't have you in harm's way,'

'Harm's way?' said the Chief, suddenly looking altogether bright, excited, his eyes twinkling, 'Do you know how long it's been since I was last in the field?'

'Which field?' said Invisible Bob.

'*The* field, this one,' said the Chief, looking fit to burst, 'and you know what, I'm going to make the most of it, I'm coming with you, Catranna.'

Cat and Smokowski exchanged a quick worried glance. They had known him during his field days, and without being cruel, neither thought of him as one of the best. A good brain certainly, couldn't argue with that – someone who was a whizz with paperwork, someone who would make a darn fine Chief Traveller one day, as was proved, but as an everyday Traveller, no. People had been genuinely ecstatic at his appointment as Chief, but mostly because it meant they had one thing less to worry about in the field.

'Are you sure?' questioned Cat and Smokowski as one.

'Never surer,' said the Chief, all smiles, 'and what possible harm can come to me with you Catranna and Beatrice by my side?'

A swift kick in the ankle, that's what, thought Invisible Bob, irked by the fact the Chief had failed to mention him.

Smokowski, on the other hand, who the Chief had also failed to mention, was more than happy. He liked being in the background and the more dangerous the task ahead the further into it the better.

'Well then,' said Cat, resigned to having the Chief along, 'a quick check to see if Tom is home, and then...'

'Done,' said Beatrice, holding what appeared to be a TV remote.

'Done?' said Cat.

'Yes,' said Beatrice, 'I've scanned for his vitals and nothings showing.'

'But that could mean...' said Smokowski, unable to put his thoughts into words.

'Oh, no,' said Beatrice, 'it only means he's not on the premises. Shall we go?'

'Time to press that hiker thingy Smokowski,' said the Chief, eager to get on, 'onwards and upwards, what?'

Cat and Smokowski exchanged another doubtful look as Smokowski reluctantly squeezed the hitchhiker.

244

CHAPTER 63

Brandy, her eyes open just enough, shifted ever so slightly on the cell's narrow bed in anticipation; she was waiting for something.

And sure enough, after not too long, what she had been waiting for dropped through the cell door's small hatch and onto the floor.

The knockout drug, administered by Beatrice's blowpipe, had done its job, but thanks to a multipurpose neutralising agent hidden in Brandy's lipstick – the twist – the effect had been greatly reduced – just enough to fool the most diligent among foe or friend into believing she was out for a very long count. Brandy had licked her lips as the dart had hit home.

Rubbing at the dart's point of origin, Brandy sat up. The need for further subterfuge not needed now that the package had been delivered, as it was also the signal that all observational devices had been disabled. Brandy now ran a hand across her belly and smiled. The amethyst had gone as she suspected it might, it being her hitchhiker, but it didn't matter. Brandy got off the bed, went over to the package and picked it up.

She opened it and tipped its contents onto the bed – a note and a small round object. Brandy read the note – an old friend wished her well. She then screwed the note and envelope into small balls and ate them. Now she picked up the small round object and, with a cherry cola with a twist covered smile on her lips, she squeezed it and was gone.

CHAPTER 64

'I say,' said the Chief, with gusto, 'must visit there again when circumstances are better. What was the place called again?'

'Milan,' said Cat, taking in their new surroundings.

'Kinda dark isn't it?' said Invisible Bob.

'Night,' said Beatrice.

'Perhaps we should come back during the day?' said Smokowski.

'Saw a nice straw hat,' said the Chief.

'Which way?' asked Invisible Bob.

'We don't even know if he's here,' said Smokowski.

'What do you think, Beatrice?' said the Chief, forgetting about hats for the moment, 'Is he here? What does that thingymacallit of yours say?'

But Beatrice was looking none too pleased. 'Sorry, Sir, but it appears it has gone on the blink. Some sort of interference – the thickness of the walls perhaps.'

'We'll never find him now,' said Smokowski.

'Yes we will,' said Cat, 'All we need is my tracker to pinpoint his position. If he's here, we'll find him.'

'Tracker?' said Smokowski.

'Yes,' said Cat, 'I popped a tracking beacon on Tom when I introduced him to Brandy.'

'But I… didn't you trust me?' said Smokowski.

'Implicitly,' said Cat, 'but one should always have a back up.' She gave Smokowski one of her smiles – her enigmatic, not to be questioned further, ones.

'Ah, right,' said Smokowski, tapping the side of his nose with a finger.

'Where is it then, this tracker?' said the Chief.

'Bob's got it,' said Cat.

'I haven't,' said Invisible Bob.

'I'm afraid you have,' said Cat, 'with all that was going on I needed to put it somewhere safe.'

Invisible Bob patted at his pockets. Then realising that he didn't have any, he demanded that Cat tell him where it was. Cat told him.

'Ouch,' said Smokowski.

'When? How?' demanded Invisible Bob, jigging on the spot.

'On our first mission, when you were drunk,' said Cat.

'When I was drunk?' Invisible Bob was horrified. 'But…'

'Don't worry,' said Cat, 'I used magic.'

'That's not the point, you could have asked?'

'We were in the field,' said Cat.

'Yes,' said the Chief, 'and what goes on in the field stays in the field, so suck it up and cough it up, young man, this instant, what?'

Beatrice smiled – she liked it when the Chief got tough.

'Cough it up?' stammered Invisible Bob, still with the horrified.

'No need,' said Cat, 'I'll magic it out. Could you put out your hand please, Smokowski?'

'But… I… why me?' protested Smokowski, not so much horrified, as mortified.

'Here,' said Beatrice,' sticking out a gloved hand, 'I'll take it.'

Cat transferred the tracker to Beatrice. 'Is he here?' said Cat.

'This way,' said Beatrice.

'We're here,' said Tom, standing before a door he thought he recognised.

'You sure?' said Darren.

Tom showed Darren the saver. It was flashing.

'What now then?'

'We go in I suppose,' said Tom, with not the faintest hint of confidence.

'But if she's not in there?'

'Then we keep on looking.'

'Couldn't we just ask the saver where she is?'

Tom stared. Why hadn't he thought of that? 'Well… you see… I thought of that,' lied Tom, who hoped it wasn't becoming a habit, 'but it sounded too easy, so I decided to keep it as plan B.' And as soon as I've had a cursory peek inside, thought Tom, we'll put that plan into action.

'Oh,' said Darren.

Tom went to open the door.

'Wait,' said Darren, putting his hand on the door, 'it might be dangerous in there. What if it's changed again – into something worse? What if the alarm's been raised and the guards are waiting for us?'

Good point, thought Tom, he's on a roll. 'Okay, give me a mo.' Tom had decided it was time for plan B.

'Tom,' said Darren.

'Hush, I'm trying to concentrate.'

'But the door.'

'What about the... oof!'

Brandy emerged from the shadows. It had been a close call. The last thing she had expected was to arrive before Cat and the others, seconds before them, but it did mean she didn't have to go looking for them. Slipping back into the shadows she set off in close pursuit. A score needed settling.

'Will you stop wriggling.'

'I'm nervous, I've never travelled in one of these before.'

'Ow! Watch where you're putting your walking stick will you.'

'Is your jacket real leather?'

'Yes, the hat is too.'

'I like the badge.'

'Anyone remember the embrocation?'

'It's here.'

'Who's got the cakes?'

'Here in the bag.' A hessian bag for life was raised.

'What we got?'

'Belgian buns, French fancies and a couple of dozen Welsh cakes.'

'Ooh, we've gone all continental!'

Laughter followed this remark. Lots of laughter. The sort of laughter heard when warriors were gearing up for the rigours of battle.

Tom could scarcely believe his eyes as not one, not two, not three, but four Da Vinci's grabbed and manhandled him and Darren, pulling them into the room. And waiting for them, casting further doubt on his eyeballs reliability, were at least a further eight Da Vinci's. Every one of them a spitting image of Leo and the Da Vinci they had left in the loo, and all shouting at once.

'What's going on?' wailed Tom, as his feet lifted from the floor.

'Who are they?' wailed Darren, as the two Da Vinci's holding his arms were lifted from their feet.

The room suddenly fell quiet as all the Da Vinci's in the room stopped what they were doing and starred at Darren. Tom gave him a sideways glance.

'I mean…'

'Darren,' said one of the Da Vinci's hanging from Darren's arm.

'Ah!' said all the Da Vinci's, bar one.

The room's earlier confusion resumed and Tom and Darren were led though to the room with the curtained garderobe. There they were bound to chairs, despite Darren managing to make a couple of the Da Vinci's cry. When the Da Vinci's were happy with their knots they upped and left, but Tom and Darren weren't alone, someone somewhere was softly sobbing.

Tom managed to move the chair he was tied to. 'Leo?' he said, 'is that you?'

The crying fellow looked up. 'Hello, Tom-Tom,' said Leo, who was looking and sounding downright miserable.

'Why are you tied up?' said Tom, assuming Leo was in league with the others.

'I'm not up to scratch,' he wailed.

'Who told you that?' said Tom, who wasn't going anywhere soon so why not.

A look of such sorrow came over Leo's tear stained face. 'The moaning lady says it. She broke my stuff and piled it over there. For the fire, she said.'

'Oh,' said Tom.

'Is that the Da Vinci you lost?' whispered Darren.

'I didn't lose him, I lost the room,' said Tom.

'What's he saying?' said Darren, not understanding a word of what was being said, 'and why can't he understand English like the rest of them?'

'Do they?' said Tom, who had missed the significance of the room falling quiet earlier.

'Seems so,' said Darren.

'Have to watch what we say then,' said Tom. 'Here, grab my cap with your teeth.' He ducked his head so Darren could take off his cap. He would be able to tell Darren what was going on then without Leo understanding. Cap off. 'He said the Mona Lisa...'

'Waaa!' wailed Leo, at the sound of the name.

'I thought you said he couldn't understand English,' whispered Tom, furrowing eyebrows.

Darren could only shrug.

'You sure we're going the right way?' said Cat, as they passed yet another piece of scenery she thought they had already passed.

'Following the tracker,' said Beatrice.

'Perhaps there's something wrong with it?' suggested a sulky Invisible Bob, who still hadn't forgiven Cat for what she had done.

'We've been walking for ages,' moaned Smokowski.

'Now... now chaps,' said the Chief, who had been looking on in wonder at everything they had passed like a child eyeing the presents beneath the Christmas tree for the first time. 'Beatrice is doing her best.' He returned to wondering and stopped at an alcove. 'Will you look at that,' he said.

'He doesn't get out much now, does he?' whispered Smokowski, to Cat.

'Not much, no,' said Cat.

That's odd, thought Brandy, as she peeped into the corridor Cat and the others had just taken, where were they? Brandy had been close on their tail until they had turned down this latest corridor, the corridor before the corridor that led to the short corridor where Da Vinci's workshop was, but now there was no one.

The corridor was long, with no turnings or arches for ages. They couldn't have just disappeared, thought Brandy. But they had. What did she do now?

*

'Ooo-ow!'

'That was bumpy.'

'Sorry about that, everyone okay?'

'A broken Welsh cake.'

'Dropped me handbag, nobody move.'

'Whoops, stepped on something.'

'Oh no!'

'What is it?'

'You've crushed me nunchucks!'

'I've seen that sconce before,' said Smokowski, remembering it because of it being slightly askew.

'They all look alike,' said the Chief, gazing at it in the starry look of wonder he had adopted since arriving.

But Cat agreed with Smokowski and called a halt. 'Something's not right,' she said, a feeling she had had for a while now, 'Are you sure the tracker is working properly Beatrice?'

'Looks fine to me,' said Beatrice, 'but give me a moment and I'll check it.'

'He could be moving,' said Invisible Bob, who had walked further than anyone else because of his short hairless legs, and so was now too tired to be peeved any longer.

'He could be,' agreed Cat, 'but we would have caught up with him by now, it is Tom we're talking about.'

'Suppose,' said Invisible Bob.

'Drat,' said Beatrice.

'What?' said Cat.

'You were right – the tracker was malfunctioning. Give me a moment.'

'Great,' said Smokowski, who had taken to sitting to give his feet a rest.

'There,' said Beatrice, 'straight ahead.'

'You said that when we set off,' said Smokowski, struggling to his feet.

'No,' said Beatrice, cocking her head, 'I said, this way.'

'She did,' said Invisible Bob, who knew which side Beatrice's gloves were sometimes buttered. He winked at her, which was a waste of time.

'Thank you,' said Beatrice, smiling at the floor, 'Would you like me to carry you?'

'*Please*,' said Invisible Bob, climbing aboard Beatrice's gloved and lowered outstretched hand.

'Whatever,' grumbled Smokowski under his breath, as he hobbled after everyone.

As Leo wailed, Tom thought back to what Brandy had said about find, observe, investigate. As he felt sure he had done his duty where they were concerned, his thoughts fell to the other thing Brandy had said – the bit about being alive, especially the, *if* part. Tom started to struggle against his bonds.

'It's no good,' sniffed Leo, who it appeared had cried himself out for the moment, 'they're masters at it.'

'What did he say?' said Tom.

'I 'on't 'ow,' said Darren, mouth full of cap.

'Oh for goodness sake,' said Tom, unable to understand what any one said now, 'here put my cap back on.' Darren dropped it on.

'Right,' said Tom, 'what did you say?'

'I don't know,' said Darren.

'Not you,' said Tom. He turned to Leo. 'And don't think I don't know your little game, pretending not to understand English.'

'I don't,' said Leo, looking puzzled.

'Yeah, well, ha-ha,' said Tom, knowing what he thought he knew, 'just tell me what you just said.'

Still puzzled, but happy to oblige, Leo told Tom what he had just said.

'Masters of tying someone to a chair?' said Tom.

'No,' said Leo, 'of knots. I have been like this for hours.'

'Great,' said Tom. But then he thought, Leo hasn't the strength of Arthur. He turned to Darren again. 'Darren, do you think you can break the ropes?'

'I've tried,' said Darren, 'but I'm pretty certain the rope is synthetic, some sort of polymer blend. Stronger than steel by upwards of forty percent, some of them you know.'

If Tom could have, he would have tapped his cap. Surely that wasn't Darren talking? Must have been an advert the telly addict had seen, but whatever, it meant they weren't going anywhere soon. Tom decided he might as well pump poor old Leo for information, you never knew.

'So,' said Tom, turning back to Leo, 'what do you know?'

It turned out that Leo didn't know a lot that was useful. He didn't even know who it was the other Da Vinci's were busy setting a trap for.

'A trap?' said Tom, 'Who for?'

'They wouldn't tell me,' said Leo.

'Why not?' said Tom.

'They say I'm not one of them.'

'That's an awful thing to say to your brother,' said Darren, who was now lying on his back, thanks to some ill advised frenetic back and forthing on his chair.

'What did he say?' asked Leo.

Tom gave Leo a knowing nod of the head. That's it old friend, he thought, you carry on playing the game, but I know different. He would have then, had he had his hands free, tapped the side of his nose with a finger. It's what old blokes did. Tom told Leo anyway.

'But they are not my brothers,' said Leo.

'Are they not?' said Tom.

'No, they are clowns.'

A door opened and several figures dressed in assorted knitwear and leather sprawled into the corridor.

'What's this, what's *this*?' demanded a figure that had followed the sprawling cardigans and jackets through the door. 'Call yourselves *soldiers*?! I've seen bargain hunters at jumble sales with more *discipline*!' The figure walked past the assorted knitwear and leather wearers and surveyed them, hands on hips. 'On your feet and form ranks, *NOW*!'

'Cor,' said one of the sprawled, as she got to her pop-socked feet, 'who died and made her sergeant major?'

'The Matron General did,' said another, dressed in heavy leather, 'but I don't think she's dead.'

'*Right* you 'orrible lot, you know why yer 'ere, so how about we get on with it and get stuck in?'

'Yes, *Sarge,*' yelled the formed ranks, as one.

'No need to salute, soldier. Pick that bonnet up.'

'Right then, by the left, *turn*!' The sergeant major looked on with pride. 'Is that your usual walking stick, Elsie?'

'Yes Sarge, just replaced the rubber tip with cold steel.'

'That is going to hurt someone.'

'I live in hope, Sarge.'

'Well done. Right you lot, by the left, quick amble. Left right left, oh all right, in your own time ladies.'

Breathing heavily with surprise, Brandy pressed her body deeper into the shadows as Cat and the others drew close. They had just appeared back where they should have been. It had been another close call.

'We're nearly there,' said Beatrice, showing the tracker to Cat.

'Right everyone, keep close.'

With Cat and Beatrice, and technically Invisible Bob, leading the way, they moved on.

A couple of corridors later, they stood before a sturdy looking door with a small barred window set in it.

'We're here,' said Beatrice, 'According to the tracker Tom is the other side of this door.'

'Right then,' said the Chief, rolling his sleeves up, 'let's get at it.'

'Not so fast, Chief,' warned Cat, 'could be a trap, let me, Smokowski and Bob go in first.'

'What?' said Smokowski, who was all for the management getting their hands dirty.

'You stay here with Beatrice, as back up.'

'But Catranna...'

'No buts, Chief, this could be dangerous, and well, you are the Chief after all.'

'Cat's right, Sir,' said Beatrice, 'Brandy is obviously dangerous and unpredictable, if you were to be hurt it would be a disaster.'

Somewhere off to the side, deep in the shadows a barely audible tut went unheard outside of their boundaries.

'If you really think so,' said the Chief.

'I do,' said Cat.

'Me too,' said Beatrice.

'Then good luck to you all.'

'The door if you please, Smokowski.'

'Clowns?' said Darren, 'They don't look like clowns. Do you think they're in disguise?'

'That's what he said,' said Tom, 'You sure you can't get yourself upright? This is killing my neck.'

'Stuck,' said Darren.

'Oh well,' said Tom. He turned his aching neck back to Leo. 'What do you mean, clowns?'

'That is what the moaning lady said,' said Leo, 'we are all clowns of the original.'

Clowns of the original? thought Tom, what the heck does that mean? He continued to muse on this as the room suddenly fell quiet.

'What's going on?' said Darren, not being able to see much from his position, but noticing the sudden silence.

'I don't know,' said Tom, they're all hiding, 'What's going on, Leo?'

'Someone's coming.'

'How do you know?' said Tom.

'Because this is what they did just before you arrived.'

Then, just like that, Tom got it, what Leo was going on about. Without a word, the Da Vinci's had acted as one. If he had had a free hand he would have slapped his thigh. He means clones, not clowns, thought Tom, clones. And that would explain a lot.

Brandy watched as Cat, Smokowski, and she guessed Invisible Bob, entered the workshop. She had expected all of them to go in. This meant she would have to rethink her next move. Beatrice was quicker than a snake and ten times as dangerous, and the Chief there as well, only made things worse.

'Left... left... left.'

'I'll give her left... left,' said Elsie, as she tapped her way along another corridor, the steel tip of her walking stick kicking up the occasional spark.

'She's keeping time to your stick and doesn't realise it,' said a lady in leather jacket and cap.'

''Ere, Elsie, don't our shadows look scary?'

'Blimey,' said Elsie, looking across the corridor where their shadows loomed, 'is that a rolling pin you're holding or are you just 'appy to see me?'

Those of the troop in earshot started giggling.

'Quiet back there,' ordered the sergeant major.

A figure suddenly loomed ahead of the ambling hopping giggling troop.

'Everyone down,' ordered the sergeant major.

'Not with my hip I'm not,' said Elsie.

There were other mumbles of dissent amongst the ranks. Someone mentioned their arthritis.

'Who goes there?' boomed the sergeant major.

'Aren't we supposed to be in silent and dangerous mode?' whispered someone.

'Think so,' said someone else.

'Just thought I'd ask.'

'Mable,' said the looming figure, answering the sergeant major's challenge. Mable was the scout sent on ahead.

'Password?'

'Do I have to?' said Mable, 'You can see it's me.'

'Yes you do,' said the sergeant major.

'Oh, okay then if I must, but I want you to know I'm not comfortable saying it, *willywarmer*, there,' said Mable, 'happy now?'

'Step forward and be recognised.'

'Oh for goodness sake.'

'Ah,' said the sergeant major, 'it's you Mable.'

'I said it was me,' said Mable, who now that she was closer, appeared somewhat out of breath.

'I take it you have something to report?' said the sergeant major.

'Yes,' said Mabel, still breathing hard, 'I've seen them, not far ahead.'

'Any sign of Brandy?'

'No, Sarge.'

The sergeant major looked thoughtful. Things were about to hot up, get dangerous. But that is why they were there. When things started to hot up, when situations were dangerous, who was it they called? The LISPS, that's who. She stood up, gathered her troops to her and told them what she knew.

'But we will fear nothing ladies,' stirred the sergeant major, 'and why is that?'

'Because we are the LISPS,' the troop responded.

'And our motto is?'

A chorus of voices answered her as one, singing the LISPS's motto loud and clear, 'Whenever and wherever danger or peril might lurk, be it in the shadows of hell or some unwholesome place of work, we of the LISPS as one shall fight, for justice, the weak, to put things right!'

'Right!'

'Thank you, Elsie, a little more practise there I think.'

'Yes, Sarge. Sorry, Sarge.'

'Right you lot,' said the sergeant major, beckoning for her troops to come closer still, 'we have them in our sights. Everyone know what they have to do?' A multitude of nods and whispered affirmatives answered her question. 'Okay then. A unit as you are. B unit ready to receive your ropes.'

'Ropes,' said B unit.

'Corporal Madge, the ropes please.'

Corporal Madge, the lady in leather cap and jacket delved into her faux zebra skin handbag and pulled out a number of ropes. She distributed them amongst B unit.

Smokowski managed a flying kick, a half spin and a karate chop, before being overpowered. Two Da Vinci's lay groaning.

Invisible Bob, who had avoided the initial skirmish, had spotted Tom and was on his way to give assistance when he inadvertently tripped a trip wire connected to a can of spray paint, an expertly hefted net of the butterfly kind, did the rest.

As for Cat, she never got in a blow. The Da Vinci's had lined up a special treat, just for her. A powerful dose of cat nip in gas form was sprayed at her as soon as she entered the room, leaving her immobilised and in her own little world. She was immediately placed in a cage that's bars hummed blue as if pulsing with electricity. This, along with a jar containing a not so Invisible Bob and a bound Smokowski, was placed alongside a horrified Tom.

Brandy had watched and waited, dangerous foe or not, it was time to move.

Units A and B went their separate ways. Unit A following Mabel. Unit B went somewhere else.

'You okay?' said Tom, as Smokowski, who had been bundled to the ground beside him, managed to sit up.

'Think so,' Smokowski replied, twisting at his bonds.

'No good,' said Tom, 'made from pollymums or something, pretty strong stuff.' His attention was then taken by something green jumping up and down in a large glass jar. 'What's that?' he asked.

'Invisible Bob, he's a BIMBO.'

'He don't look very invisible.'

'He was when he came in.'

'Aargh!' yelled Leo, when he saw what Tom was looking at, 'a goblin!'

In the jar, the goblin had accidently banged his head on the side of the jar and was now sat rubbing at his forehead.

'Did you see what happened to Cat?' said Smokowski, who had been otherwise engaged when she had been captured.

'She's behind you,' said Tom.

Smokowski wriggled round until he could see the cage. His face dropped when he saw it and Cat. Cat was out for the count on the floor of it. 'It's a magic containment vessel. She won't be getting out of that anytime soon without help.' Smokowski wriggled back again. 'They were waiting for us Tom, I'm sure of it.'

'Is that you, Boss?' said Darren, who was missing most of what was happening.

'Is that Darren?' said Smokowski, wriggling the other way.

'It's him,' said Tom.

'How?' said Smokowski.

'Long story,' said Tom.

'Sorry I didn't sell anything,' said Darren.

But before Smokowski could lie and tell Darren that it was okay, a buzzing filled the room, the buzzing of excited chatter. The Da Vinci's, who had been busy going about their business again, now stopped what they were doing and congregated in a gaggle in the middle of the workshop, eager anticipation coursing though each of them.

'What's happening now?' said Darren, the chatter reaching his ears.

'I don't know,' said Tom.

But a few seconds later he did as Brandy strode through the dividing arch, the Chief, his hands tied behind him, beside her. 'Put him somewhere safe,' she ordered.

'Cream tea to coffee morning, do you copy, over?'

'Is that you, Sergeant Major?'

'This is cream tea – I repeat, *this is cream tea*, over.'

'Oh, only you sound just like our sergeant major.'

The sergeant major covered her walkie talkie, sighed, counted to ten, and started again – if you can't beat them... 'Where's Madge?' she said, 'and when you've finished talking, say over – over.'

'She's spending a penny, over over.'

'Over!'

'*I don't know,* whatever she can find I suppose.' A heavier sigh, this one not hidden, sounded through the walkie talkie. 'You all right, Sarge? Over over.'

'Just tell Madge I called.'

'Sarge, over over.'

'Yes?'

'You didn't say over over.'

There was a pause.

'Over over.'

'Brandy?' exclaimed Tom.

'Tom, so nice to see you again, I don't think.'

'Aargh!' yelled Leo when he saw her, 'My Mona Lisa has come back to haunt me.'

'Shut up you idiot,' said Brandy.

Suddenly, Tom realised that the inkling that he had had back with Leo when first shown the crayoned picture of the Mona Lisa wasn't only because he recognised the picture, but because he also recognised the face. Give Brandy a brown wig and...'But... why?' he asked.

'Enough!' snapped Brandy, 'Get rid of them.' As some of the Da Vinci's advanced, eager to do their master's bidding, one of them went to Brandy's side and spoke to her. 'Wait!' she said. She then strode over to where Tom was sitting. 'Where is he?'

'Where's who?' said Tom.

'Da Vinci.'

Tom made a show of looking around the room.

'The *real* one! The original.'

'I don't know what you're talking about?' said Tom, which wasn't entirely a lie. She could mean the young one, but he doubted it as he now realised exactly who it was he had locked in the loo.

Brandy grabbed Tom's lapel. 'Yes you do. He was hanging around with Darren, remember? Now, tell me what you've done with him or it'll be the worse for you.'

Tom, even though he was cacking himself, managed to hold his nerve. 'Thought you'd already decided that,' he said.

Brandy raised her fist.

'Wait! Don't, I know where he is.'

Brandy lowered her fist and released her grip on Tom's lapel. She looked down and glowered at Darren. But before Brandy could ask him where, there came a knock, knock, knocking on the workshop door.

'Coffee morning to cream tea, do you copy, over?'

'At last, cream tea here, over.'

'Sorry about earlier,' said Madge, 'shouldn't have had that cuppa before we went, over.'

'Apology noted, are you in place, over?'

'In place and ready to swing, over.'

'Well done, swing on my command, over.'

'Wilko, over.'

*

260

The Da Vinci's looked at Brandy. A puzzled Brandy wandered to the archway.

'Who's there?' asked a Da Vinci.

'Delivery for Leo Da Vinci,' a muffled voice replied.

Brandy stared daggers at Leo and wondered what the fool had done this time, she then snapped her fingers. A Da Vinci stepped forward. 'Answer it.'

'Go... go... go!' shouted the sergeant major down her walkie talkie. The time for over, was over.

On the other end of the line Madge gave the order. 'Swing!' she bellowed, 'Swing like you've never swung before!'

The Da Vinci who answered the door, was now tumbling backwards across the floor, his assailant striding after him.

'Brandy?' said Tom, as the Da Vinci assailant came into view. Beside him Leo, on seeing two Mona Lisa's, gurgled, dribbled and then fainted.

'Get her,' screamed Brandy, the one in charge of the Da Vinci's.

'Now,' shouted Brandy, the one not in charge of the Da Vinci's.

Suddenly the room was in chaos as wearers of leather, wool, some crinoline and an assortment of pop-socks, stormed into the workshop. Some through the open door, others swinging on ropes through the arched windows.

Mayhem ensued. Welsh cakes, hardened slowly at gas mark two and finished at five, flew through the air with lethal effect. Belgian buns, stale and stiff, rained from above. French fancies, their icing like iron, were lobbed, exploding on impact. A walking stick, with iron end, bounced on skulls.

Battle raged, leather and woollies pitted against Da Vinci. Brandy against Brandy. While on the sidelines, Tom, the Chief, Invisible Bob, and a woozy Cat, looked on, shocked, bemused and befuddled. Darren was the same only listening.

Then it was over. The tide of battle that had turned and turned again finally ebbed for the Da Vinci's. Cowed and beaten, they were rounded up and bound. But though the battle was won, the war continued, as

Brandy still fought Brandy. Blow for blow they struck, a maelstrom of fighting fury, techniques new and ancient used.

Away from the fight, skirting round them travelled an elderly lady with a walking stick, her bonnet awry. She edged to where Cat, released from the cage, sat. 'You've got to do something, Ma'am,' she said, when she got there.

'And you are?' said Cat.

'I know,' said Smokowski, 'she's the lady who kept hitting me outside my shop.'

Ignoring Smokowski, the elderly lady introduced herself. 'Private Elsie, Ma'am,' she said, going to salute, but changing her mind, 'motorised division, when I can get the blasted thing going.'

'LISPS?' asked Cat.

'Yes, Ma'am, and proud of it.'

Cat was fairly done in, the containment cage she had been placed in, along with the concentrated catnip, taking their toll, but she saw something had to be done before the two Brandy's killed each other and left them with a whole lot of questions and no one to answer them. 'Okay,' said Cat, 'I'll give it a try, but I can't promise anything.'

'Bless you, Ma'am, because you see,' Elsie whispered, 'one of them Brandy's is our Matron General. We've been secretly following her orders. Don't tell the Chief.'

Cat starred at Private Elsie in disbelief. Brandy? Head of the LISPS? If that was true then Brandy *wasn't* the culprit, her surmising had been wrong. It also meant she would have to do a little bit harder than just try. Cat wrinkled her cute little nose, closed her eyes, and swished her tail. Everything in the room was immediately engulfed in a bright white flash.

The room fell quiet. Eyes blinked. People groped. And in the middle of it all, lay the two Brandy's, stunned and groaning.

'Oops,' said Cat, 'not quite what I'd had in mind.'

Those of the LISPS that had not been that affected by the flash ambled over to the stricken Brandy's. Cardigan clad arms grabbing hold and keeping them where they lay.

'Right,' said Cat, her exertions leaving her way below par, but determined all the same to find out what was going on, 'let's see if we can get to the bottom of all this.'

'Catranna? Is that you?' The Chief had stumbled through the archway.

'Grief,' said Tom, on seeing him, 'it's the coach driver from my trip.'

'What?' said Cat.

'Don't know what the fellow's going on about?' said the Chief.

'*Chief*?' said Cat, in a low no nonsense tone.

'She'll know if you're lying,' reminded Invisible Bob from his jar, 'and if anyone is interested, I could do with a hand getting out of here.'

No one was, not for the moment, as the Chief's reply was waited for.

'Oh, all right, we wanted to keep an eye on him, him being a newbie and all, and as I was the only Elder Traveller with a PSV license, it followed that I should drive the coach.'

'But you were in court?'

'Let's just call that a sleight of hand and leave it at that shall we?'

Cat shook her head. 'And I suppose the LISPS were in on it as well?'

'Always are.'

This prompted Tom to cast an eye over the lady's of the LISPS, who were now tidying up and talking about tea. He instantly recognised a couple as being on the coach with him. He pointed them out. They in turn smiled back at him and waved. The one with dandelion hair winked. 'What the heck are the LISPS?' he asked.

'Ladies Institute Special Participatory Services,' said Cat, 'their version of the SAS and just as hard.'

Tom whistled through his teeth. 'But don't you mean the Woman's institute?' he queried, 'Never heard tell of the Ladies Institute.'

'Leave it Tom.' warned Cat, 'Some things are best left.'

Tom left it.

Smokowski then got in on the act when he noticed that two of the LISPS bore an uncanny likeness to the two leather clad ladies of whom he had made the acquaintance of while in the bookshop queue.

'Corporal Madge and Private Doris,' said the Chief, 'two of the best.' Doris and Madge, their leather jackets and faux skin handbags covered with icing and stale cream and the odd current, looked up on hearing their names mentioned, and they too smiled and waved.

'Do you have a finger in every pie?' asked Cat.

'Better safe than sorry,' said the Chief, who had the decency to at least look a little bit embarrassed by it all.

'And what about me?' said Cat, 'Was I observed?'

'Only from a distance.'

'Beatrice?' said Cat.

'Yes,' said the Chief, 'she volunteered.'

'I bet she did,' said Cat, believing that she now knew who the real brain behind everything was.

'What *do* you mean?' said the Chief, frowning at her.

'Well, I don't know about you, but I'm wondering where she is? The last time I saw her she was with you.'

'Good grief!' said the Chief, sporting a genuine look of surprise, 'I'd forgotten all about Beatrice.' He turned round and stared into the workshop. 'I… she said she thought she had heard something behind us in the corridor. She told me to stay by the door while she went to look. Next thing I knew Brandy had me by the arms and was pushing me through the door. The rest you know. Where can she be?'

Cat meant to tell the Chief her suspicions, but held fire for the moment as the sergeant major was heading their way; perhaps it was better if he learned the truth himself.

The sergeant major joined them and announced that the Brandy's had recovered their wits.

'Wait a minute,' said Tom, as the sergeant turned to go, 'I know you too, don't I?'

'Me too,' said Smokowski.

'Checked those books you returned, all in good order, but next time please use your library card, there's a good fellow.'

'But…' stammered Tom.

'And you Mister Smokowski, should keep a lower profile when tailing your friend, banging your head like that, gave me quite a start.'

'I… I,' stammered Smokowski.

'Oh, and I was wondering,' whispered the sergeant major cum stern looking lady librarian moving closer to Smokowski, 'where do you get your stockings and leather wear from?'

264

'What did she say?' said Tom, just out of earshot.

'Nothing,' said an ashen Smokowski, 'nothing at all.'

The sergeant major winked at Smokowski and then went back to the troops holding the Brandy's.

'And what did she mean when she said you were following a friend?' said Tom, all suspicious.

'Tell you later,' said Smokowski.

Cat who was still eager to get to the bottom of things went to follow the Chief, who had followed the sergeant major. 'Are you two coming?' said Cat, heading for the workshop.

When they got there the Brandy's were standing glaring at each other. LISPS were holding their arms. Other LISPS were standing by, armed with tasers and heavy duty rolling pins.

The Chief had stopped a few feet from them, arms crossed. 'Okay,' he said, 'I don't know what is going on here, but would the real Brandy please take a step forward so we can clap you in irons.'

Neither of the Brandy's made a move. One, because it was a stupid request, and two, they couldn't. The sergeant major took a step forward instead.

'I think you're making a mistake, Chief,' said the sergeant major.

'Mistake, what do you mean?'

'Brandy is on our side, she's Matron General of the LISPS, trusted to the full. We alerted her to what was going on when we heard about the unfelt ripples and she told us to keep a discreet eye out for anything suspicious, we were following her orders. Whoever the other Brandy is, she is the villain of the piece.'

'Her orders? Head of the... Impossible.' The Chief turned to Cat, who nodded. 'Really? Then who... *no*.' The penny had taken it's time, but it was finally beginning to fall. The sergeant major quickly grabbed a stool and placed it behind the Chief. He plopped onto it.

'It makes sense,' said Cat, 'Beatrice had the opportunity. We just need to discover the motive.'

'Blimey,' whispered Tom, to himself more than to anyone, 'Brandy head of the Ladies Institute? Would you Adam 'n Eve it?'

The Chief, suddenly full of anger, stood up. 'Is this true?' Is one of you really Beatrice?'

'Yes,' said one of the Brandy's, 'she is. Didn't know she was a shape changer did you, Chief?'

'She would say that,' said the other Brandy, 'I was watching you and Beatrice from the shadows, waiting for the LISPS to show up. I saw her change and push you into the room.'

'That's a lie!' said the other Brandy.

The two Brandy's squared up to each other again, but arms made strong through cake mixing, bread kneading, and arm wrestling, held them apart.

'So it wasn't Lucy that kidnapped me,' said Darren, catching up.

'I knew it,' said Tom, 'a doppelganger.'

'Well, that's me done, Catranna, I think we've moved into your territory now,' said the Chief, sitting down, 'I believe you've heard enough to know which of them is telling the truth.'

A multitude of expectant faces turned towards Cat, the Brandy's amongst them.

But Cat was spent, drained. 'I'm sorry,' she said, 'but I haven't the energy. I tried as they were speaking, but nothing. I doubt I'd even be able to tell if Invisible Bob were lying at the moment.'

'Wahoo!' sounded from the room next door. Followed by a, 'Sorry,' as Invisible Bob realised he had shouted out loud.

'That bad eh, Catranna?' said the Chief.

'That bad,' said Cat.

'What now?' said Smokowski.

'Perhaps I might be able to help,' said Tom, stepping up.

'Tom?' said Cat.

Tom walked over to where the Brandy's were being held.

'What's he doing?' asked the Chief.

'I haven't the slightest,' said Cat.

'You holding them tight?' said Tom. LISPS knuckles whitened in response. 'Good, just let me…' Tom went up to the first Brandy and sniffed at her.

'He's gone mad,' said Smokowski.

'I always thought he was,' said Darren.

'Hush,' said Cat.

Tom did the same with the second Brandy – then stood back. 'This is the real Brandy,' he announced.

'Are you sure?' said Cat.

'I'd know that perfume anywhere,' said Tom, eyes watering, but now glad he had forgotten all about buying her a different scent.

'Ha!' snorted the other Brandy suddenly, 'betrayed by cheap perfume and an idiot, but you haven't got me yet.' Beatrice now dropped her guise and changed back, and in doing so she managed to slip from her captors grip.

She was at the windows in the other room before anyone had moved and was ready to throw herself through when she suddenly hesitated. The Chief was shouting after her.

'Why, Beatrice, why?' he wailed.

Some say her face softened. Some say she had been about to change her appearance again, but whichever it was, her gaze in that moment had fallen on the Chief.

'Because,' was all she said. And then she was gone.

CHAPTER 65

'Well... well,' said Tom, 'if that doesn't take the biscuit. It was you who snaffled my jammy! I hadn't imagined it after all.'

Smokowski laughed. 'Yeah, don't know what I was thinking to be honest.'

'And you never saw him?' said Tom.

'Not a hair,' said Brandy, 'I thought I saw the gate close, but Mister Smokycoughski here has still got it.'

Smokowski reddened.

Tom, Cat, Smokowski, Brandy, and Invisible Bob, were in Tom's kitchen, mulling over recent events. There were questions asked. How did Da Vinci's workshop change? Why had Tom not used the saver when he was taken by the Da Vinci's? Why had Beatrice done it? There were some answers. Leo's room was simply a time bubble created by Beatrice to contain her clones and cause Da Vinci mischief. Tom forgot he had it. Rumour was, it was because of Beatrice's secret love for the Chief. Some things though remained unexplained, like why the loo had refused to budge when Tom had Da Vinci. Cat thought the loo, which has a mind of its own on occasion, knew something they didn't, but she didn't know for sure.

'So how did you escape from headquarters?' asked Cat.

'The LISPS slipped me a hitchhiker,' said Brandy.

'Thought so,' said Cat.

'Oh,' said Brandy, reaching for her handbag, 'Almost forgot, when I took your clothes back to the museum Tom, I picked this up for you.'

'My backpack,' said Tom, taking it.

'Not yours I'm afraid,' said Brandy, 'yours wasn't where you said you'd left it when I went back to the dungeon. This is a brand new one, straight from a shop in Milan.'

'Milan?' said Tom.

'It appears someone called Vincenzo started making them back in Da Vinci's time. Making them has been a family concern ever since.'

'Oh,' said Tom.

'*Tom*,' said Cat.

'Can't we go back and get it?'

'Too complicated, but don't worry, not too much damage done.' Brandy uncrossed her long tanned mini-skirted legs and stood up, 'and on that note I'm afraid we must be going.'

'Must you?' said Tom and Smokowski, crossing theirs.

'Sadly, yes,' said Brandy, putting her handbag on the table.

'*Oh*,' said Tom.

'*Oh*?' said Cat, grinning.

'Don't worry,' said Brandy, leaning forward and planting a cherry cola with a twist smacker on top of Tom's head, 'I won't be forgetting my favourite Traveller in a hurry. I'll make sure to drop in and say hello the next time I'm passing. You ready, Bob?'

'Aw,' said Invisible Bob, who was sat on a sheet of kitchen towel in the middle of the kitchen table tucking into a bag of chocolate peanuts, care of Smokowski.

'Aw, nothing,' said Brandy, smiling, 'time never stops and nor do we. Hop in.'

Dragging his bag of chocolate peanuts behind him, Invisible Bob, with a little help from Brandy, climbed aboard. He gave everyone a wave, and this time everyone saw him do it, thanks to sticky chocolaty fingers. Everyone waved back.

''Bye then,' said Brandy, squeezing the jewel in her bellybutton.

''Bye,' said Tom, Cat and Smokowski.

It wasn't long after Brandy and Invisible Bob left that Smokowski bade his own goodbye. He wanted to get back to the shop to see how Darren was getting on. Tom fared him well and started filling the kettle up for another cuppa, a half full packet of jammy biscuits, courtesy of Smokowski, on the table waiting to be dipped.

'Sorry about the backpack,' said Tom.

'Happens,' said Cat.

'Couldn't we have done the same for the Da Vinci's, or at least for Leo, he wasn't a bad sort? Did it hurt them?'

'No,' said Cat, 'clone Da Vinci's are a little different than a backpack and no, they never knew they existed once we went back and stopped the cloning.'

'Is the real one all right?'

'All the real ones are all right.'

Tom laughed at this even though he had a hard time getting his head around the concept of counting one person as many because of the different times you could drop in on them. He put the kettle on the work surface and had another go. The Tom today is one, Cat had said, the Tom yesterday is another, the… no, enough. 'Any news on Beatrice?' he said, reaching for a clean cup.

'Still the same I'm afraid,' said Cat, 'dangerous and delusional. But she does have moments of lucidity, which is encouraging.'

'It's a good job the LISPS put that polywhatyercallit net outside the windows just in case,' said Tom adding the coffee.

'Yes,' said Cat, 'it is, goodness knows what she would have got up to if they hadn't.'

'Cat?' said Tom, pouring water on the coffee granules in his cup.

'Yes?'

'Is it really true what Invisible Bob said about Beatrice?' said Tom. He added the milk and stirred it.

'About her doing it for love, you mean?'

'Yes.'

'So she said.'

Tom carried his cup to the table and sat down. 'Funny way of going about it, I say. All that trouble just to be with him.'

'Yes,' agreed Cat, 'but it's how her mind worked, she thought he would never leave the Travellers so she set out to woo him away.'

'By conjuring up an unfelt ripple to get his attention.'

'No, from what she has told us, by conjuring up a nonexistent unfelt ripple. Therefore creating something only she would be able to solve. The Chief would then notice her as being more than an assistant, and they would live happily ever after.'

Tom did some frowning. 'I thought the Da Vinci's were the unfelt ripple?'

'No, she created the Da Vinci problem as a ripple solely to give you your next mission and keep me busy – she could keep an eye on me then – thought I might be a spanner in the works – but she hadn't figured on the Chief calling me in on the unfelt ripple business straight away. She and her plan went a bit awry from there on – she became desperate – and here we are. But from what I hear, she need only have had to ask the Chief. That's love for you I suppose.'

'Complicated. Women for you, I say.'

'Brandy's a woman, didn't hear many complaints from you there.'

Tom coughed and quickly changed the topic. 'Invisible Bob also said that there wasn't a code after all.'

'No, the "up yours" was her little joke it would seem, planted, along with the seven red herring ripples, when the Chief called me in.'

'How is the Chief?' said Tom.

'He's fine. Shame he had to retire though, but with his identity revealed, he didn't really have a choice.'

'Yeah, shame that.' Tom went to take a sip of coffee.

'Oh, and before I forget Tom, where is it?'

'Where's what?' said Tom, cup stopping short of his mouth.

'The crayoned Mona Lisa.'

'Don't know what you're talking about?' lied Tom, knowing full well that Cat would know he was.

'Darren...'

'Darren! Why that little... Arthur!' Tom put his cup down and reached for his jacket.

'That should have been destroyed,' said Cat, as Tom removed the picture from a pocket.

Tom unrolled it and put it on the table. 'No one will know,' he said.

'Darren knows,' said Cat.

'Aw,' said Tom.

'But it's all right,' said Cat, smiling, 'I glamoured him, where are you going to put it?'

'I thought the smallest room might be a good place,' said Tom.

'Good choice,' said Cat.

A happy Tom finally took a sip of his coffee. 'Ugh!' he said, his face creasing in disgust.

'Didn't turn the kettle on, did you?' said Cat.

'No,' said Tom.